L ou was always searching.

Always seeking.

Magical blood—as anyone knew—flowed through the heart of Ilsnare. It was only a question of finding.

With a brisk nod, he dismissed the boy and turned his eyes to the horizon once again. And, for the first time in weeks, a smile appeared on his lips.

It had been a long time before he had had reason to feel positive about anything.

But the return of two trusted companions merited soaring spirits.

The Kingdom of Shellacnass
stands on the brink of war.

A war only one man can stop:

Louson Dorf.

But the years have been unkind to Lou.
Many doubt he retains the strength of his youth.

And the most doubtful among them?

Himself.

An action-packed fantasy adventure.

HITCHKING

THE SEVENTH CRYSTAL KINGDOM NOVEL

- RAYMOND S FLEX -

DIB
books

Hitchking

ISBN-10: 1-78532-048-3

ISBN-13: 978-1-78532-048-4

Published by DIB Books, 2016.
www.dibbooks.com

THE CRYSTAL KINGDOM SERIES

The Webbing Trilogy

The Webbing Blade
The Webbing Bow
The Webbing Cloak

The Four Corners Quartet

Crow's Mind
Heart of Flame
Galleries of Justice
Hitchking

Collections

Blood & Guts & Hexes

HITCHKING

THE SEVENTH CRYSTAL KINGDOM NOVEL

- RAYMOND S FLEX -

JOURNEY'S END

Syre Dorf felt her whole body racked with tension as she eyed the pit-black City Walls of Ilsnare. The Crystal City. She had returned.

Whether or not she would be welcomed was another question altogether.

It was as if invisible hands laid a heavy weight across her shoulders as she turned her back on the city. Feeling herself begin to sweat beneath her rugged traveller's cloak, she slipped it off over her shoulders, revealing the thin material of the tunic she wore beneath.

She looked to the Glyph, tending to the campfire.

With its grey, furry body; its round eyes; the floppy, velvety ears; she couldn't help but feel slightly tickled by the sight. The Glyph seemed such an innocuous Creature . . . so light weight; its spindly limbs which seemed as if they might snap at the first sight of hard work. As Syre well knew, however, those limbs were rubbery in texture and far hardier than they appeared.

Perhaps far hardier even than her own.

She wouldn't *ever* fall into the trap of judging someone—or *something*—based solely on their appearance.

Smoke billowed up from the campfire as the Glyph worked to get it going.

The Glyph had promised to her that it would have breakfast ready and served within the hour. Syre had to admit that, throughout her travels with the Glyph, she had been somewhat spoiled by its cooking. Even if her brother Lou would have her back in the Palace—and that was a *big* if considering how they had left things ... considering the fact that *she* was supposed to be in exile—she couldn't quite imagine the quality of the cooking measuring up to that of the Glyph.

Then again, perhaps the Glyph could find a place among the kitchen staff.

If that was what it wished for ...

Somehow, though, the Glyph having travelled all this way with her and Sully, all the way down from the Winter's Moan, she couldn't help but imagine that it might have somewhat *grander* designs than simply preparing meals for Mortals.

Albeit *royal* Mortals.

Sully had left camp at first light, headed across the plains to go and meet with her brother Louson, the King of Shellacnass. They had decided that it would be better for Sully to be the first to go and meet with Lou, considering that Sully was the one he had sent away on the quest in the first place; and so, it followed, the one who he expected to come back.

Later on in the evening, Syre and the Glyph would await Sully and the response from Lou.

To see whether the two of them would be welcome within the City Walls.

Or if they were to remain outside.

As Outcast.

The reason that Syre had made the journey at all was so that she could give her brother Lou fair warning about the Horrox charge. That the Horrox army would be arriving from the Winter's Moan, looking to lay siege to Ilsnare, and so to Shellacnass; the Crystal Kingdom.

Syre felt a quiver pass through her to think about another magical war brewing.

This time, though, it would be far more bloodying.

The Horrox would be looking to install a fresh regime . . . one of their own devising. And, from the stories of torture which she'd heard from Sully, based on his time incarcerated by them, the Horrox were not particularly fond of Mortals. Sometimes she wondered how it was that nobody else could see the cyclical nature of these things. And that the only answer for all Shellacnass—*for all of the world*—was for Creatures and Mortals alike to live in peace and harmony.

Yeah, and it was as if she could *feel* the impossibility of that tumble down upon her like a downpour. Those times—times for peace—had been consigned to the previous decade.

Now, once again, it would be time for war.

She felt a sigh building in her chest as she turned back to the— now-blazing—campfire.

Was it just her or could she already hear the tramping of horses' hooves on the wind?

The advancing Horrox army?

She was worried that it was too late.

And that so many—*too many*—would die because of it.

If only her brother Lou would take her back . . . if only Lou would allow her to help . . . she was *certain* that she could resist them.

But, first, she had to wait for Sully to return.

A MAGE'S PATIENCE

U p on the ramparts of Ilsnare Palace, King Louson Dorf could feel the warm, tropical winds rolling up from the south of Shellacnass. They blew against his cheeks and caused his pit-black robe to flutter out behind him like a flag unfurled.

His heart beat a sedate, percussive rhythm against his throat. It sent the ice magic throbbing through his veins, offering him no respite. He felt the ice bite and scratch beneath the surface of his skin; a disease which was slowly consuming him, which was chewing him down to the bone, leaving no scrap of flesh untouched.

One day it would destroy him.

Of that he was sure.

It was only a matter of time.

Earlier today, he had tried eating, but had been unable. When the kitchen staff at Ilsnare Palace had laid the plate of roast pork before him, drizzled in the honey-flavoured sauce which so often set a fire burning in his stomach, he had only picked at the meat— got nothing much more than a *taste*—before his gut had begun to quiver and he had felt a sickness rise up in him.

Lou turned to the north.

The overcast sky stretched to the edge of the horizon; its frumpy-bottomed clouds seeming to bring the moisture oozing up through the plains. The humidity hung in the air, impossible to disperse. He wondered if the weather was the reason for his nausea, for his weariness.

The weariness which had been hanging over him for days.

From what he could tell of the weather so far, he thought that Shellacnass was in for a long, hot—*humid*—summer. He didn't envy those who would be offering their labour throughout the summer; those who would be tending to livestock or else working the fields.

His gaze traced the foothills to the north—the purple haze which hung down over them, making it almost impossible to make out any of the finer details. His scouts would have their ears to the ground. As always. Watching for any signs of the approaching Horrox army.

The Horrox would come into range any day now.

They would arrive expecting war.

There was nothing Lou could do about that.

All he really *could* do was have the Royal Guards train for the coming siege.

But, hopefully—he couldn't *help* hoping—the war would be over before a single arrow or crossbow bolt was fired in anger.

Before a single sword was brought *screeching* from its sheath.

Before a single hex was thrown *crackling* through the air.

He turned his attention away from the hills, and back down into the courtyard of the Palace. He could see the Royal Guards in their wispy grey uniforms, standing to attention, their scimitars sheathed at their waists and their spears held upright in their grasp; pointing to the heavens as if *that* was where the attack would come. Their morning's training was done with, and these men had been left on patrol until the night-time session.

Lou heard footsteps on stone.

Behind him.

He turned to look.

A young, male member of the House Staff was approaching.

He had light-brown hair; that mousy colour which half the population of Ilsnare seemed to share. He couldn't have been more than seven or eight summers old. His skin was slightly bronzed and Lou wondered if the boy had perhaps spent some time out in the fields before he had managed to find this job indoors.

In a way, that was much like the trajectory Lou's own working life had followed.

As with all junior members of the House Staff, the boy was anxious about approaching the King. This in itself was nothing to be ashamed of. There were many senior members of the House Staff who were just as nervous around the King. In fact, there were many administrative members of Ilsnare who, if they had had a choice, would spend as little time in the company of the King as they could possibly manage. How many times Lou had used that knowledge to his advantage . . .

The boy's voice wavered; ducked and dived as he addressed him. "Your Highness," the boy said. "There's a pair of men here to see you."

Lou stared back into the boy's blue eyes for several moments.

He reached out to him, with an invisible hand.

Into the boy's blood.

He felt his fingertips within . . . dipping into the veins.

Sensing . . . *waiting* . . .

After a few seconds—and finding *nothing*—Lou released his invisible touch.

Lou was always searching.

Always seeking.

Magical blood—as anyone knew—flowed through the heart of Ilsnare.

It was only a question of finding.

With a brisk nod, he dismissed the boy and turned his eyes to the horizon once again.

And, for the first time in weeks, a smile appeared on his lips.

It had been a long time before he had had reason to feel positive about anything.

But the return of two trusted companions merited soaring spirits.

OLD FRIENDS
TOGETHER AGAIN

Lou could feel his heart squeezing tightly as he descended the stone staircase, down toward the Throne Room where his House Staff always instructed his visitors to await him. If Lou had had his way—if there hadn't been such matters as 'protocol' to be bound by—he would've had the staff lead his friends into the kitchens so that they might have something to eat. But, as King, as Louson had learned over and over again, there were Ways of Doing Things . . . and woe betide him to *try* and change the Way Things Are Done . . . goodness knew, he had broken enough royal 'rules' for a lifetime. How nobody ever seemed to see through him—to see that he simply wasn't *kingly* material—often perplexed him.

Already, before he had so much as set foot in the corridor which led to the Throne Room, he could hear the warbling tones of Rut, interjected, at times, with a muttered comment from Sully.

A smile crept onto Lou's lips, and he could already feel the blood rising in his cheeks and sending warming notes through his blood.

These past few weeks, he had felt so alone in the Palace. He had no one to confide in save his House Staff—his *servants*—and since they didn't believe themselves Lou's equals, as Sully and Rut did, despite what Lou's 'official' role might dictate, they were the only people with whom he might discuss matters of import.

And there were *so many* matters to discuss.

Lou stepped in through the large oak doors of the Throne Room, ready to welcome Rut and Sully; to embrace the two of them . . . or whatever it was that he believed he might do.

However, when he felt the sole of his boot tread the marble, emerald-green floor of the Throne Room, his gaze slipped past the spry, raven-headed Sully and the rotund, blond-haired Rut, falling, instead, onto Hilda . . . *Hildie* . . . the daughter of Ma'reygar; the fire mage who, among others, Lou had defeated in order to claim the Throne of Shellacnass.

For a long moment, Lou could hardly breathe.

His eyes were fixed onto hers.

A sparkling *green*.

He felt himself stunned, as if she had cast some sort of enchantment over him.

It was only after a couple of seconds that he realised his ability had far exceeded hers; that, even now—*a reflex*—Lou held a protective charm over himself.

He couldn't even recall moving his lips.

But he *had*.

When he gathered his wits back together, he took in the rest of Hildie; that red hair of hers which hung loose about her shoulders. How she wore a leaf-green tunic to draw out the colour of her eyes. And how she had on a fire-red sash about her waist to bring attention to her hair.

Finally, he turned his attention to the stump of her left hand concealed beneath her sleeve. . . what remained of her encounter with Herimyre. Ten years; that was how long it had been, though it seemed as if centuries had gone by since they last laid eyes on one another.

It was a wonder they remembered one another at all.

As if the heavens themselves stood reverent to this moment, the sunlight streamed down through the windows above, setting Hildie in the centre, with Sully and Rut—her noble steeds—standing at either side.

"Your Highness," Hildie said, finally breaking the silence in the Throne Room.

She gave a curtsey too, although Lou wasn't alone in noting the wry smile which clung to her lips when she straightened up. A good thing that no members of the House Staff were present at that moment, otherwise Lou might have had been compelled to have her head chopped off just to maintain order about the place.

He blinked away his daze then turned his attention to Sully and Rut.

He realised that the two of them wore smiles, as if they had been awaiting this meeting—as if this was some sort of *entertainment* for them.

Lou had expected it . . . he *knew* that his and Hildie's past would be the cause of elbows nudging ribs, the sly exchange of winks, but that couldn't be helped.

For what he had in mind, it was imperative that she be here.

That she be nearby.

He could feel the stirring sensation in his stomach, and he knew he had to put his feelings away, he had to push them down into some part of himself where they would never again be raked up.

Was that even possible?

. . . With *control* everything was possible.

Lou approached the trio, smearing a grin across his face.

And mostly meaning it.

As he closed in on them, he had to admit that he was somewhat astonished at the state of their dress, that, considering the journeys they had each been on, they should have turned up in not much more than soiled rags hanging off flayed skin.

A few paces from them, Lou halted, cast them with a glance, then said, still smiling, "You all look . . . *clean.*"

There was a profound pause before Rut spoke up. "Well, you didn't think they'd show us to the Throne Room without scrubbing behind the ears, did you?"

Lou gave a dry chuckle; one of those which seemed to stick in the throat, and to rattle his chest. It had been so long since he had laughed . . . almost as if he had to learn how to do it all over again.

He looked over the face of Rut—his doughy cheeks, and his blond hair hanging down about his ears. He could see a hardness to his expression now; some unplaceable detail which told Lou that Rut had been in battles . . . and that—most important—he had overcome them all.

He was here, after all, wasn't he?

Forgetting all the kingly customs at once, Lou lurched forward and threw his arms about Rut, drawing his sizeable bulk into him, and feeling the gentle heat of his body. He breathed in his soap-scented skin too, and vaguely wondered at what other tasks the House Staff assigned to be done behind his back. Perhaps they *did* have his guests fed before meeting with him after all . . .

When he was through with his hug on Rut, he turned to Sully, for a moment avoiding Hildie who stood upright, gazing about the Throne Room.

Sully looked just as he had done before—just as he surely had done throughout his life.

Skinny to the bone and with ragged, shoulder-length black hair.

Stubble speckled his cheeks and Lou could tell that, although the House Staff had clearly given him a shave, Sully's hair wasn't willing to accept defeat gracefully.

It would keep on growing.

Finally, because Lou knew he couldn't put off the moment any longer, he turned his attention onto Hildie. Only onto Hildie. He drew her in, already smelling the scent of lemongrass.

He wondered if this was an innovation of his House Staff or if it was her natural odour. It had been so long he couldn't possibly stretch his mind to remember.

Even when he stood right before her, he held back for another few moments, as if he wanted to savour the moment for some seconds more.

Then he leaned forward and wrapped an arm about her.

It happened as soon as his hand first brushed the exposed, feather-white skin around the back of her neck. He felt the churn—the *ember*—of fire magic which coursed through her veins. And which brought out a reaction from his ice magic . . . that biting, thawing sensation which Lou felt while out in the sunrays.

As he felt *now*, standing in the sunlight which poured in through the roof windows.

It was Hildie who backed away first, out of the embrace, and Lou couldn't help but wonder if she had felt the same unpleasant reaction from her own magic.

Had it been like pouring ice-cold water over glowing coals?

Lou reconciled himself with the fact that he would never know—*exactly*—just what it felt to have fire magic in his veins. Perhaps in another life.

When he turned his attention back to Sully and Rut, he couldn't help but notice the slight looks of concern which crossed their faces.

It was Sully who spoke.

"Lou, we need to talk," he said.

Lou allowed himself another few seconds to savour the moment—to savour this sensation of having these three people back in his life . . . and then the smile slipped from his lips.

He turned his mind to what needed to be done.

To the fate of the Kingdom.

WATCHERS

F lucknor could only trust his guide—Brotsboore's—instincts. The long grass of the plains swished up against his kneecaps as he trudged through it. On the horizon, he could already hear mumbling thunder. He smelled rain in the air. It wouldn't be long before a storm broke out . . . and with Flucknor and Brotsboore in the middle of nowhere; stranded in this marshland.

They were already weeks out from Ilsnare, and yet he had the lingering sensation that, all the while, they had been travelling in circles.

Whenever he raised this possibility with Brotsboore, he was met with the simple reply that Brotsboore could 'sense' his race nearby: The Horrox.

Brotsboore, too, seemed to understand the current condition they found themselves in, as he peered upward, to the heavens, as if scrutinising the thunderclouds; as if he might be able to make them disappear simply with a vexed look.

Like Flucknor, Brotsboore wore the dingy brown robes of a hobblesman. They had decided, between themselves, that it would be the most unsuspicious outfit they could muster. For where they were going—where they were headed—it was important for them to stay unnoticed.

Unremarked upon.

There was no question about what they were doing—about what they intended; that they were in search of the Horrox army advancing on Ilsnare; the army which Brotsboore had informed Flucknor of . . . and what seemed to be the only hope for a peaceful future for Shellacnass.

One day.

But if they were discovered by, say, a wandering group of Royal Guards; those who Flucknor knew, for a fact, Lou kept in all parts of the landscape which surrounded Ilsnare, they risked nothing short of execution.

Lou might've let Flucknor pass through the City Walls, but if he found out the exact nature of Flucknor's intentions; that he wished to join with and abet the Horrox—*the enemy*—he knew that was something that not even the strongest friend-ship in the world would be able to forgive. And there was little doubt that Lou and Flucknor's friendship had taken a dive in the recent past . . . Lou's exact feelings toward Flucknor were nothing but a mystery . . .

Flucknor felt the light, warming spray of drizzle fall against his cheeks. He felt the water tangle and dampen his blond hair—now stodgy with sweat and dust from travel and barely recognisable from his well-conditioned, cleanly kept appearance of before.

Flucknor breathed in the thick, damp scent of rain, and turned to Brotsboore. "I think we'd better get out of this," he said. "It wouldn't be well for either of us to catch our death out here."

Brotsboore again turned his attention upward, to the sky, and to the constantly falling drizzle.

Flucknor watched the raindrops collecting and dribbling their way down his face, clinging to his jawline for mere seconds before dripping down.

Even in the dying light, Flucknor observed the scar which ran down Brotsboore's left cheek . . . the scar which he himself had made. He was surprised that Brotsboore hadn't made any attempt to better conceal his scar, but, then again, Flucknor supposed that, compared with humans, the Horrox had very differing views when it came to aestheticism.

Flucknor took in Brotsboore's rash-red skin, his lizard-like form . . . that *lizard-like* snout of his. As with the rest of the Horrox grouped together in Ilsnare, Brotsboore had refused to use his innate shape-shifting powers so that he might blend into the Crystal City. Brotsboore, and the underground community he had attached himself to, believed in equality—*freedom*—for all Creatures. And it was this belief which also spurred Flucknor on, because, despite his Mortal appearance, Flucknor often thought of himself as closer related to Creatures than Mortals due to the ice magic which flowed through his veins.

Too long had magic—*all types of magic*—been relegated to the shadows.

Now was the time to *take* that equality—to *take* that freedom— and the only way that it would be achieved was by force.

Brotsboore turned to Flucknor and gave an almost imperceptible nod.

Flucknor took this as the cue to properly examine their surroundings.

Over, on the horizon—perhaps a journey of ten, fifteen minutes—he could make out a copse.

Nothing more than a trio—a quartet?—of trees.

But it would be enough so that they might see out the on-coming downpour.

There was no need for words as Flucknor led Brotsboore through the long grasses and toward the tree. With every footstep, it seemed almost as if the thunder was getting louder; rumbling on their heels, as if it was reacting to their own journey. As if it was some demonic pursuer dead-set on chasing them . . . on inspiring *terror* in them.

The rain was falling harder still—*warmer still*—when Flucknor and Brotsboore eventually reached the copse. Flucknor wondered what good getting out of the rain had actually done, considering that he was already soaked to the skin.

His dingy-brown robe clung to him. Now beneath the welcoming canopy of the elm trees, he began to peel the material away. Back at Ravensbark—back when he had been a monk—it had been instilled in them very early on that no monk was to wander about the monastery in wet clothing. Up in the Sable Mountains that was, quite simply, a recipe for death.

Even all the potions, all the subtle enchantments concocted by the monks, wouldn't be able to save one who'd become badly afflicted.

And, despite having left Ravensbark behind for good over a decade ago now, Flucknor had clung onto some of the more base teachings, unable to shake them from his consciousness.

Flucknor leaned his back up against the smooth tree bark. He peered out across the plains, watching the rain coming down in sheets. He listened to the drops splatter down through the leaves. Felt the odd splatter of water up against his cheeks.

Flucknor slowly swivelled his attention to take in Brotsboore.

Even in profile, he could make out Brotsboore's pit-black eyes, and the almost unerring determination which gripped his features. Brotsboore stared out hard across the plains as if he might be able to see the advancing army—the Horrox—from where they stood.

Brotsboore's powers of perception might well be several marks higher than Flucknor's own, but he knew that his eyes could no more strain themselves to take in all the land of Shellacnass all the way to the Winter's Moan than Flucknor's could.

No, often Flucknor believed that, most of the time, Brotsboore merely *feigned* the extent of his powers as a means of keeping Flucknor in check.

As a means of preventing the constant flow of *awkward* questions.

Those questions about *just where* they were headed.

As these thoughts tumbled through his mind, Flucknor was surprised to hear Brotsboore speak aloud—as if Brotsboore had been paying attention to his thoughts all along.

As if the protective charm which Flucknor maintained about his mind all day, and all night, was nothing of consequence.

"They're here," Brotsboore said, clearly, succinctly.

Flucknor felt the wrinkles embed themselves in his forehead.

He took in their surroundings once again.

Of course they were just as barren as before . . . not accounting for the pouring rain.

However, just as Flucknor brought the word 'Where?' to the tip of his tongue, he experienced the rising motion surrounding them.

Flucknor shifted away from the sturdy trunk of the elm tree, took a couple of numbed steps forward. And then he examined their surroundings.

Caught sight of the dozens of rising bodies.

Raw-red skin.

Lizard-like appearances.

Pit-black eyes.

All of them wearing dark robes—as Flucknor and Brotsboore did . . . and all of them with a red-tinted glow.

Ready to attack.

Flucknor turned back to Brotsboore, with about a million questions on his lips. But, before he could say anything at all, Brotsboore jerked his head around to him and—a note of panic in his voice—said, "Don't move. Don't move a muscle."

SETBACK

Lou could still feel the vibrations rattling his bones.

It was difficult to get the realisation through to his brain—*really through to his brain*—that Hildie was back ... that she had returned to Ilsnare Palace; or, perhaps more accurately, that she had *been* returned to Ilsnare Palace.

He stood in one of the Palace courtyards—a small affair designed for the use of the King whenever he had private matters to attend to ... whenever the company he kept demanded a sort of *discretion.* He preferred this particular courtyard above all others.

He enjoyed listening to the playful *trickle* of fresh water moving through the smooth apparatus of the marble fountain. He adored the miniature pine trees which were dotted about the courtyard in their terracotta pots; their soil a rich, dark brown which turned almost black when given a good soaking.

Off, over on the horizon, on the plains approaching Ilsnare, he could hear the *peals* of thunder. He knew, in a matter of minutes, the rains would be here. This stifling humidity which hung in the air would be vanquished. A freezing-cold chill would cut right through it with the subtlety of a knife.

Lou breathed in the steady, ever-fresh scent of the pines, and turned his attention to Sully.

Since Sully had demanded that he speak with him, Lou had sent Rut and Hildie off to find their quarters; where they would be located for the duration of their stay at Ilsnare Palace.

Lou could somehow tell when there were matters better discussed one-on-one.

As he trudged about the circumference of the fountain, he eyed Sully, who had taken his place on one of the marble benches. The way that Sully perched on the edge of the seat had the effect of making Lou nervous. It showed Lou that Sully feared his reaction.

If he had really wanted, of course, he could've merely read Sully's mind, and seen the very thoughts which troubled him. But that wouldn't be entirely friend-like. He understood better than most that a mage spent an inordinate amount of time attempting to gain the trust of others . . . and a cheap parlour trick such as mind-reading could easily put paid to all of that.

Sully finally broke through the silence, flashing a nervous smile. "As I'm sure you can tell, I failed in my quest to track down Lumbswich."

Although it was true to say he had expected *this* particular statement to be coming, he couldn't help but feel a touch disappointed to have his suspicion confirmed. He really had hoped Lumbswich would be the answer; that he would have accompanied Sully back to the Crystal City.

Lou turned to face Sully. "Go on," he said.

Another fleeting smile tugged at the corner of Sully's mouth. "He was dead, Lou."

" '*Dead*' ?"

Sully gave a solemn nod by way of reply.

"How?"

31

Sully went on to explain that—during his voyage into the Winter's Moan—he had come across Lumbswich's abode and found him within it.

Dead.

Sully continued to say that he had given Lumbswich a respectful burial, as if this was here or there, and then he got even more fidgety than before.

Lou wondered if Sully worried about making him angry . . . if he would turn all his magical strength upon him, determined to teach him a lesson for his obvious insolence.

But, of course, there was nothing Sully could do about this.

He could hardly bring people back from the dead.

In actual fact, Lou couldn't help but feel a slightly guilty *joy* that Lumbswich was gone; he had never been the most likeable of types. After all, he *had* been a member of the Magical Council, the one which had backed Ma'reygar in waging war on Ilsnare.

One of those responsible for having put Lou on the Throne of Shellacnass.

Lumbswich had been the only member of the Magical Council Lou had known to still be alive. Like the others, he had been living out in obscurity, keeping out of the limelight for obvious reasons. There were few things more shameful than losing a war.

Especially when all those mages had been so confident they would win.

That they would bring about misery for Mortals all throughout Shellacnass.

. . . Even so, he had needed Lumbswich . . . just as he *had* needed Hildie.

Did this make his plan still workable, or was it an unrecoverable mess?

He supposed that only time would tell . . . but, meanwhile, he would have to make contingency plans.

"There was another thing," Sully continued, apparently not finished with the bad news. He paused for a long moment, one of those pauses which sent a tingle skittering down Lou's spine. "It's about your sister," Sully said. "About Syre."

Lou felt his chest tighten.

His heart rapped against his ribs.

Too soon.

It was *much* too soon.

RIDICULOUS REQUESTS

Once **Sully** had delivered *that* particular blow, about his sister—*Syre*—that she was lurking outside the city, waiting to be asked back in, Lou found himself wandering aimlessly about the Palace, trying to force a solution to the situation. But, in truth, no matter how much he forced himself to think it through, to see how he might jiggle things to his advantage, he couldn't quite get past the stumbling block . . . the mere *shock* that Syre had returned to Ilsnare.

He had thrust her into exile not more than a season ago, and he had hoped that she would spend at least a year out in the wilderness . . . he supposed that it all threw up the question of just what she had been doing in the Winter's Moan at all . . . and then, as Lou happened upon the Library, where he had instructed the others to meet with him, it struck him.

Syre—*his sister*—had ventured up to the Winter's Moan so that she might meet with Lumbswich. So that she might ask him to be her master?

No, it seemed almost too far-fetched.

Too difficult to comprehend.

Why would she go to Lumbswich, one of those who had enabled Ma'reygar?

One of those who would've stood by and smiled at the Mortal screams of pain and anguish.

One of those who would've—*quite happily*—sat beside Ma'reygar and tortured their frail, exposed bodies himself.

Lou, though, could see no other explanation.

As he strode through the doorway into the Library, he eyed Hildie and Rut standing within. He had informed Sully that he could retire to his quarters for the evening, and that a member of the House Staff would be up later to cater to his needs. Lou had chosen the boy with the mousy-brown hair since he had been getting under his feet at the time.

Already, Lou felt the tension racking his muscles, just to think that Syre was *out there*, waiting on the plains. Hoping to be asked back in.

What did she expect?

What did she *expect* from returning?

Lou took in the Library.

All things considered, his House Staff had done a good job of repairing the space.

He had found himself locked in a magical battle with a Horrox and Cyclops as Flucknor had made his 'daring' escape . . . how little did Flucknor understand just how he had played into Lou's hands . . . and especially now—*now that Syre* and *Hildie had returned* . . .

Not that it would matter all that much with Lumbswich dead.

The stone etching which'd once concealed the entrance to the Catacombs was gone, of course, and it had been replaced with the *far* more practical solution of a sturdy door.

Although not without Lou administering a rigid protective charm to it, of course.

The shelves of the Library, too, had been repaired as far as had been possible, and the least-damaged tomes had been given a cursory cleaning job before being slotted back in their places. The worst-afflicted had been sent off to a bindery across town where they were being expertly patched up by those who knew books best.

Hildie and Rut were each browsing the shelves, although Lou had to admit—just from looking at them—that Hildie was doing a far more convincing job of appearing enraptured by her particular piece of reading material. It was all too obvious that Rut, frowning as he peeled back the pages of his own tome, was waging a fraught battle within his own mind.

The two of them shifted their attention away from the books and onto Lou.

Both gave Lou a somewhat sheepish smile . . . for what reason—considering that they didn't seem to be up to any hijinks—he couldn't quite say.

Convinced that he had their attention, he found himself speaking without so much as thinking.

How nice it was to be in the company of friends once again . . .

"Do you know what they call me?" Lou asked.

Rut and Hildie both offered him a blank look.

"The Hitchking," he said, feeling an uneasy smile creep onto his lips. "You know," he went on, "as if I just *turned up* here, in Ilsnare, saw an opportunity and *hitched* away the throne."

Already feeling foolish for having spoken aloud, he turned his attention upward, to the Library windows. He eyed the sunlight—turned golden by the thick, overcast skies—and he wondered, as he did most days, what the world would be like if he had never been named *King* of Shellacnass.

If someone else had taken it upon themselves to accept the burden.

Neither Rut or Hildie said anything in reply, and Lou decided that they—most likely—believed that he was looking for their sympathy; that he wanted some sort of *cooing, cloying* words of condolence for the responsibility that he had to bear.

But, if this was what they took from his words, then they didn't reveal anything of the sort.

In the end, it was Hildie who spoke first. "Lou?" she said.

Distracted, if just for a moment, by the spine of a nearby book, he turned his attention away from the gilded lettering; and the somewhat vague title of *People & Power: A History of Shellacnass*.

He fastened onto Hildie's brilliant green eyes, already feeling as if he might be falling under her spell . . . all over again.

"Why did you bring me here?" she said, her voice firm, and yet with a touch of vulnerability about it . . . as if she was nursing some sort of a minor—*yet nagging*—physical affliction.

Then again, over the past decade, Lou hadn't much paused to think about what Hildie's mental state might be . . . that, as the daughter of Ma'reygar, the mage who had attempted to overthrow Shellacnass, she wouldn't suffer from such trivialities.

And then there was the truth that *she* had been the one who had decided to leave Ilsnare when—in actual fact—she would have been just as welcome to stay.

"I . . ." Lou began, and, already, found his tongue becoming tied.

He shifted a glance in Rut's direction.

Rut seemed to catch the clue.

Cheeks reddening slightly, Rut replaced the book he'd been feigning an interest in back on the shelf and then padded toward the exit of the Library. When he reached the doorway, he lingered for a moment, before saying, "I'll . . . uh, see you at dinner?"

Lou gave a nod, and flashed a smile.

Rut did the same—albeit with a little more blushing than Lou—before skittering off around the corner and up off along the corridor.

Lou smiled to himself to think that he had instructed the mousy-haired boy to run a warm, lemon-scented bath for Rut . . . that would be the perfect way for him to relax.

If only the foremost matters on Lou's mind had been hot baths . . .

He turned back to Hildie who, in the meantime, had taken steps toward him.

She wore a nervous smile.

"You know," she said, getting closer still, "it doesn't *feel* like a decade, does it?"

Lou shook his head, then averted her gaze, again looking out of the windows to the cloudy skies which hung above. "No," he said, "no, it doesn't."

For several long seconds, he listened to the sound of her breathing.

Even despite the enormous Library, it felt like a somewhat intimate moment . . . as if he and Hildie might be the only ones in the Palace.

Finally, Lou knew that he couldn't put off the matter any longer.

"I'm afraid," he began, "that I've got a series of ridiculous requests to ask of you."

He slipped her a sidelong glance, as if she might be able to cause him some irreversible harm if he looked her directly in the eye.

Hildie looked back into his eyes now . . .

"Go on," she said.

Lou felt the words stick in his throat, and then his heart flutter in his chest. "Really," he said, "there's so much—I don't really know where to start."

"That's okay," she replied, "I've got time."

When Lou finally did properly take her in, her pale, feather-white skin; her glittering, perfectly green eyes . . . the adorable sprinkling of freckles all over her cheeks, he wondered to himself how he had *ever* let her go.

Had he always been such an idiot?

CAMPED

S yre could feel the rain beginning to fall.

Working on instinct, as she always did following the weeks and months of travel, she reached for the tarp and worked to hang it between the branches of the tree above her head.

As a chill cut through the air, she reached for her traveller's cloak which she had washed earlier in the day and then left to dry at the end of an offcut of wood. It was mostly dry when she drew it around her shoulders and felt her own warmth reflected back at her.

Smoke wafted up from the campfire and the Glyph, at least for the time being, wasn't anywhere to be seen. She supposed that it had ventured off to go and catch them something for their dinner . . . an unsuspecting rabbit, or—*better*—a nice and fat boar.

As she listened to the raindrops drum away on the tarp over her head, she turned her attention to the pit-black walls of the Crystal City. If the skies hadn't been overcast, then she would've seen the light from the sunset catching the glass roofs, setting them ablaze. As it was, though, tonight the rooftops remained dampened by the weather.

Just like the campfire which, Syre witnessed, with a series of futile *hisses*, was in the process of being extinguished by the fledgling downpour.

She had imagined her return for so long—almost every day and every night she had been away. She hadn't planned on returning for the longest time; that she would be away for much longer than she had been. She had hoped she might be able to solicit some sort of counsel from Lumbswich, that she might be able to seek out her own master.

Learn more about the magic which lingered in her veins.

And about her alignment.

There were very few mages she knew of throughout the world who would be able—let alone *willing*—to help her nurture dark magic.

Often she wondered about her alignment; about what it meant.

Of course when she had first picked up that book of her mother's: *A Practical Understanding of Dark Magic*, she hadn't had any sort of concept what might be meant about *magic*, let alone by *darkness* . . . and, at the time, it had seemed a fair way of protecting those who remained.

One of the only potent weapons they—as survivors—possessed, out in the wilderness.

She had used her power to keep everyone safe.

To guard their encampments from the invading magical army as it'd swept through the foothills of the Sable Mountains, en route to Ilsnare . . . the *Crystal* City.

And then she'd used it again, in Ilsnare Palace, when their butler Tineoots had shown his true form, that he was a shape-shifting Horrox. She had turned her power on him.

Destroyed him.

It still sent a thrill through her blood to think of the force she held within her; how, if she only put her mind to it, she might easily be able to crush the entire world beneath her little finger.

Why should she focus on control when there were so many opportunities available to her, so much potential running through her veins?

She felt herself calm and at peace looking through the veils of rain, so much so that she was greatly startled when she heard the gruff voice behind her.

" 'Ello there, sweetheart."

She turned to look.

Standing there was an elderly man, with long grey hair; a bushy, grey beard which bristled over the entirety of his chest. He stood beside an aged mule which had its saddlebags packed full to bursting. Like her, the man wore a traveller's cloak. She could see that there were several holes in it. He also wore a battered, wide-brimmed hat.

It was arguable whether or not the hat had more holes in it than the cloak.

"Mind if an old man takes some shelter?" he said, already spreading out a blanket he had—*apparently*—produced from one of the mule's saddlebags.

"Sure," Syre replied belatedly, "go ahead."

The man smiled at her, showing off his yellowed—almost *gold-coloured*—teeth.

He spread the blanket across the long grass at the base of the tree beside her, and then, with much scowling and mumbling to himself, settled down on top of it.

"So," the man said, looking off across the plains, to Ilsnare, "you fleein' the Crystal City too?"

Syre felt her heart beat a little steadier now.

Her muscles relaxed a touch.

"No," she replied, and then wondered if she should've lied . . . judging by the man's response, she probably *should* have.

The man narrowed his eyes and grinned, leaning in toward her. "You what?" he said. "You ain't heard yet?"

Syre shook her head, this time taking care to lie.

"Not about them *Creatures* on their way . . . on their way *here?*"

Again, Syre shook her head.

"Aye," the man said closing one eye, "ain't I seen you before—you look familiar to me."

Syre felt the colour rise up in her cheeks.

A strong, warming glow.

She turned away and hoped the elderly man wouldn't notice.

"You're Syre Dorf, aintcha? Princess of Shellacnass?"

Even though Syre was still turned away, she realised that it was futile to try and hide her blush. She had never been any good at lying and it seemed that this man served only to prove the point. "Yes," she replied, finally, seeing no point in hiding it now.

"So this's where you've been hiding out, hmm? I mean, after your brother decided to chuck you into *exile?*"

"Yes," she said, wanting this conversation to end.

She looked out through the rain and couldn't help wishing that it would stop.

That it would *just* stop . . . so that she could get away from this old man.

"Tell me," the man continued, either trying to get on her nerves, or unaware how *annoying* he was being, "have you been hiding out here this whole time, in this copse here, or have you just returned to the city?"

"Just returned," Syre replied, looking around and hoping to see the Glyph approaching.

Already, she could feel a tingle through her blood, and at the tips of her fingers. She knew that if she didn't concentrate all her energy she was liable to lose control . . . to simply have the magic *pour* out of her. During her travels, she had got slack with her control.

With *forcing* herself to control.

It had seemed irrelevant when there were no longer Mortals around.

Kind of like a twist on that old saying:

If a mage casts a spell in the middle of nowhere, does anybody else notice?

In truth, she had hoped Lumbswich might be able to offer her further guidance; to pitch in some specific advice on how to control *dark* magic . . .

She was glad for the silence which followed between her and the old man, but it seemed it wasn't to last.

"Feel good to be back?" the man said.

Syre counted to ten in her mind, hoping that the rain would ease off.

But, if anything, it only grew stronger.

She felt her patience give way and turned on the man feeling a severe anger rising in her. "Listen," she said, "do you think you could just keep your jaw still for a while? I'm not interested in answering questions."

The old man held up his palms, as if in surrender.

Then he remained where he was, kneeling up on the blanket. He stayed like that for several minutes before rising up, going over to the saddlebags of his mule and then fishing through the flaps for something or other.

Syre turned her attention back on the plains stretching out ahead, and willed the Glyph to return . . . the Glyph would provide moral support, and it would be reassuring to know that there was another magic user nearby.

"Magic user, eh?"

Syre jerked around, looked to the old man.

She locked onto his grisly, grey eyes.

He had just . . . he had . . .

"Read your mind?" the man put in, and then chuckled. "Funny the things that elderly travellers can get up to, hmm?" He paused for a long moment, reached up and tipped the rim of his hat a little. He mumbled something else to himself.

"What was that?" Syre said, staring at him now.

The man glanced up, a look of feigned surprise in his eyes. "Oh," he said, "don't you mind me, bad habits, you know—*elderly habits* . . . you spend so much time out on the road—so much time alone with nobody else to talk to—that you get into the habit of conversing with yourself."

"What did you say?" she said, resilient.

"Oh," he replied, "just thinking of shoving off . . . don't wanna get on your nerves or nothing."

Apparently true to his word, the man continued to fiddle about with the saddlebags on his mule.

Syre couldn't allow this to pass as if nothing at all. "But it's still *pouring* down," she said.

The man flashed his eyes and shrugged. "To be sure, but it's nothing out of the ordinary for one like me . . . I've a slick, waterproofed skin." And with that, he tugged on the rim of his hat, unharnessed his mule from where he had tied it up to a knot on a tree trunk and headed on down the hill; out into the rain.

Syre stared after him. Rather than relief at the elderly man's departure, she felt anxiety. Almost as if she was allowing something to slip by . . . an opportunity?

But before she could think of anything else, she heard the elderly man's voice again; but this time his words appeared inside her mind.

— *You come along now, Syre. If you want to learn that which Lumbswich never had the chance to teach you. About the darkness.*

Syre felt her chest tighten.

How could this traveller know about Lumbswich?

Before Syre could so much as think to reply, though, the old man spoke into her mind again.

— *Lumbswich was my brother. The two of us served on the Magical Council. My name is Ems'plot.*

A shudder passed through her body.

She knew that she should remain behind.

That she should wait for the Glyph to return.

That she should wait for word from Lou . . . from Sully . . . that she would be allowed to return to Ilsnare . . . to the Palace . . . and yet, she couldn't help but cast her mind back to all that had happened, to how Lou had cast her out like a mangy bitch . . . why should *she* go crawling back to him all over again?

With a final glance around, and not seeing any sign of the Glyph, Syre rose up off the ground and made to follow the elderly man.

Ems'plot.

ORDERS

After dinner was over and done with—radish stew with beef casserole—Lou allowed Hildie to make her way to bed, to retire to her quarters, while he held both Sully and Rut behind.

Although Lou was aware that his face might not do a good job of showing it, he knew that this was the happiest he had been in the *longest* time. He could still taste the salty goodness of the stew and casserole, and he felt a merriness had descended over him like a thick, smoggy cloud when he had taken a cupful of brandy wine . . . it was probably the first time in a decade that he had so much as *touched* the stuff . . .

The air was still thick with the homey scent of wood smoke, and the flames of the fireplaces were dwindling and crackling as they worked to break down the remainder of the logs. The warmth wafted about the Banquet Hall, sending soothing notes through his blood while—at the same time—it caused a prickly reaction from his ice magic; giving him a sort of itchy sensation just beneath the surface of his skin.

He wondered if walking with weakness had ever been so delightful.

With Rut and Sully seated on the wooden bench opposite, both of them with their own flask of brandy wine before them, and the two of them with glowing, red cheeks, a slight weight made itself felt on the spirit of the conversation.

The two of them surely knew that there was a sombre purpose to this evening.

A *consequence* for Sully having been unable to bring Lumbswich to Ilsnare.

It seemed almost as if Lou had spun through a hundred thousand other options and—each time—come up short. He simply couldn't think of any other means of protecting the Crystal Kingdom than that which confronted him right now.

Feeling the steady gaze of Sully—his skinny face and black hair—and that of Rut—with his doughy cheeks and blond tufts sticking out at all angles from his scalp—Lou knew that the time had arrived. And even as he admitted it to himself, he felt his heart sink in his chest. Because he well knew that the two of them had only just arrived back from a pair of perilous quests . . . and that which Lou now had to ask of them was the most perilous by far.

He breathed in deeply, feeling the air prickle his lungs. Then he said, "I need the two of you to bring me the contents of the Webbing Armoury."

At first, neither Sully or Rut reacted.

The two of them sat stunned.

And then they spoke over one another.

In the end, it was Rut who managed to get the first word in.

"You're *sure?*" Rut replied, arching his eyebrows.

Lou nodded. "There's no other way." He glanced to Sully. "If Lumbswich is really gone then I see no alternative—no other way for us to see off the invasion of the Horrox."

He thought again about how Sully had seemed *so* glad to bring him the news of the coming invasion after the blow of finding Lumbswich dead.

Sully gave a shake of his head. "I don't like it," he said, "I mean, you said it before, the Webbing Armoury should only be used as a last resort . . . it might destroy you this time." He met Lou's eye uneasily. "Are you certain that you'll be able to control it?"

"Look," Lou said, "I don't want to sound like a martyr—nothing like that—but when I arrived here, to this city, when I was *made* King, it was on the basis that I would be able to protect Ilsnare and its people from any and all invaders." He paused for a long moment and then added, "If it takes my death to help protect them then that's a sacrifice that needs to be made."

Another long silence passed between Sully and Rut, and then, as if it was a previously agreed gesture between the two of them, they both broke out into a smile.

Then Rut said, "You do realise that what you just said makes you sound *exactly* like a martyr? In fact," Rut added, jerking his thumb over his shoulder, "I'm sure that if you picked out a dictionary from the Library you may well find that you repeated, by rote, the definition of 'martyr'."

Despite the situation, despite the *seriousness* of what was about to happen to Ilsnare, Lou couldn't help but nurse a wry smile. Then he shook his head.

He couldn't control the world any more than he could predict the weather.

And there was nothing else to be done . . . the Webbing Armoury had to be brought.

Did it make him seem like a martyr when this was clearly the only thing to be done?

A WOULD-BE ASSASSIN?

L ou found it impossible to sleep.

He had ordered Sully and Rut to leave Ilsnare immediately, for them to set out on their way to fetch the Webbing Armoury. He had even stood up on the ramparts and watched the pair of their horses slip out through the City Gates. He had waved to the two of them as he had observed their paths split . . . seen as Sully had headed to the west while Rut had gone to the east. They would each go to fetch their half of the keystone which would unlock the Webbing Armoury stored beneath the city.

Soon after Lou had taken control of Ilsnare—soon after the magical war which'd gripped Ilsnare—he had enchanted the stone vault where the Webbing Armoury was kept, and then created a keystone which he had split in half. He had wanted to free his hands of the responsibility of being the one to preside over the Webbing Armoury; over the Webbing Blade, Bow and Cloak . . . and so he had divided that responsibility up between his two oldest—and most trusted—friends.

In theory, at least to his mind, it made the location of the Webbing Armoury incorruptible.

Or maybe he was just fooling himself.

But the way he saw it, he simply couldn't imagine anybody managing to get to either Sully and Rut—let alone *both* of them—and manipulating them to their own bidding.

When Lou had returned to the Throne Room—and his quarters—he had felt something strange in the air. Something which'd immediately attracted his attention.

There was somebody *there.*

As the moonlight streamed down through the ceiling windows of the Throne Room, he felt his ice magic stir and groan within his veins. He felt it pump through his heart; filling him with fresh vigour, and a strange, almost uncontrollable sense of power.

But he *had* to control.

Otherwise he would be destroyed.

He would end up like so many others . . . history was scattered with the mages who'd become enraptured by their own power only to have that which they loved most brought down upon them. *Crushing* them.

After Lou had searched the entirety of the room—including his four-poster bed and en suite bathroom—and had found nothing, he allowed himself to retire to the throne where he slumped down. He felt drained even though it was Sully and Rut who were putting their lives on the line . . . the ones who had *yet more* great hardship awaiting them up ahead.

Lou tilted his head back, peering up through the glass, and to the moon. He closed his eyes and allowed himself to drift off . . . to feel the moon's rays caress his face in the same way that he—as a lowly field hand, stripped to the waist—had once enjoyed the warmth of the sun.

As he felt himself slipping away to sleep—as he felt his entire mind begin to unstitch from the present—he couldn't help but notice something.

From the corner of his mind.

No, it was *more* than that.

It was a sound.

A slight *scuff* of the sole of a boot.

He snapped an eye open.

His night vision was exceptionally clear; aided by his ice magic, and the energy which he harnessed from the moon.

He saw the figure right away.

Small.

Waif-thin.

Just the right shape for an assassin.

He remained where he was, a snake lying in wait, ready to strike.

His heart beat steady and full.

No fear.

Only preparation.

He studied the form's movement, and realised that it was moving *away* from him rather than toward.

Deciding that he should act now, lest the person—and he was *certain* it was a person—should escape.

Working his ice magic to keep his movements silent, so that he wouldn't make so much as the *creak* of a muscle, he rose up off the throne and crept across the emerald-green marble floor.

For the longest time, he stood right behind the small form.

Studying all its aspects.

How it didn't shift to a higher pace when it closed on the door.

Apparently *wary* of making any sudden movements.

Right as the intruder reached for the door handle, Lou grabbed the intruder's shoulder and grasped it firmly. He felt the quivering reaction pass through his fingertips.

He gripped harder still.

The intruder tried to squirm free but it was too late.

As helpless as a mouse in the firm grip of a serpent, Lou had him.

He spun the intruder around and—in the moonlight—studied his features.

The boy with the mousy, light-brown hair.

His eyes were wide.

Lips slightly parted.

He shook all over in shock.

Lou had no idea what the boy must be thinking . . . well, in actual fact, he could hear every single thought twitching through the boy's head . . . but none of it was of any coincidence.

Just the rambling, excited *fright* of a child.

Right away, he was certain the boy hadn't meant anything malicious by his intrusion of the Throne Room.

He could tell, from the pattern of the boy's thoughts, that he was merely curious.

With a cynical tone, he thought of all the previous Kings of Shellacnass and what they might've done in such a situation.

. . . Without a doubt, they would've called for the Royal Guards long ago, and the boy would've been the first to the chopping block come the morning light.

He couldn't help but feel glad that he had very little in common with the previous Kings of Shellacnass.

"What're you doing here?" he finally asked the boy, keeping his tone firm—*even*—while taking great effort not to sound angry.

The boy quivered some more, apparently finished with his attempts to escape Lou's clutches. It seemed that either the boy had made peace with the fact that he was to be executed for his lack of judgement or else that he was still too much in shock to realise what it was that awaited him.

"Please, Your Highness," the boy said, "I'm *so* sorry . . . I was told to come in here and run a warm bath for you." The boy gulped at the air, then went on. "It's just . . . it's just, I seem to have fallen asleep a little time after . . . the steam . . . it was . . . was . . ."

"*Comfortable*?" Lou put in, hoping to help out.

The boy nodded vigorously. "That's right, sire, that's exactly it."

Lou studied the boy's tone, and realised that there was still something which he couldn't quite put his finger on. He could tell, without a doubt, that the boy wasn't telling the complete truth . . . then again, he supposed any self-respecting schoolmaster might've been able to say the same thing.

"You do realise the seriousness of what you've done?" Lou said.

He enjoyed the effect of hearing his voice reverberate about the Throne Room . . . he knew that there were certain spots which were *intended* to create this effect, to make the King sound like a wild bear . . . and still others which were meant to make visitors sound as inconsequential as mice.

The boy continued to twitch beneath Lou's grip, but Lou held firm.

Finally the boy responded, in a downbeat voice, almost too quiet to hear, "Yes, sire."

Lou allowed this reply to float about the Throne Room for a moment, and then he said, "What's the real reason you were here?"

"I . . . I . . . that's the truth, I swear it! I . . . I . . ."

But Lou cut the boy off before he could jabber through any more of his lies.

"It's okay," Lou replied, "I just want to know the truth . . . I promise you won't be in trouble."

The boy stared back at Lou, his eyes seemingly growing wider by the second, as if he expected the killing blow to come. He found his voice again. "I . . . I heard about . . . about the . . . the . . . *legend.*"

When Lou replied, he was surprised to feel a smile in his voice, "The Webbing Armoury?"

The boy nodded, and then, almost out of place, chanced a grin.

Lou saw that the boy had several missing teeth. He wondered if this was the natural way of things or because the teeth had been left to decay. Although the House Staff of Ilsnare Palace were held to very high standards of hygiene, the younger members of the House Staff tended to be kept back till last . . . never *truly* given the benefit of such attentions until they were adolescents, when it was more of a sure thing that they would be around the Palace for a while.

"What did you hear?" Lou said, his tone now lighter—*softer*—than it had been any time before.

The boy held his silence for a few more seconds. And then he glanced about the Throne Room, as if there was somebody else with them, as if—perhaps silently—some Royal Guards had managed to sneak in.

But there was nobody here except for Lou and the boy.

Finally the boy said, "I heard it was the *most powerful* thing that anybody in Ilsnare has ever witnessed; that, with those weapons, you killed two mages. And a fearsome Mortal."

Lou gave the boy a slight smile by way of reply.

For some reason, the boy reminded him a little of Guilknot . . . the boy who'd been his manservant until his murder by Sheilds—the assassin who had been employed by Tineoots.

Guilknot, too, had been very curious about the more blood-thirsty elements of Lou's past.

But, then again, were there really any *other* elements to his past?

It was then that Lou felt a melancholy settle down over him, and when he looked to the boy again, he couldn't help but lose the smile which he'd been wearing before.

The boy, too, seemed to sense this shift of mood.

"Sire?" the boy said. "Shall I leave you?"

Lou stayed still, silent, for the longest time.

And then, without a word out loud, Lou felt a single tear roll down his cheek.

Ice-cold.

As he reached up to wipe the tear away, he gave a subtle nod of his head.

The boy glanced about himself once more, and then, with a nimble reflex, reached out and turned the door handle. He disappeared into the night-time Palace.

PRISONERS ON THE MARCH

F lucknor could feel his heart thrum in his chest.

It knocked against his ribs.

And made his blood well up in his temples.

For the first time since he had left Ilsnare, he felt as if he might've made a mistake. As if following Brotsboore out of the city—having come *here* to search out an advancing army—had been a big mistake. And one which would be impossible to correct . . .

Although Flucknor did his best to keep his mind alert, to keep himself aware of the stodgy marshland which he trekked over, he couldn't help but note the fatigue which rippled through his muscles, and which now made every single one of his footsteps something like agony.

He shifted a glance about him.

Noted the many Horrox who surrounded him on all sides.

They had been caught a little after first light, and it was night now.

Each of the Horrox gave off a slight, red glow.

They illuminated the way just enough so that Flucknor wasn't completely blinded.

More than anything now, even despite his situation, despite being a—*prisoner?*—Flucknor wished for nothing more but to be allowed to rest a while.

It seemed as if his feet might catch fire if he didn't put them up.

One of the things which made Flucknor most uneasy about being among the Horrox was that he wasn't entirely sure of his own status.

The Horrox stood sentry around him. Neither Flucknor or Brotsboore wore chains, or any other markings of prisoners. And neither had the Horrox spoken to either of them, said in so many words that they were captured now.

That had been assumed.

However, as the Horrox had closed in on them from all sides, as they had risen up seemingly out of nowhere and surrounded Flucknor and Brotsboore, Brotsboore had had the presence of mind to let Flucknor know these were the Watchers . . . scouts which the Horrox sent on ahead of all others.

Pathfinders.

So, it seemed to follow, the Watchers were leading the two of them back to their main camp. And, Flucknor could tell by the position of the moon and stars that they were headed *away* from Ilsnare. They weren't yet part of the advance on the Crystal City.

Part of the *revolution.*

As they trudged through the marshland, Flucknor hearing the gentle suckle of the soaked clods of earth beneath the tread of his boots, he shifted a quick glance over to Brotsboore, hoping to catch his eye. But Brotsboore continued to stare straight forward.

Flucknor knew better than to try and speak directly into his mind, as if that might protect the privacy of their conversation. He knew that every single Horrox surrounding them would hear the words just as clearly as if Flucknor had bellowed them at the top of his lungs.

Up ahead, Flucknor noted the flaming orange light.

It lit up the night-time sky.

Illuminated a semi-circle.

Like a half-shell.

It took him a few seconds to realise that there were many forms within the illumination, that there were *tents—an encampment—* beneath.

This, it seemed, was the centre of the Horrox advance on Ilsnare.

They had arrived.

A hard stench of rotten eggs twisted through the air.

Flucknor expected their advance to pause, perhaps for one of the Horrox to turn on Flucknor and inform him where he would be staying the night.

But, as if unaware of the surrounding tents, the Horrox simply continued their advance.

Until they arrived to the largest of the tents.

And Flucknor felt his heart *hum* in his chest.

A chill passed through his blood.

He felt . . . *something* . . . although Lou had been extremely sparing in the magical knowledge he had relayed to him, he knew enough of magic to be able to sense it . . . and he felt that it was *extremely* strong here.

That although the Horrox which surrounded him held their own magic, their magic was as nothing compared to that which lay ahead.

Flucknor wondered if there was something he might do to prepare himself.

If he had known any protective enchantments then he might've uttered one beneath his breath. Or if he had known what he might do to prepare himself to attack, then he might well have done that. But, as it was, he was nothing more than a Mortal—*a piece of meat*—with a channel of ice magic running through his veins. Then again, wasn't that how all *mages* started out?

The Horrox, as if they had prearranged it with themselves, began to fan backward from Flucknor, to form a channel through which he now moved.

It left only Flucknor himself and Brotsboore.

This time—the first time since their capture—he managed to catch Brotsboore's oily black eyes.

If some message passed between the two of them then Flucknor wasn't aware of it himself.

Would Brotsboore protect Flucknor against the sure-fire danger which waited ahead?

Or would he simply allow Flucknor to be dealt with . . . whatever that might entail?

As Flucknor and Brotsboore stood surrounded by the Horrox Watchers on all sides, another Horrox emerged from within the tent.

Flucknor hadn't much practice in separating the red-skinned, scabby-textured Creatures one from the other . . . except for Brotsboore who he could easily tell apart from familiarity above all else; and because he had a spindly—*almost withered*—body.

This Horrox, Flucknor could tell right away, clutched something in his fist.

Down at his side.

Flucknor had to force himself to shift his attention away from the Horrox's side, and up to his face. He held the Horrox's gaze as if they might be having a staring competition.

And then the Horrox spoke into his mind:

— *Mortal.*

Flucknor held onto that word for a long while, not really sure what to make of it. And then, realising there was *nothing* to be made of it, he answered simply:

— *Yes.*

The Horrox continued to stare at Flucknor long and hard, and then spoke, again, into Flucknor's mind:

— *You are far from Ilsnare.*

"Yes," Flucknor replied, but this time aloud, instead of within the eerie surroundings of his own mind.

The Horrox spoke once again:

— *And you have now entered the realm of the Horrox . . . you have left behind that which Mortals may call their own, and have moved into our thralls.*

This time Flucknor hadn't any idea what he should say by way of response.

So he remained silent.

The Horrox, apparently sensing this silence, brought its fist up from its side and—*slowly*—finger by finger, unravelled his clutched fist.

On his palm, Flucknor saw, there was a strange, button-sized object.

It was made of glass.

A sky-blue colour.

Something which Flucknor might've been able to acquire from one of the many market stalls on the Crystal Causeway, the road which ran alongside the River Ils and which led to the Palace.

The Horrox again spoke into Flucknor's mind, and all Flucknor could do was *feel* each of the words appearing within his brain.

— *You shall be useful, when the time comes, when we plan on entering the city. That is why I determine to keep you alive.*

Flucknor felt his spirits raise a touch. But then, as he surveyed the glass, button-like object which lay flat on the Horrox's palm, he felt a strange, out-of-place skitter of pain pass up his spine . . . entirely unexpected. And it was gone as soon as it had begun.

Flucknor was certain that—*just for a moment*—he had seen a dark mist descend over the sky-blue shade of the button sitting in the Horrox's palm.

Could this be related to his brief bout of pain?

It was now that the Horrox smiled wryly, speaking into Flucknor's mind again:

— *But the difference between alive and dead, that says nothing about discomfort.*

Once more, Flucknor felt a sharp sting.

This time sustained.

Deep down in his gut.

It seared his veins.

Brought a burning sensation to the surface of his skin.

As if his blood itself was coming to the boil.

Before long, the pain was too much to bear.

Too much for Flucknor to keep himself standing.

And he felt his knees buckle.

He collapsed to the ground, between the Horrox.

Felt their joined gaze on him.

As he felt the darkness begin to seep into his vision—the world begin to dim—he heard the Horrox speak into his mind again:

— *I am Arfklan. King of the Horrox. Eliminator of Mortals.*

NIGHT-TIME SENSATIONS

Although Lou did his very best to sleep, he found it almost impossible.

As it had been almost every night since he had come to Ilsnare Palace, ever since he had beaten Ma'reygar, Auch'ray and Herimyre, in one fell swoop.

Even though he had got himself as far away from the Webbing Armoury as he could safely place himself, he still felt its effects. The constant skitter of ice bit at his veins.

It was especially strong—*impossible to stand*—during the night.

That was why, almost every night since he had inhabited the Palace, he would walk aimlessly through the silent corridors until he saw the first rays of sunshine rising up on the horizon. Then, and only then, in the dawning hours, he would be granted some sleep.

Before the day would begin again.

Before the matters of *State* made themselves felt in the Throne Room.

His night-time stroll had brought him—as it often did—to the ramparts. So that he might look out over the plains which surrounded Ilsnare. Some nights, he found himself hoping to spot an

enemy camp on the horizon; some sign that there would be someone out there, in Shellacnass, willing to ease the burden of power
from his grasp.

But there was never *anybody* . . .

Never any movement.

Only the odd bunny rabbit here and there.

However, this evening, it seemed that Lou wasn't alone at all.

That he had company.

Even in the darkness, with only the vague illuminations of torches from the courtyard, down below, he could make out her form:
Hildie's form.

Her long red hair unfurled over her shoulders as she rested her
elbows on the stone ramparts, peering out over the plains. Her attention fixed on the horizon—just as his own was.

There really hadn't been any point in bringing Hildie here; back
to Ilsnare.

Now that Sully had failed to bring Lumbswich to the Crystal City,
none of it mattered.

None of Lou's plan mattered.

How he had ever thought this coming war could be resolved by
anything but bloodshed

escaped him . . . but he supposed he had always been a dreamer.
Even back when he'd worked the fields, he'd strived for something
bigger—*something better.* What he'd learned, during his tenure as
King of Shellacnass, was that there would be no controlling the
whims of the world.

When the world demanded blood, blood it *got.*

Apparently sensing his approach, if not reading his thoughts
themselves—Lou hadn't thought to cast a protective charm—
Hildie turned to him. Her green eyes skirted over his own, and a

slight smile turned up the corners of her mouth. "Good evening," she said.

Lou said nothing as he arrived beside her.

He propped his elbows up on the stone ramparts, glanced at her briefly, able to meet her smile, before shifting his attention back over the City Walls; out and down onto the plains below. "I had an intruder tonight," he said, skipping the greeting as if the two of them had slipped back into the easy companionship of a decade ago.

"Really?"

"Mm, a young boy." Lou rolled his shoulders, hoping to ease the tension which'd grown there from the many hours he'd spent on the throne during the day. "He wanted to know about the Webbing Armoury—no doubt he wanted me to regale him with stories of the Magical War—stories which his family had talked about."

"And did you?"

Lou shook his head. "No, I . . ." But his words, almost under their own steam, trailed off . . .

He *was* speaking about the death of Hildie's father, after all.

Hadn't he any tact?

Hildie made no attempt to prop up the conversation, and the two of them continued to stare out over the ramparts, to look over the plains which surrounded the Crystal City. Finally, after what might've been minutes or hours, Hildie broke the silence. "Listen, Lou. I was moving through the city streets the day I arrived, before you asked me to perform the duty I am now."

That was right.

Lou thought again of the instructions he had fed Hildie; how he had had to conceal the true nature of his bringing her here . . . he couldn't allow *that* fact out of his head until the time was right.

Even now—even though he had implored Sully and Rut to bring him the keystones so that he might unlock the Webbing Armoury— he held a hope that he still might be able to unite the Magical Field . . . that he might be able to fend off war . . .

Though how he would be able to do it remained something of a mystery.

Because, without Lumbswich, it would be impossible.

Even with all the other pieces neatly slotted into place.

Lou had told Hildie that the reason he had brought her back to the Crystal City was because he wanted her to aid him with his spy network; the Eye . . . he wanted her to simply move through the city and inform him of any great, untapped sources of fire magic. She, after all, daughter of the most fearsome mage of their times—Lou aside, of course—would be the prime candidate for such a task.

Hildie continued, "It was while I was pacing along the Crystal Causeway, when I was coming up through all those market stalls, through the vendors, all of them barking out various things . . ."

Lou turned to her, making it clear that all his attention was focussed on what it was she had to say. He stared deep and long into her green eyes and wondered how—*in another life*—things might've worked out differently. If only Hildie didn't have fire magic running through her veins.

If only Lou hadn't had ice in his own . . .

Hildie went on, ". . . I stopped by one of the stalls selling fine fabrics, you know, the ones which can create great cloaks; the sorts of clothing that the shepherds in the foothills might wear?"

Lou nodded. He knew just the ones she meant. Thick, fleecy robes which swayed down elegantly—covering the whole of a person's body. Keeping the cold out . . . keeping the warmth *in*.

"Well, it was while I was speaking with the vendor of this particular stall that I felt . . . uh . . . a *presence* . . . a *sharp* presence . . ."

Lou turned on Hildie. Although it was true that he had appointed her this task, in truth he hadn't expected her to actually find anything of use from it. He had specifically designed her job to be one which would pass the time before Lou could know for certain whether or not his plans were truly scuppered. "Fire?" he said, arching his eyebrows.

Hildie shook her head. "No," she said. "*Not* fire." She paused for the longest time, and then, when she spoke the word it was almost with a biting frost on her tongue. "*Ice.*"

Lou pondered this then turned back to look over the ramparts. "Ice mage?"

Hildie replied quickly, without pause. "I can't think of any other way to explain the strength of magic emanating from the man—an *elderly* man . . . it was something . . . more powerful than . . . than . . ."

Although she didn't finish, he knew that she was going to say that it was the most powerful magic she had felt since Lou had wielded the Webbing Armoury—since he had channelled all the power within him to destroy Ma'reygar, Auch'ray and Herimyre.

Now feeling his chest tighten, he couldn't help allowing her to see all the passion in his eyes. "Where?" he said. "Did you see *where* he went?"

Hildie gave a slight nod, and then a vague shake of her head. She sunk lower down on the stone ramparts, resting her weight over her arms. "No," she said. "He was travelling with a mule . . . on his way out of the city . . . on his way *out* of Ilsnare."

Lou felt all the enthusiasm leak from his body. His heart continued to beat rapidly before sinking down in his chest. What Hildie had described had served only to raise his hopes before bringing them back down to Earth with an almighty *thump.*

"Did you . . ." Lou said, staring down at his hands now, "I mean, had you seen him before, did you know who he was?"

There was a long pause and Lou shifted a sidelong glance at Hildie, hoping that he might be able to garner the truth even if she didn't wish to be forthcoming in dispensing it.

She remained impossibly still. And then said, "Yes." Another pause, and then, "Ems'plot." She shook her head, and then looked back at Lou, tears glittering in her eyes. "I'm sorry. If I'd known before—known what it was that you brought me here to do then I would've told you right away . . . I would have held him back. Stopped him from leaving."

But Lou, already, felt his mind getting away from him—setting once more into fantasies that, quite simply, could never . . . *would never* . . . come to pass.

It seemed as if the gods themselves conspired against him.

And why shouldn't they?

What *right* did Lou have to be King?

What right did Lou have to believe that *he* knew the right way forward for Shellacnass?

As he felt Hildie beside him, the gentle glow of her body, warmed by her fire magic, he was surprised to hear her speak to him again . . . cut through the heavy silence which lagged over them as if it was nothing at all.

"The boy," Hildie said, "he has a name, you know."

"Hmm," Lou said, turning to her, caught out by her sudden change of subject.

"Veerna."

With that, she straightened up and trudged back across the ramparts, apparently headed off to go and get a decent night's sleep.

After a long while—*an impossibly long while*—Lou imitated her.

The sting of his ice magic churning through his veins.
And frustration almost crushing him to dust.

EMS'PLOT

Syre could feel the clouds rolling in overhead.

The air was thick, and moist, and it pressed up against her skin.

From her time travelling, she knew that it would only be a matter of minutes before a downpour commenced. But, from the looks of it, this fact didn't seem to bother the elderly man, Ems'plot . . . the ice mage who had promised to show Syre the way.

And not only that.

He had promised to lead her into the darkness.

To aid her in understanding it.

That was all she wished for . . . all she had longed for through all these years.

And *finally* it seemed she had found her mentor.

On their first day out from the copse, she had surveyed the landscape, certain that she might see the Glyph appearing nearby . . . that it would crop up at any given moment.

But she had seen no sign of its slick-skinned, grey form.

Those floppy, rabbit-like ears.

The large, round eyes.

Already, despite knowing that she had had no choice, that she had had to follow her destiny, she felt great regret at not having at least waited for the Glyph to return to the camp. She felt as if she had deserted it. Then again, she supposed a magical being with powers such as it possessed, wouldn't find itself in too much trouble on the plains which surrounded Ilsnare.

The very worst it might find itself embroiled with was the bug-eyed surprise of field hands, or of merchants, shifting from one village to the next; perhaps on their way to Ilsnare and the Crystal Causeway where they hoped to flog their goods.

She eyed Ems'plot, took in his ragged traveller's cloak, and observed his bedraggled mule lugging along the saddlebags.

She felt a slight pang in her heart to take stock of the mule. She had always had an affection for horses . . . anything with four legs, really . . . and she couldn't help but think to herself that the mule was deserving of a rest; that it had surely done enough work for one day.

However, when she turned to Ems'plot, the thought soon vanished from her mind.

Ems'plot tilted his head back.

Observing the sky.

Perhaps now he would bring their advance to a halt.

Perhaps now he would allow them to rest.

However, when Ems'plot brought his chin back down to his chest, when he gazed about himself, he looked to Syre—gave her a slight smile—and then stared off at the horizon.

From the position of the sinking sun, she could tell that he was looking off toward the east. The pose which Ems'plot struck made her feel almost as if he was sniffing something on the wind. It reminded her of how a deer might look, turning its concentration to smelling danger which lurked in the shadows, nearby. Did danger await them?

"This way," Ems'plot muttered, beneath his breath.

He hadn't spoken into her mind since the day he had invited her along with him. She had got used to him speaking aloud . . . in fact, the only reminder that she could sense from Ems'plot that he was a magical being at all was the gentle, low-level *thrum* of his ice magic. Even she, as raw as she was in her magical education, could sense the brute force—the *strength*—of the magic which pumped through his veins.

They staggered on like that until nightfall, when Ems'plot tilted his head back and sniffed at the air once more. When he turned back to Syre, she could see he had deep, black bags dragging down from each of his eyes. He was surely weary.

In need of rest.

But it seemed that some external urge tugged him on.

Wouldn't allow him to ease off the pace.

In the end, Syre decided that she couldn't stay silent any longer, and she spoke up.

"Excuse me, Ems—"

Acting swiftly, Ems'plot arched his body around, his finger extended, seemingly lined up with brutal accuracy at the very tip of her nose. "*Master*! You must call me *Master*!"

Syre felt her chest tighten.

She felt the prickle of her ice magic beneath the surface of her skin.

"Master," she said, a touch begrudgingly. "*Where* are we going?"

Ems'plot's finger remained outstretched for several more seconds, pointed at her, but his nose seemed to distract him. He shifted his gaze all about the landscape, again turning off to the east.

Beneath his breath, he muttered—*seemingly to himself*, "Faster . . . moving *faster* . . . faster than I thought."

"*Who*?" Syre got out.

Ems'plot mumbled something else, something which she couldn't distinguish. Finally, Ems'plot looked her in the eye and a thin-lipped smile made his mouth crooked. "Nearby," he said, "I believe there's a village—is that so?"

Syre examined her surroundings.

As far as she could remember, she hadn't been here before ever in her life.

She began to shake her head, and to part her lips to reply, but Ems'plot moved quickly, shunting that same finger he'd used to point at her to press her mouth closed.

"No," he said, "I don't *care* about Mortal memories . . . I want you to sense their souls . . . I want you to *hear* their movements . . . their day-to-day complaints; their *mundane* utterings they believe no one else can hear."

Syre couldn't find the strength to change the route of her thoughts while Ems'plot held his finger to her lips, and so she waited until he finally broke off contact.

Then she closed her eyes.

And turned her concentration to doing what Ems'plot instructed.

She reached out.

With her mind.

At first, she felt nothing but stillness—the calm, empty wastelands.

Plains . . . as far as the eye could see . . . still not sown with crops, or grazed by animals, the people of the surrounding villages still superstitious about the curse which'd plagued Ilsnare before re-turning . . . returning to claim anything they might attempt to grow . . . to turn any animals they left out in the mists into *cursed* beasts.

She felt the swaying grasses, caught by the gentle breeze, and she felt almost as if the grass took root within her mind; as if she herself might be sinking deeper into the earth beneath the soles of her boots.

"No—*no!*" Ems'plot said, his tone scolding. "Not *down!*"

Syre flinched a little at the reprimand, but then she reminded herself that she was here to learn. That she was *supposed* to be paying attention to Ems'plot's instructions.

She did as he told her.

Moved her focus.

Shifted it upward.

And *across* . . .

Her mind skipped over the land with as much ease as a flat-bottom pebble might have skimmed over the surface of a still lake. She felt the ripples that each of her thoughts made, as she exerted her effort . . . as if her thoughts themselves were leaving a trail that she might be able to follow.

In the distance, almost to the periphery of her consciousness, she heard Ems'plot's voice.

"Yes," he said, "*yes* . . ."

She continued her exploration.

Over the land.

Faster now.

Much faster.

Finally she saw the village coming into view.

Surrounded by a rudimentary stone wall.

A tiny temple at the centre.

No more than a dozen houses.

Everything still.

No sign of so much as a soul.

It was then she felt the presence—*something unflinching . . . almost* impossibly *strong.* She tried to resist at first . . . but it was almost as if she was attempting to wade upstream in a gushing river . . . she was knocked back time and again till she simply no longer had the strength to keep on going.

To continue her resistance.

With biting fatigue setting in, she felt her thoughts—*her mind's eye*—being wrestled away from the overview of the village . . . from the structure of the place . . . her thoughts—*her perspective*—was wheeled around . . . around to the other side of the village.

Buildings with arched roofs.

A paddock marked with another stone wall.

Horses standing.

Tied up.

Their hides rippling with their shudders.

Stables.

All of a sudden, she caught a copper taste in her mouth.

The taste of *blood* . . .

She fought back again . . . against the control of her thoughts . . . the invisible hand guiding her mind's eye . . . and then, all at once, she was free.

She opened her eyes.

Saw once again.

The golden sunset.

Sunrays splashing all around.

Warming her skin.

Making her blood prickle through her veins.

She reached up to her lips on instinct, felt with her fingers.

Damp. It was damp.

When she brought her hand down she saw that her fingertips were laced with crimson blood. That, during this exercise, while she had reached out with her mind, she had sunk her teeth into her lower lip. She turned to Ems'plot, as if seeking explanation, but—*already*—he had set off at a fair pace; striding across the plains, his shuffling stride.

Apparently convinced of their destination.

His mule, too, plodded along.

Syre remained standing there for several moments, and then turned around, sure that somebody had been watching her from the shadows. *Sure* that somebody had brought her back from her thoughts. However, when she turned back to follow Ems'plot, she reached the conclusion that only one person had broken free of the hold which Ems'plot had exerted over her mind . . . and that was *herself.* She could control. If she wished. And with control would come great power.

. . . Or so she hoped.

MORNING MATTERS

Lou made a point of asking after Veerna, of having him personally assigned to him as his manservant. Although Lou noted the scepticism in the housekeeper's face when he requested this of her, he also saw that she would not presume as to second guess the King.

Sometimes Lou found himself getting all too swept up in the unquestionable power which accompanied his role as the King of Shellacnass.

Nobody would question him if they could get away with it.

It was the first time he had had a manservant since Guilknot . . . since Guilknot had been brutally murdered by the scoundrel Sheilds . . . the one who his sister Syre had eventually crushed with the aid of her black magic . . . the act which had told Lou that he could no longer permit her to remain in Ilsnare . . . not for the time being.

Not while she could not control.

There was only room for one loose cannon about town, and, as the King of Shellacnass, Lou could hardly desert his people. And, after all, he was the one who absolutely *had* to be here if his plans for unifying the Magical Fields were to have any chance of coming to pass.

If there was to be any chance of *peace* coming to pass.

When Veerna was delivered to him on his first day of service, Lou couldn't help but notice the boy's new clothes . . . how he had been granted a wispy-grey set of robes; the colour favoured by the Royal House of Ilsnare, and the one which everybody from the House Staff to the Royal Guards wore. He had been given a good clean, too. Whereas Veerna's teeth had been almost green before, they were now shone up to a sparkling white.

Lou knew, from experience, from when he had had housekeepers attempt to change *his* appearance, that this whiteness was achieved from a rare root . . . one which grew over in the foothills of the Sable Mountains; and one which was brought to Ilsnare, at great expense, so that the wealthy—or those who *served* the wealthy—might have clean, white teeth.

Veerna's breath smelled lightly of mint.

Not an unpleasant odour.

Since it appeared that the House Staff hadn't given Veerna instruction beyond having to present himself at the Throne Room, for the King, Lou had him cart an armload of the piled-up tomes off to the Library. All the books which Lou had read through and made use of.

He gave Veerna instructions on which books he should bring to the Throne Room.

Veerna, with a slight smile, acquiesced.

Lou *had* been counting on getting in a little sleep before going about the day's business, but, as often happened around mid-morning, he found his doze interrupted by a sharp series of knocks on the oak Throne Room doors. Although he was sure that other Kings of Shellacnass—kings *far* better suited to the role than he—would have ignored such interruptions, he couldn't help but ask for the knocker to enter. He supposed that it was something of the pleasant—*polite*—country bumpkin which continued to inhabit his soul.

Perhaps another decade or so of service to the Kingdom of Shellacnass might cure him of that particular affliction . . .

In the doorway, Lou made out Leona—the former Speaker of the Council of Wisemen. The one who now occupied the role which Flucknor had chosen to desert when he had fled Ilsnare Palace.

His High Representative.

Formerly, the High Representative, as Lou had envisioned it, would serve as a sort of go-between for the King and the Council of Wisemen . . . almost a *negotiator* . . . a person who was supposed to act the *disinterested* party in any dispute which might crop up.

However, since Lou had made it so that the King was responsible for appointing the High Representative, he would be first to admit that the *neutrality* of the High Representative could be very easily called into question. And since there was no longer a Council of Wisemen—for reasons which were also inextricably tied into the King of Shellacnass—the role of High Representative could, understandably, have been believed to be a redundant one.

But Lou had other matters in mind.

He was all too aware that with his sister Syre in exile if anything was to happen to Lou then it would plunge the Kingdom into chaos. He needed a proxy . . . and Leona filled that role to perfection. She had become his closest aide in the city. And, what was more, she had seen Lou up close—she knew what he was capable of . . . that he had chosen to save her above all other members of the Council of Wisemen.

That—if it hadn't been for Lou—she would have been roasted in the fire at the Great Hall with the others.

He took in her eyes; a rich blue colour. He absorbed her grey hair.

She wore the emerald-green robes of the High Representative, the ones which Flucknor before her had worn, and which matched the marble floors of the Throne Room; as Lou had thought to himself when he'd made the decision at the time, a means of subtly establishing the High Representative's special relationship with the King.

She bowed and then took several steps forward.

Today she wore a slight smile.

Lou could still recall when she had been a nervous wreck.

When she had been unable to so much as look him in the eye.

And although Lou could tell that she feared him still, he also realised the power which she held over him. That if anything *did* happen to Lou then she would be the *de facto* ruler of Ilsnare . . . for so long as all the matters and complications could be worked out.

"Good morning, Your Highness," Leona said, greeting him.

Lou nodded in recognition.

Down at her side, as she always seemed to, Leona gripped a scroll tightly. Whenever she spoke with him, she would often bring the scroll up and consult it, as if she needed to give her mind a nudge to recall some fact or other. In reality, though, Lou knew that Leona was an expert on all matters which pertained to the Crystal Kingdom.

She had no need to consult with her scroll.

The only reason she did so was as an excuse to break away from his gaze.

This morning, though, she continued to hold the scroll down at her side, apparently not requiring its use as a prop. "The Royal Guards are awaiting you, sire."

Lou cocked his head to one side. He could feel the gentle fatigue of sleep tugging at his mind, and he would've liked nothing more than to slip off his throne and go lie in bed for a couple of hours. He would sleep with the sunshine. He could walk with weakness later.

" 'Awaiting me' ?" Lou replied.

"Yes, they wish for your inspection."

"An 'inspection' ?" Lou said, realising that he was again echoing Leona's words.

Leona nodded. "You said yesterday you wished to see the forces with which Ilsnare has to defend itself."

Lou held himself very still for several moments and then it returned to him.

He *had* said that . . . and yet, he had completely forgotten about it.

He blinked several times, hoping that he might be able to clear the daze which'd clearly settled down over his mind. He did feel as if things were somewhat *clouded* today . . . and he wondered if it was anything other than his own perception.

He gave a flap of his hand, an almost-wave, and Leona took this as her cue to slip out.

For the longest time, Lou sat upright on his throne, elbow set on the armrest, his fist crutched beneath his chin.

Was he beginning to lose his mind?

A ROYAL INSPECTION

Lou felt his heart thudding in his throat as he ascended the several stone staircases up into the Royal Garrison. When Lou had ventured down to the stables and ordered a horse to be saddled for him, Leona had once more appeared out of the woodwork and informed him that the Royal Inspection was to take place in the Palace itself.

In accordance with his instructions.

Again, he had felt that frail, flapping feeling—that sensation of his stomach sinking, as if he might be about to fall down from a great height.

That *was* what he had ordered.

Lou quickly re-centred himself, bringing his mind back under control, and he had duly followed Leona to the Royal Garrison. He panted his way up to the top step now, wondering how he had ever allowed himself to get *this* out of shape . . . and yet he was so skinny.

He supposed that his muscles had all atrophied.

Sure enough, as Leona had informed him, the Royal guards all stood spread out in neat rows.

Still recovering from the breath which'd quickly departed his lungs, Lou surveyed the ranks, counting them out; column by column.

Thirty to each column.

A hundred columns.

Three thousand men at his disposal.

Lou gripped the stone ramparts tighter in his fist, and watched on as the sun emerged from behind one of the thick clouds which'd been hanging over the city for days.

In a single, *dramatic* moment, sunlight poured out through the gap and sent the spears and swords of the Royal Guards glimmering. The reflection was so painful to Lou's eyes that he had to hold up his forearm to shield himself from the glare.

He felt his ice magic bubble through his veins.

Itch at his skin.

Wishing to escape.

And, for the first time in *years*, he felt as if he might not be strong enough to control it.

That he might fail to keep his magic *within.*

He bowed his head.

Staggered against the sure, stone rampart, but managed to keep his balance.

"Sire? Sire?" Lou heard Leona saying from beside him.

Lou felt the sweat oozing out of his brow, and rolling down the side of his face.

It formed thick, ice-cool droplets.

He felt each one of them trickle down his cheeks, hang on his chin for moments, and then drop down . . . *splashing* on stone.

When he felt Leona's hand on his shoulder, attempting to steady him, he shrugged it off.

She immediately let go.

Lou straightened up, using the stone rampart to steady his dizzy mind, and then cast a glance at Leona. Even from her expression alone, how she eyed him closely, lips tightly pressed together, he knew that she had *felt* it . . . that she had felt the strength of the magic which dwelled within him; and she had realised that it was threatening to emerge.

And that—when it *did* emerge—it would destroy him.

Did she understand his secret?

If she did, she said nothing aloud.

"I . . ." Lou managed to utter, ". . . need *rest* . . ."

It was all he could do to drag himself away from the ramparts, away from the Royal Guards all spread out down below. As he turned his back on them all, he couldn't quite shake the feeling that each and every one of the Guards—*his Guards*—were lining up their bows and crossbows so that they would shoot him between the shoulder blades.

Pierce his heart.

The fear only faded—but didn't disappear—when he had found the reassuring shadow of the corridor, of the stairs which led back down to the Palace.

And to the Throne Room.

As he trudged across the stone floor, he couldn't help but feel like he was a weary warrior, having escaped from a battle his army was certain to lose.

He had saved himself for another day, but how many more battles might his body be able to resist? How many more before he buckled at the knees again and failed to rise up?

And, more to the point, could anyone else see his weakness?

. . . That defeat was only around the corner . . .

PAIR OF TRAITORS

F lucknor felt as if a spider's web wrapped itself about his body.

And that *each strand* of the web was a searing hot thread.

Slicing into his skin.

As if its intention was to cut him right down to the bone.

He could see nothing for the tears which bleared his eyes.

They ran down from his eyes no matter what he tried.

He couldn't suppress them.

He had *given up* trying to suppress them.

It was only when Flucknor sensed a presence lingering over him, only when he sensed that Horrox from before—the one who had self identified as Arfklan, 'King of the Horrox'—that he felt the pain wane slightly. Just enough so that Flucknor's mind was no longer so consumed by pain that he couldn't tilt his head upward. Up to see the scabbed, rash-red skin . . . and breathe in the stinking, rotten-fish smell which seemed to smother all Horrox.

Arfklan spoke into Flucknor's mind:

— *You have been most giving. With your thoughts. Your brain has offered us* untold *delights. Before we were walking in the darkness, truly blind, but now we can see . . . and—my!—what a wondrous sight it truly is.*

Flucknor had no idea what to make of the words which tumbled about his brain. As he had lain on the ground—as he *still* did—as he had felt the soaking-wet mud press up against his body, and the night-time rains pound down on him as he'd been left among the long grasses, imprisoned in his own gaol of pain, he had felt as if invisible fingers had prodded and poked at his mind . . . going into places which even Flucknor himself couldn't have identified . . .

Arfklan went on:

— *Through your brain we can see the innermost thoughts of your King, of Louson Dorf, your own mind presents us with a gateway to his plans. All of those* logical *ideas linked by a delicate chain.*

Arfklan cocked his head to one side as if he expected some sort of a response from Flucknor—Flucknor, though, could not raise so much as a *modicum* of an idea which might suggest what Arfklan was getting at.

Arfklan, apparently sensing this, continued:

— *He wishes to take up the magical artefacts, is it not so? He believes that he can vanquish us, the Horrox, just as he vanquished those mages from before . . .*

This time Flucknor did manage to raise a reply, but not within his own mind.

He couldn't summon the strength to so much as imagine the words within his mind's eye.

Instead, they tumbled on out from between his lips.

"He *will*! He *will*! . . . You don't understand . . . his power . . . his *ruthlessness* . . . he will destroy . . . destroy . . . *everything*!"

Flucknor had hardly uttered the final word when he felt the intense pain return to rack his body. He felt himself writhe all over the ground, his body convulsing in each and every direction. Several times, he tasted blood in his mouth . . . and then, strangely, in his nostrils.

He breathed in the thick stench of *ash* . . . of *cinders*.

It choked him.

Arfklan spoke into his mind again:

— *I have learned so much from you, Flucknor. That you have ice magic running through your veins.* Throbbing *through your veins. It makes me wonder, gives me pause for thought, whether or not you ever learned to harness that power of yours. What does it serve us to keep you alive now, to keep you from death, when you might rise up and attack us once you have regained your strength?*

This time Flucknor did manage to pool enough strength to reply to the Horrox, to these threats, within his own mind:

— *Because . . . because . . . I don't stand beside Louson . . . I . . . escaped* him!

It seemed as if Flucknor had to use every remaining scrap of energy in his body to jerk his head around, to search for Brotsboore. But he couldn't see him.

He had believed that Brotsboore might be lying on his side, like Flucknor, balled up in agony from the button-like object Arfklan used to inflict pain.

But he was nowhere in sight.

Flucknor turned his attention back upward, to Arfklan, standing over him.

He spoke into his mind once more:

— *Please. I can help you. I can help you with the invasion. Help you to Ilsnare. You can still make use of me; I promise.*

Flucknor lay still on the ground, continuing to feel the pain dance over the surface of his skin. The feel of the razor-sharp, spidery legs. He expected the pain to continue at any second. He gritted his teeth, tasting enamel, and wondered when it would return.

It *would* return.

He was certain . . . and yet, it stayed away for longer and longer . . . and the memory of the pain became more and more distant. Thrown more and more into the shadows of recollection.

Finally, he heard Arfklan's words in his mind:

— *Stand up, Flucknor. It's undignified for any being to die while lying down.*

RECOVERY

Lou **stared up** into the darkness above.

His whole body was itching with ice magic.

More than anything, he wanted to stand up; to escape the stifling-hot, arid air of the Throne Room where he lay . . . but he couldn't summon the strength. It wasn't like before; it wasn't for lack of physical strength . . . it was because his mind wouldn't cut him free.

It seemed to be fatigued.

Too tired to deal with his body any longer.

In the darkness, he was certain he could make out an odour, something which wafted up his nose. The odour reminded him of grass . . . of breathing in a field of long grasses in some distant place . . . somewhere far—*far*—from Ilsnare.

He turned over, feeling his undershirt sticking to his sweaty body.

His heart hammered in his throat.

And his mind felt as if it might be coming unstitched.

He managed to prop himself up onto his elbow and to peer out into the gloom, his curiosity now overpowering the sense of fatigue which racked his body and mind.

He breathed in more deeply . . . and then he better recognised the odour.

Elderberries.

He recalled them from the Sable Mountains.

When he had gone to meet with his master—with *Auch'ray* . . .

There was so much beauty which the thought of the Sable Mountains brought to Lou's mind, and, at the same time, there was a huge deal of sadness—sadness because Lou knew that he would never again see those things; that, as King of Shellacnass, he would never be allowed to ever go anywhere again unaccompanied. He was no longer an individual. He was a figurehead.

A *symbol* . . . for an entire people.

How had this happened?

If—back in the fields, in the Northern Villages—someone had offered him the role of King of Shellacnass would Lou have accepted?

. . . If they had told Lou what he knew now?

That the price of becoming royalty was one's own personality . . .

Then again, he supposed he had never really *had* a personality back when he'd been a field hand. Things had been so simple . . . he had been almost an extension of the elements when he had worked the land; an extension of the *soil* . . . now, though, he was an extension of Mortals; and, as he often thought of it, one more step removed from nature.

Lou breathed in deeply, summoning yet more strength into his blood, into his muscles.

After all the exertion, Lou finally managed to sit himself on the edge of the mattress, and to gaze out across the Throne Room. He could see the stars blinking down through the glass rooftop, and the sallow *sheen* of the moon dribbling in. For some reason, as hypnotically as he might've been drawn to sunlight after weeks of overcast, thundering skies, he lifted himself up off the mattress and trudged toward the emerald floor of the Throne Room, where the light pooled.

As he walked toward the spot, the scent of elderberries grew sharper still.

Almost irresistible.

He felt as if he had only to open his mouth and his tongue would come alive with flavour. As he stepped closer to the moonlight, he allowed his eyelids to droop shut so they were nothing more than slits.

He lost himself in the odour.

Felt it lapping against the inside of his mouth.

Finally, around him, he sensed movement. He thought that he cottoned onto the soul which shared this space with him. "... Veerna?" Lou got out, his throat dry and his tone wavering . . . surely unbefitting of the King of Shellacnass.

There was a long silence which opened out from the darkness like a yawning mouth, and Lou felt a slight flash of temper pass through him, to think of the boy's previous attempts to skulk about in the shadows of the Throne Room in the afterhours.

But, before he could say anything at all, there was a reply.

"No, it's Hildie."

All at once Lou felt his body seize tight.

His muscles burned and then froze . . . his ice magic working to protect him.

To keep him from danger.

Or was it only acting to protect itself?

. . . If the magic made a point of protecting its conduit then—*in turn*—it protected itself too.

Would he never be shot of his magic until the day he died?

NIGHT-TIME IN THE THRONE ROOM

L ou opened his eyes, although he had no need to do so.

He could see just as easily with them shut.

He could *sense* his surroundings just as easily . . .

For some reason, though, Hildie had remained veiled to him, he hadn't been able to tell who it was until she had said her name out loud to him. It caused him consternation for a great many moments; he wondered what it might mean. If Hildie had used some sort of an enchantment to protect herself from his knowledge. Or if Lou's magic was merely weak . . . *worn out* . . .

The other alternative, that Hildie's powers were far greater than he had anticipated, he quickly discarded . . . because, even if that was so, by the time Sully and Rut returned to Ilsnare with the pieces of keystone to open the Webbing Armoury, that would only be a matter of semantics.

Nothing could face up—let alone *destroy*—the Spider Warrior.

"Tea?" Hildie said, emerging from the darkness, and into the moonlight where he stood.

Although Lou saw that she did her best to hide it, he noted the slight flinch when the moonlight touched her skin. Just as with his ice magic and the sun; she suffered the same from the combination of her fire magic and the moon.

But she was no stranger to 'walking with weakness'.

He turned his attention downward, to the cup of tea which she enveloped in her hands. He saw how the steam rose up off the surface. And, once more, he breathed in the thick scent of elderberries. Without another word, he took the mug from her and felt the warmth from the cup passing through his fingertips. As he sipped at the delicious, refreshing concoction within, he eyed her over the rim of the mug.

Tonight, she wore a flame-red gown to match her hair, and a grass-green tunic underneath which matched her eyes. Then he noticed something which he hadn't seen before.

A golden chain about her throat.

A pendant—*glass*?—dangled at the end of it.

When the moonlight met with the glass, Lou noted the slight sparkle embedded within.

Somehow, it made him think of the night sky stretched out above them.

If it was filled with *golden* stars.

He continued to stare at the pendant several moments before switching his attention back onto Hildie. It was a good thing that she spoke to him, because he wasn't certain he could raise the strength to make his own voice heard.

"I see that you've been putting together a garrison," Hildie said.

Lou was taken off guard by the question. Throughout her stay in Ilsnare, Lou had made a point of keeping Hildie at an arm's length when concerned with the *real* matters which were going on. Then again, perhaps he had been a fool to underestimate the daughter of Ma'reygar—the most fearsome mage of their times . . . Louson Dorf aside, of course.

Lou nodded in reply and then sipped at his tea. He glanced into the layers of darkness, and to the pile of books which leaned up against the wall. He had left them out there—*exposed*—for Veerna to return to the Library. He shifted his attention back onto Hildie.

"There's a war coming, then?" she replied, meeting his eye.

Again, he nodded.

He knocked back the rest of the contents of the mug, and then handed it to her, as if she was nothing more than a servant. She took it from him with no complaint, though. He half expected her to shift off into the darkness, to slip on out through the doors of the Throne Room.

To leave him in peace.

But she hung around.

Spoke to him again.

"You've been avoiding me," she said, "haven't you?"

Lou allowed these words to stir through his mind, and then he gazed upward once more, through the glass rooftop of the Throne Room. To the stars beyond.

This time, he did manage to find his voice.

"I avoid *everyone*," he said.

"Well, that makes me feel *quite* common."

Lou turned his attention back to Hildie, to those glittering green eyes of hers.

And he managed to raise something resembling a smile.

Her expression, though, continued to resemble stone.

She grasped the emptied mug tight in her grip.

"What're you *doing*, Lou?" she said. "Why'd you bring me back here? Why'd you have Rut go all that way to track me down?"

Lou continued to stare back at her . . . he felt as if he should tell the truth—if he was going to tell *anyone* the truth then surely he should tell it to her . . . and yet, he felt to do so would be to betray himself in some way . . . he couldn't simply *say out loud* that which'd plagued his mind for so long.

And that which was, now, most likely impossible.

Seizing the perfect excuse, he nodded to Hildie's necklace. "Where did you get that?" he asked. "From one of the stalls on the Crystal Causeway?"

Hildie reached up to the glass pendant, wrapped her fingers protectively about it as if Lou might be able to snap it off its golden chain and have it float through the air into his own fist. Even in the darkness of the Throne Room—even with only the aid of the moonlight—Lou could tell that her cheeks flushed ever so slightly.

"It's . . . nothing," she replied, and then, apparently realising what a vague—*floaty*—response this was, she continued, "Some stupid little trinket I picked up on my travels."

Lou pouted a moment, and then shifted his attention back to the books piled up against the wall of the Throne Room. What could he lose by telling her? The plan wasn't even *feasible* any longer . . .

As he looked to Hildie, feeling his heart swelling in his throat, ready to betray his secret for the first time, he became aware of the skittering sound of approaching footsteps echoing all about the corridors outside the Throne Room.

He turned to the doors and saw Flucknor standing there . . . staring right back at him.

Already, even before Lou could properly process the image, he knew there was something wrong, that this couldn't be . . . that he *couldn't* be seeing Flucknor . . . not like *this . . . as a boy.*

It took him another few seconds to note the obvious differences; that the boy had mousy-brown hair while Flucknor's hair was blond . . . and that this boy—again, unlike Flucknor—had skin which was a deep-bronze complexion.

Veerna.

When Veerna spoke to him, his voice was hurried, and it skipped about.

But Lou got the message.

That he was to go to the ramparts at once.

PILFERED BEASTS

S yre felt as if her entire body was on the brink of being racked with a cold. Her sinuses felt blocked and she could feel her heart thrumming against her ribs, as if it wished to depart her body before the sickness set in.

The night had closed in long ago, and the only light present came from the moon shining up above. The crickets and endless—*perhaps nameless*—other bugs croaked and chirped out from the long grasses which surrounded the road.

Something about the whole situation reminded Syre of when she had been a young girl . . . but, then again, she supposed that she had spent so much of her childhood among nature—*so much time on the move*—that those sounds had become almost like a bedtime lullaby.

One which her parents might've sung to her before their deaths.

On the back of the horse that she'd stolen from the nearby village—the one she had sensed from a long way away with Ems'plot's assistance—she swayed from side to side, every muscle within her body seeming to ache with fatigue. They had walked a long way before reaching the village.

Before stealing in through the inadequate walls which surrounded it . . . and past the dozing sentry curled into a ball in some of the
long grasses, his spear comically clutched to his chest as if it had
been some sort of child's pacifier.

When Syre had reached the stables, she had followed the instructions which Ems'plot had delivered directly into her mind. He had
remained well back from the village, fobbing her off with the excuse that his 'old body' would be no good at running away—if that
was what the situation came to. Meanwhile, she had gone about
saddling the pair of horses, taken several of the feeding bags, and
then she had led the two of them out through the sleeping village
and away into the night. When she'd returned to where Ems'plot
awaited her—an unsuspecting copse to the periphery of the village—he had only had a small barrel of ale to offer her by way of
sustenance . . . but she had been so hungry and so *thirsty* that she
had been unable to resist drinking.

Almost immediately, she had felt the entire world sway about her.

She had never had a head for spirits . . . and, to be quite honest,
had never quite seen the point of them. All those who enjoyed consuming ale—*brandy wine*—more often than not ended up in some
drunken stupor; puking their guts out in some back alley.

Syre turned in the saddle now, even though she felt as if a giddy
spell might strike her at any second, and send her tumbling to the
ground.

She looked to Ems'plot, mounted on the other horse which she
had stolen, and leading that long-suffering mule of his along on a
rope behind him.

When Ems'plot caught her eye, he smirked.

She turned back around, already feeling—*knowing*—that this
had been a great mistake. That she should've stayed with the

Glyph . . . that she should've shrugged off Ems'plot when she had believed him only to be an elderly hobblesman. But that was all very well in retrospect.

Had there even been a choice?

Wouldn't he simply have taken her by force if she hadn't chosen to go with him?

In any case, there was *very little* she could do about it now.

Syre could tell, from the position of the sunsets and sunrises, that they were headed from west to east. When she had broached the question of just where they were going—had directly asked Ems'plot just exactly *where* they were going—he had done his best to silence her with claims that they were going someplace which would *infinitely* strengthen her powers.

To say that Syre was unconvinced as to the veracity of these claims would have been an overstatement, and, already, she found herself constantly looking around, hoping that she might be able to catch sight of the Glyph somewhere . . . perhaps skulking about in the shadows, a matter of footsteps away . . . or else up ahead of them; anticipating their every move.

But, the more she thought of the Glyph, the more she was convinced it would've seen she had gone and begun the melancholy trek back to the Winter's Moan . . . headed on its way back home.

Just the thought of *that* image sent an unimagined sadness jangling through her.

A sadness which was only cut off by Ems'plot's chiding remark.

"My dear," Ems'plot said, from the horse he plodded on along behind her. "You should really put such silliness as Magical *Creatures* out of your mind."

Syre felt a shudder pass through her.

She often forgot that Ems'plot could read every thought which passed through her mind.

She couldn't help noticing that—of the powers which Ems'plot had taught her so far—he had given mind-reading a decidedly wide berth.

How else would he hold his advantage over her?

"Ah," Ems'plot said, not much more than a croak from the back of his throat, "yes, *mind-reading* . . . a very useful skill, and, please do not be worried, one which we shall certainly get around to dealing with . . . but everything in its own time, my dear. Patience, as they say, is a *virtue.*"

Despite her tiredness, despite feeling she wanted nothing else but to leap off the horse and curl herself up in the long grasses at the side of the road, she managed to get out a reply to him.

"When?" she asked.

"Everything in its own time."

Here, while she continued to eye him, she noticed him tilt his head back and sniff at the air. He jerked his head forcefully back behind them, and then off in a perpendicular direction.

The smirk which he'd worn previously straightened out.

He kicked his back leg out and over the saddle of his horse, and then, with another neat flourish which again belied his elderly appearance, he hopped down to the ground, taking the reins of his horse and that of his mule in his fists. "Come. Get down—*off* your horse!"

Syre thought long and hard about squeezing her horse with her heels—about doing her best to kick on along the road and away from Ems'plot. She was certain, all things being equal, that she would be able to outrun him on horseback. She had made sure that she had picked out two horses of similar stature from the stables in the village, already—*no doubt*—subconsciously believing that if it came down to a race her horse-riding ability would win out.

But that was just it.

It wouldn't be a simple matter of horse-riding ability which would decide the success, or failure, of her escape. Ems'plot—if he so wished—could surely stop her heart beating with the merest twitch of a fingertip. She expected another of Ems'plot's quips, but he remained preoccupied.

When Ems'plot did speak to her, it was with a snap to his voice. "Come on! *Off* that horse!"

Acting out with some sort of adolescent disobedience, she took her time in getting down. When she was finally on the ground, with the reins bunched into her fist, she followed Ems'plot over to the few trees growing out of the side of the road.

Ems'plot remained fixed, staring on through the trunks, at some aspect in the distance which Syre—*apparently*—had no chance of seeing.

"What's happening?" she asked, intentionally failing to keep her voice to a whisper . . . let alone speaking into Ems'plot's mind, as he surely would've preferred.

The annoyed expression on Ems'plot's face was obvious, even in profile, but he kept his frustration out of his voice. He calmly turned back to her, away from whatever it was that'd caught his attention. Then he gave her a slight smile—that *ever-present* smirk making a return.

"Tonight we bed down here, my dear."

DISTANT LIGHTS

Lou felt the warm winds blowing about the ramparts.

They sent a shiver down his neck, and caused the hair to rise up on the backs of his arms.

A tingle passed through his veins; the most subtle of protests from his ice magic.

That *tiny* warning of danger on the horizon.

But his ice magic didn't speak of any physical—*Earthly*—danger, but that of the sun which would be rising shortly.

Already, even without the thought consciously passing through his mind, Lou felt the profound quiver tickle the pit of his stomach to think of that day when he had gone to inspect the garrison . . . the day when the sunrays had struck him down. Some days he couldn't help but wonder if up there— *up in the heavens*—the gods might be looking down on him and laughing . . . that they might be intentionally attempting to have him destroyed.

That they wished to see him *suffer*.

That for the crime of aspiring to be a lesser god he was to be brought to a painful death.

But Lou only wondered that on the days when he believed in the gods at all.

Today, he wasn't sure.

He peered out over the ramparts, Veerna on one side, Hildie on the other. He could see the encampments, of course; or, more exactly, he could make out the glow of the campfires among their number. The fiery-red glow which crept its way up, pushing back the darkness.

He thought he could smell the ash on the breeze . . . but that might just have been because Hildie was standing in close proximity to him. Just the gentle warmth of her fire magic making its effects felt on his skin. As Lou looked out to the encampments—to the *Horrox* encampments—he spoke quickly, with great urgency, to Veerna beside him.

"You haven't told anyone else?" Lou said.

Out of the corner of his eye, Lou saw Veerna shake his head. "No, Your Majesty."

Lou felt a cool sensation drip through his bloodstream. "Good," he said, "that's good."

There was a lingering silence before Hildie broke through it.

"But they'll see at daybreak," she said. "The *garrison* will see."

"It's okay," Lou replied, "by then I will have spoken with Leona—I'll make sure that not one soldier crosses through the City Walls."

Another silence, and then, to Lou's surprise, Veerna spoke up.

"Your Majesty?" Veerna said.

"Hmm," Lou replied.

"Why don't you want to send the soldiers out there, to the encampments?"

Lou held himself still, the *fizz* of ice shifting through his body.

Up through his arms.

Down through his legs.

"Because that's what they want," Lou replied. "They're expecting us to send soldiers along there, to their encampments; that's why they made their camp right on the periphery of our vision, to tempt us into attacking them."

All the while, Lou was aware of Hildie's tight, uncontrolled movements.

Nothing more pronounced than the tucking of a strand of hair behind her ear, or a series of rapid blinks. But Lou noticed all the same.

He turned to her. "What?" he said. "What is it?"

She held herself still. She tried to ward Lou off with a smile, as if it was nothing at all.

But Lou wouldn't accept it.

Even if it was only to his own mind, Lou had been on the point of telling Hildie about the plan; about how he hoped to save the whole of the Kingdom without so much as a single *screech* of metal-on-metal, when the first scimitar was drawn from its sheath.

He continued to stare at her until she broke.

"It's just," Hildie said, her eyes twitching about the horizon, about the encampments, "I'm sure that I've seen this before—that I've seen something *like* this before."

Lou held her gaze even though it set a fire raging in his stomach.

He could hear Veerna's heavy breathing and realised that the boy was just as enraptured by whatever it was that Hildie had to say as Lou himself was.

Lou guessed that Veerna had truly set his mind on becoming a hero . . . or a *knight* . . . the realms of his imagination were the limit.

Hildie continued, "When I was in the tropics, where Rut came for me, there was a village, Nor'tarth, which was under siege by the Horrox."

Lou felt he was losing himself in her green eyes.

He made the conscious decision to draw himself back.

He couldn't allow himself to get sucked in again . . . not when there was so much at stake.

So many *lives* at stake . . . an entire *kingdom* at stake.

"The Horrox," Hildie went on, "they were all camped out just beyond the limits of the village. We thought . . ." she paused for such a long while that Lou thought he might have to prompt her to continue . . . "We thought that they were about to attack—that they were *preparing* an attack—and so we sent the town garrison after them . . ."

She trailed off before finishing.

Lou felt a tightness in his chest, knowing that the rest of the story would be somehow tragic, and yet he had to know. "And then?" he said.

Hildie turned into him, her eyes a touch dewy now. "The soldiers, they arrived there, and they killed every last Horrox in the camp . . . *every last one of them* . . . all but the one they kept alive, the leader—*Inta* was his name."

"What did they do to Inta?" Veerna said, again surprising Lou by his insistence of entering the conversation . . . perhaps his parents hadn't instilled in him enough of a sense of reverence—a sense of *fear*—for royalty.

"They brought him back," Hildie said, answering as if it'd been Lou to ask the question, "And they *executed* him in the middle of the town—before all the town's people." Hildie shook her head. "We heard the screams as we left the town behind—the citizens rejoicing in his blood being spilled." She looked Lou back in the eye once more. "It was a *massacre* . . . nothing less . . ."

Lou breathed in deeply, taking the air right down to the very bottom of his lungs. "Well," he said, "then I suppose we shouldn't mention that to the garrison here—it might give them ideas."

Hildie remained still for a long time.

Lou realised she was shaking slightly.

And that she'd gone a touch pale.

She tweaked her lips into an unconvincing smile. "If it's okay with you," she said, "then I think I might . . . uh . . ." Her eyes drifted off along the ramparts, and then, quite suddenly—at least *Lou* didn't expect it—she lost her balance and fell into his arms.

Lou reached out and caught hold of her.

He grasped her tightly.

Found himself staring down at her closed eyelids.

She was out cold . . . wrapped in sleep . . .

Thinking quickly, Lou turned to Veerna. "Fetch a servant," he said. "Ask them to bring something warm to drink, have the fire lit in her quarters."

With a nod, Veera skittered off along the ramparts, then disappeared from sight.

Lou turned his attention back to Hildie.

He looked down upon her, and realised, before hearing the words, that her lips were moving. He tilted his head down, bringing his ear so close to her mouth that he was certain he could feel the stirring embers of her fire magic.

". . . Lou," she said.

"Yes," Lou replied, a note of insistence in his voice, "I'm here."

He pressed his ear closer still, afraid that he might miss an important word.

"I'm . . . I'm . . ." she continued.

"You're what . . . ?" Lou said, his own voice at a husky whisper.

"I'm so afraid of you."

ON THE MARCH

Flucknor felt himself swaying from side to side on the back of the horse which'd been assigned to him. On a horse near-by, he could make out Brotsboore. Like himself, the Horrox hadn't bothered to shackle his wrists.

Flucknor moved his attention forward, to Arfklan—the leader of the Horrox.

As with the rest, Arfklan was mounted on a horse.

Flucknor was all too aware of Arfklan's clenched fist down at his side.

And, more to the point, the button-like object he held concealed within. The one which was painted a sky-blue, and yet which could transform—*in the blink of an eye*—into a pit-black shade.

He continued to feel those skittering pangs of pain dancing across his skin.

It was almost a ticklish sensation now.

And each time he found his mind cast back to the pain, he felt his heart leap in his chest.

As if his body was prepared to submit to the torture once again.

Unlike a Mortal procession, where the generals of the armies—and most certainly the *kings*—never would've made it past the belly of the column; Arfklan made a point of riding out in front of them all. Then again, this procession was hardly one fit for meeting another army in a battle. There were only about a dozen of them, if that . . .

Flucknor had woken with a start, early that morning.

He had found Arfklan, flanked by a pair of Horrox guards, standing over him.

Flucknor's first reaction had been to look to Arfklan's clenched fist, and to search for the button-like object he held. And Flucknor had stared for the longest time at the clenched fist, certain that at any given second the pain would start again.

But it had held off.

Nothing had happened.

Even when the Horrox had helped him to his feet, Flucknor had hardly been able to stand. His whole body was so worn out by the constant pain. He had been taken aback by the sudden tenderness, by how the two Horrox guards had taken care to help him find his balance, so that he wouldn't simply topple back over onto the ground. He couldn't help but wonder at the treatment which might've been meted out to Horrox at the hands of Mortals.

As the days had gone by, Flucknor couldn't help but wonder if he'd been born beneath the wrong sort of skin. Born into the wrong heart and bones.

Almost as if Flucknor had barked out his thoughts at the top of his voice, he noted Arfklan turn in his saddle and glance back. He gave a nod to one of the mounted Horrox guards at either side and then dropped away so that he rode alongside Flucknor.

"Mm," Arfklan said, his red skin caught up in the mid-morning sunrays. "An interesting proposition—being born into the *wrong* body." Flucknor observed Arfklan's eyes, surprised to find that they were just as inky-black in direct sunlight as they were by torches. "Would you like to know what has so stoked the ire of the Horrox?"

Flucknor turned to look to the front of their procession.

The dozen or so mounted Horrox.

He glanced briefly over to Brotsboore, caught his eye for a second.

He analysed him for a long moment . . . wondering if he might be trying to communicate some sort of warning to Flucknor. In the end, Flucknor decided—warning or no—it really didn't matter. If Arfklan and the rest of his Horrox underlings had taken it into their heads to have him put to death then there was very little he would be able to do about it.

Finally, Flucknor turned his attention back to Arfklan.

Flucknor managed to summon a dry-throated, "Why?"

Arfklan's face creased with a smile.

His inky black eyes turned back to examine the direction of their procession.

"To the south of here," Arfklan said, his voice sounding a touch whiny—*frail* almost when spoken out loud . . . when Arfklan spoke into Flucknor's mind it was another prospect entirely; like speaking with another Creature. "Near the tropics"—Arfklan brought up the claws of his hand to indicate the direction—"there is a town, Nor'tarth."

Flucknor wondered if he was supposed to draw something from this name.

But he caught onto nothing.

He shifted a glance in Brotsboore's direction, checking that he wasn't missing anything obvious. But Brotsboore was already staring out between the ears of his horse, to the landscape ahead.

"The Horrox there," Arfklan continued, "like so many of us, grew tired of living among the Mortals . . . living lives of *lies*"—Arfklan really *hissed* his *s's*—"and they took to encampments, surrounding the village."

Flucknor felt his heart slow to a gentle pulse.

Perhaps for the first time since he'd been captured by the Horrox.

He wondered if this was all some ploy . . . that Arfklan wanted Flucknor to relax totally so he might hit him with pain once again. However, when Flucknor looked to Arfklan, he noted the wrinkles which'd formed in his forehead . . . an expression which, at least to a cursory glance, seemed to be filled with concern.

Arfklan continued, "Now, my people, I shan't lie to you, they waged attacks outside the village, they wanted to make it known they were *there* . . . that they were *liberated* . . . but these attacks were never anything more than the death of some merchant; some wandering lamb from the fold."

Flucknor felt himself begin to shake at the thought that the Horrox might've had some similar device in order to wreak havoc on the 'wandering lambs' from Ilsnare.

Arfklan blinked a few times, and Flucknor wondered if he had been reading his mind.

But, if he had done, he continued with his story all the same, "One night, it was decided, by—I *believe*—a member of Louson Dorf's court that they should take care of the 'Horrox Problem' once and for all; that they should lay waste to the camps."

When Arfklan finished speaking, he stared off into the near distance, focussed on some point which Flucknor couldn't see for himself. Finally, feeling the warm wind blowing against his cheeks, Flucknor decided that he should prompt Arfklan to finish the story.

"And did they?" Flucknor replied.

Arfklan held himself still for several long moments, and then he gave a doleful nod.

They rode along the plains for another few minutes, neither of them saying anything at all. Flucknor wasn't quite certain what he was to gather from this story . . . of what it might mean for his and Arfklan's relationship. As if out of nowhere, out of the yawning silence, Arfklan brought his hand up from his thigh. He showed Flucknor the clutched fist. And Flucknor found himself staring at the clenched fingers, unable to stop the searing-hot sensation from swirling through him.

From *piercing* his skin.

It took him a second to realise that there *was* no pain . . . that Arfklan was holding out the sky-blue button-like object flat in his palm. "Take it," Arfklan said. "I *want* you to take it."

Flucknor stared long and hard at the object on Arfklan's palm, unable to quite believe what was happening. And then, deciding that he shouldn't take this opportunity for granted, he reached out and took the object.

It was smooth—just like the button it'd always appeared to him.

He allowed it to lie flat on his palm.

Afraid that doing anything else might set it off.

"Do you know what this is?" Arfklan said. "Do you know what its name is?"

Flucknor shook his head.

"It's an ancient device, forged by Horrox, long ago . . . our people have no written history—we exist only on oral legend . . . all that is really known of this object is its name."

"And what's that?" Flucknor said, lifting his gaze to Arfklan.

"The Plarstark."

Flucknor took a moment to allow the name to echo about the hollows of his skull.

"It's okay," Arfklan said, a slight smile peeling back his lips, "you can put it in your pocket. It needs *magic* to be activated . . . and pain can only be dispersed when you clutch it in your palm."

Flucknor continued to hold onto the Plarstark tightly, unsure just what he should do with it. Something within told him to simply toss it away, into the long grasses . . . so that it might not harm another soul. But what would that achieve?

Arfklan would, undoubtedly, send one of his guards to go and fetch the Plarstark.

And Flucknor would be back to where he started.

No, it was better for him to hold onto it for now.

Forever . . . if he could.

He turned back to Arfklan, feeling that—*somehow*—their relationship had thawed.

Still facing forward, Arfklan spoke to Flucknor. "Would you like to know the only reason why you're not dead?"

"Why?" Flucknor replied.

"Because you said you wanted to aid us in defeating Louson Dorf . . . that is the only reason."

Flucknor felt his whole body go rigid.

He clutched the Plarstark tightly in his fist.

That made him feel just a little better.

That Arfklan at least couldn't hurt him with it again . . . if what he said was the truth.

As Arfklan gave his horse a kick, as he headed back to the front of their group, Flucknor realised that he had to speak now . . . that if he wanted answers then he needed to ask them *now* . . . who knew how Arfklan would be feeling toward him in the morning?

"Where're we going?" Flucknor asked. "Why did we leave the encampments behind? The rest of the army behind?"

At first, Flucknor thought Arfklan hadn't heard him—or that he was feigning not to have heard. When Arfklan was near the front of their group, though, he turned back, a slight smile on his lips.

This time he *did* speak into Flucknor's mind:

— *One thing at a time, don't you think, Mortal?*

A SICKLY GUEST

As Lou stood in the corridor, outside Hildie's quarters, he couldn't recall a time when he had felt so tense—*so nervous.* And, more to the point, he couldn't quite understand *how* he had come to feel this way.

When he and Hildie had said goodbye, more than a decade ago now, he had believed that it would be the end; that they would never meet again. But Lou had had the Eye continue to file reports on her; even after she had disappeared off on her own journey. Why had he done that? Did he believe that he could keep her safe somehow . . . or that he could give himself peace of mind knowing that she was far away from the Crystal City?

Far away from his Crystal Kingdom.

. . . And then he had decided that he'd needed her.

He'd brought her back here.

And, whatever the details, she *had* returned.

Didn't that count for something?

Didn't that *show* she cared?

. . . If not for the cause—if not for Shellacnass—then . . . for what?

. . . For *him?*

Lou turned side-on several times to allow various members of the House Staff to sidle by, on their way to go in to see Hildie; to bring her all sorts of goodies: tea, buttery slices of cake, chicken broth, a leg or two of lamb . . . and, Lou couldn't help noticing, a flask of ale; though he did stop that particular member of the House Staff and ask after the efficacy of such an item. He had been told in no uncertain terms, though, that this was a thing of miracles.

And who was Lou to argue?

He knew next to nothing about remedies.

And even less about that which afflicted Hildie.

As he stood in the stone corridor, leaning up against the firm surface, he thought about what she had told him before she'd fainted . . . that she was *so afraid* of him.

Had she simply been delirious?

Or had that been the truth?

When the door to Hildie's quarters swung open, he caught a glimpse inside. He saw how the flames appeared to lurch up the walls. Even standing out here, in the corridor, he couldn't help but feel the radiant glow; almost a searing *sting* of the flames up against his skin. It was bringing his ice magic to the surface . . . suggesting that it might *thaw*.

But nothing would thaw his ice magic.

Nothing.

. . . Only death could do that.

For about an hour now—the hour that he'd been lurking in the corridor outside Hildie's quarters—he had been flirting with the idea of popping in to speak with her.

But the influx, and outflux, of House Staff was almost constant.

In the end, he wondered if he should just give up. He supposed that, by now, a decade into his rule, he should've twigged that there was no such thing as privacy in *his* palace. Finally, he spotted a gap in the constant flow of people moving in and out. He took his opportunity. He wedged himself in through the door as the latest member of the House Staff stole out of the room with a kettle grasped in her hand. When Lou stepped in over the threshold of Hildie's quarters, he felt a sudden flush rise up in his cheeks. His ice magic became almost unbearable. It graduated swiftly from a stinging sensation running all about his veins to being something more like a thousand razorblades being slowly slid beneath the surface of his skin.

His heart hammered in his throat.

He felt the flickering flames of the torches which hung off the walls—the *fire* which blazed away in the stove—as if they were scolding waves of lava . . . intent on burying him alive beneath their molten, impossibly hot weight.

Before advancing into her quarters, he casually reached back and shut the door; drawing the bolt so that only the most determined member of the House Staff would be able to pass through.

He turned to take in Hildie.

Of course, she was tucked into the four-poster bed, the sheets drawn up to her chin.

At first, Lou was certain she was asleep. It was only after he'd taken several steps toward her that he realised her eyes *were* open but that the lids were so far lowered that she might as well have had them closed. "Hildie?" Lou began, taking another few steps to her bed; already feeling that his entire body was afflicted with agony.

Hildie managed to raise a smile to him.

Her complexion was still pale—*as pale as it had been up on the ramparts*—but at least she was conscious now.

He noted her hand, lying on the bedspread, and he reached out for it, entwined her fingers with his own even though he knew that it would bring pain to both of them.

Lou met her beautiful green eyes—*still* beautiful, even beneath her heavy lids. "You should've seen the looks I got when I asked about all this." He widened his eyes to indicate the whole of the room; the torches which hung up on the walls and the fireplace which was blazing away—half a dozen logs all stacked up.

Hildie gave a slight smile.

A shake of her head.

When she spoke, her voice was flimsy.

Almost too quiet for Lou to hear at all.

"Suppose it helps when you're the king—they expect you to be mad."

Lou smiled back at her, and he felt her give his hand a squeeze.

He couldn't prevent a smile from breaking out over his lips.

It felt like it'd been so long since he'd had something so simple as this; with another human being. Just *warm* human contact . . .

He had to keep everyone else away.

That was his condition.

His *affliction.*

Hildie set her eyes on him once again. "Lou?" she said, her voice seemingly weaker than before. "What was it . . . what was it you were going to tell me?"

Lou thought about the question for the longest time.

He second guessed himself.

Wondering if he had been wrong.

Perhaps it was better to keep his plan to himself . . . the plan which would never come to pass. And yet, when he stared into those gleaming green eyes, he couldn't help but do anything that she asked. "I . . . uh," Lou started, unconvincingly.

Over his shoulder, he heard a fist up against the door of Hildie's quarters.

But he paid it no mind.

He shifted his attention back to her.

"I've been doing lots of reading. About *Ravensbark*."

" 'Ravensbark' ?" Hildie replied.

"That's right," Lou continued, "and, you see, I've come to better understand the balancing of the Magical Fields"—he paused for breath—"how to organise the Four Corners."

Hildie's eyes widened slightly—almost indiscernibly.

But she squeezed his hand all the tighter, clearly encouraging him to continue.

"And," Lou went on, "I thought that it might be the solution—the way that we could prevent a war this time."

Hildie narrowed her eyes.

Wrinkles appeared in her forehead.

She parted her lips but no sound came out.

Lou knew that he should leave her soon.

That she needed strength.

Time to recover without all these . . . *outside* stresses.

But he had to finish what he had started.

"When your father—Ma'reygar—when he decided to attack Ilsnare, he had to take care of Ravensbark first; he needed to take out the monastery, that which held the Four Corners of the Magical Fields in check, before he would be able to harness all his power."

Hildie continued to stare at him.

"And," Lou went on, "he succeeded in doing so . . . which meant that he could launch an attack on the Crystal City . . . what I propose is that we try doing it again—"

This time Hildie did manage to break through what he said, albeit with a voice almost too quiet to understand. "... You mean to rebuild ... to rebuild Ravensbark ... *here*?"

"In a way," he said, "but, from all the research I've done, I've found that the building itself would be unnecessary—that's just a *symbol* ... the one who really stood at the centre of Ravensbark, the one who the monastery *really* depended on, was Damon."

Lou allowed Damon's name to float about the room for several moments, so that Hildie might be able to absorb all that it meant . . . all that *Damon* meant.

Lou thought back to when Damon had arrived in Ilsnare; and how he had had to cast him out. In his mind, Lou had explained to Flucknor a million times just *why* he had had to do so .... why he had had to cast Hildie out ... and then—*finally*—and with his heart wrenching, why he had had to do the same to Flucknor.

Perhaps after all this was over, if Lou's plan actually *did* come off, then—*then*—he might be able to explain everything to Flucknor.

It would all make perfect sense.

Lou stared back into Hildie's eyes, and he saw that her eyelids were almost drooped all the way down; that she was nearly asleep. "Listen," Lou said, "I promise that you're an integral part of this ... of what I hope to achieve in uniting fire, ice, dark and light. You will see by the end." Realising that Hildie had now shut her eyes, and that her breathing had become profound, Lou silently repeated to himself, much quieter, "You'll see by the end."

THE HIGH REPRESENTATIVE ADVISES

L ou had hardly brought the door to Hildie's quarters shut behind him when he heard the familiar voice of Leona; his High Representative.

He turned to look at her, in her emerald-green robes.

She wore a slight smile.

Nervous.

As was everyone around him.

Already feeling tired, having been up for most of the night, and now most of the day, Lou set off walking; headed for the Throne Room. He knew, without even having to give her so much as a glance, that Leona was following on his heels at a reverent distance.

Perhaps she thought that she left enough space between the two of them so that she wouldn't get hit by any hexes which might manage to fling free of Lou's fingertips.

Then again, he supposed that, if he hadn't had magic running in his veins himself, then he would've been just as afraid as any other

Mortal . . . then he thought about Hildie, and how she was afraid of him. And it made him wonder how many other Magical beings secretly—or not so secretly—feared him.

"Your Highness," Leona said, her voice, as usual, businesslike and to-the-point, "I've been meeting with the Captain of the Royal Guards and he has informed me that his scouts have news of an invading force camped just on the periphery of the City Limits."

Lou felt himself still coming down from the meeting with Hildie.

The fire burning all around him had had a fatiguing effect; and that, coupled with the sleepless night, and having been up half the day, wore him down. But he continued to pace along the corridor, determined not to allow any sort of weakness to show. Even though his legacy as the Spider Warrior was still very much pertinent throughout not only Ilsnare but the whole of Shellacnass, he couldn't bring himself to entirely rely on that past event. Because, as Lou had learned over the years, people tended to forget about the past very quickly indeed.

"Your Majesty," Leona continued, "the Captain would like your permission to launch a sneak-attack on their camps."

She paused for a long while and Lou soon realised that it was because she'd run a little short on breath from their brisk pace along the corridor.

Sensing this, Lou consciously upped his pace, hoping to leave her in his wake.

"I . . . I . . . Your . . . *Highness!*"

Lou turned the corner, leaving Leona entirely in his wake. He eyed the doors to the Throne Room ahead, and, as if he had commanded them with only his mind, they shifted open. Veerna stood in the doorway, peering out, having already learned the familiar pattern of his master approaching.

Of his *king* approaching.

Almost without pause, Lou was right through the doorway, and back in his Throne Room. The sun streamed down through the glass ceiling, and he examined the way the light played on the throne itself; setting it in a flaming pool of natural glory.

Before he had even had the time to properly get his bearings, he slumped down on top of the throne and—*somewhat reluctantly*—awaited Leona.

About half a minute later, Leona passed through the doorway; rosy-cheeked and with several beads of sweat rolling down her tanned, yet still-youthful face.

Lou turned his attention onto her, and she took several moments to compose herself.

"As I was . . ." Leona drew in several more deep breaths, and then went on, "As I was *saying*, Your Majesty, the Captain believes that if we're to strike the camps now we shall catch the enemy off guard"—here, seemingly *spontaneously*, she broke into a wide grin—"it might be a chance for us to end the war before it's even started."

Lou stared back.

He felt like stone inside; as if he had become solid.

Frozen.

The flaming surroundings of Hildie's room were nothing but a memory now.

His ice had hardened once more in his veins.

When he spoke, he took care to keep his voice clean and clear.

Crisp.

"I can't say I think it's a good idea," Lou finally replied.

It seemed as if Leona's eyes might bulge from their sockets. "*Sire?*"

Lou focussed his attention on a spot about an inch above Leona's head. "These are magic users, yes?"

Leona tilted her head to one side, met Lou's eye for the briefest of seconds and then acknowledged this fact with a nod.

"So," Lou said, "what the *Captain* proposes is to send in a whole group of *Mortals*—with Mortal weapons—to attempt to capture the Horrox in their beds?"

Leona continued to stand before him. And he saw now, even from these few comments of his, that he had taken the wind out of her sails somewhat. Just because he felt like he had to press his advantage, he added, "And you can see nothing wrong with that plan? Nothing at all?"

Leona held still for several seconds, apparently processing how quickly this discussion had swung around . . . and *not* in her favour. "Your Highness," she said, "with *all* due respect, what do you expect us to do?" She took several steps toward him, a far braver move than Lou had ever witnessed from her. "To simply sit back— to allow the Creatures to attack *us?*"

He eyed her, flashed a smile. "That's *precisely* what I expect," he said.

As Lou raised his head, he noticed that Veerna was staring at him; apparently just as struck with disbelief as Leona herself was.

But Lou held firm.

He was the *King.*

"Do I make myself clear?" Lou said, finally.

Lou was certain he could see Leona visibly trembling . . . but not with fear . . . with something else . . .

"Very good, *sire,*" Leona replied, and then, with a curt bow, she left the Throne Room.

Lou listened to her footsteps echo away down the corridor.

As she left him behind.

He glanced up, met Veerna's eye, and saw the incredulous expression there.

He gave the boy a slight smile.

"Sometimes," Lou said, "you just have to have belief."

As Lou allowed himself to sink down on his throne, already feeling weariness and sleep begin to overwhelm him, he couldn't help but wonder to himself whether or not he *had* just lost the war . . . before it had even started.

TRAVELLER

Syre woke with a start in the middle of the night.

At first, as was often the case when she found herself suddenly awake following a dream, she didn't immediately realise what it was that had woken her.

She propped herself up on her elbow, feeling the damp long grasses surrounding. The dew had soaked her tunic, and she felt it chill the surface of her skin. Her heart beat steady and full.

She cocked her ear to the air; listening out for something.

Anything.

As she gradually took in the campsite—where she and Ems'plot had bedded down for the night—she noted the flaming torch, stuck into the soft ground. It illuminated the small area where they had laid down their bedding, and showed off the silhouettes of the horses and mule quietly sleeping on their hoofs. Neither of the horses, or the mule, stirred under Syre's gaze.

And she knew it hadn't been them who'd woken her.

She shifted her attention out beyond; past the immediate glare of the campsite—of the *torches*—but, still, she could see nothing much at all.

Only darkness.

Slowly, taking care not to make a sound, she rose to her feet.

She could hear the constant *grinding* of crickets, and the *chitter* of the other assorted bugs which made their home in these long grasses of the plains.

Neither had it been them who had woken her.

The sound was constant.

Consistent.

Those sorts of sounds were only ever soothing—they tended to lull her into sleep.

She trod silently over the crushed grasses, and snuck her way between the pair of sleeping horses.

She stood between them, feeling the warmth from their bodies.

She looked out into the darkness, into the moonlight which streamed down across the plains; and she waited for her eyes to grow accustomed to the sight.

She wanted to see Ems'plot.

That was what concerned her first and foremost.

She found it *greatly* unsettling to not know where he was.

It was only then when the solution occurred to her; when she decided that she should do that which she had been frightened of doing in the company of Ems'plot.

Still between the sleeping horses, she turned her concentration inward—to her own thoughts. She listened to her heart drum away in her ears. And felt each one of her heartbeats twitch percussively through her veins. In her mind, she pictured the crow . . . the animal with which she shared so much in common—the animal which she *believed* to be her kindred spirit.

Her whole body was still for a long, long moment.

She wondered if—after all this time; after she had expended this much effort—whether or not she would have the energy to go through with the transformation.

She supposed that she would soon find out.

Her mind sharpened down into a single focus.

Just *one* image.

A single, pit-black feather . . . gleaming dully like coal.

She pictured it so clearly.

And gradually—*so smoothly*—she felt her skin slipping away from her.

The feathers gliding out from who knew where.

Her body shrinking.

Legs becoming so thin as to resemble knitting needles.

And her toes becoming sharp as the edge of a Royal Guard's spear.

Talons . . . highly apt for tearing flesh . . . if it came to that . . .

For no longer than a couple of seconds, Syre hobbled about in her crow's body—on the ground. Picking her way between the gargantuan horses' hoofs. And then, with a series of natural, sweetly smooth motions, she made herself airborne.

She floated up above the campsite.

The flaming torch down below.

Then switched her focus—her sharp, beady *crow's eyes*—onto the plains which surrounded them.

Already, she made out the shape in the darkness.

The hunched-over figure of Ems'plot.

Even in her crow's form, she felt the anger swell in her chest.

For several moments, it felt as if she might explode from it.

Why had she been so *stupid* . . . how had she allowed herself to be taken in?

It took all of her restraint not to dive bomb the man right away . . . and perhaps she would've done if it wasn't for the shred of sense which leaped up at her; which nudged her in the ribs, reminding her that Ems'plot was many, many times stronger than she.

Her attacking him now—in her crow's form—would be tantamount to suicide.

She held herself aloft.

Floated about on the thermals.

Just as the clouds did . . .

She recalled how, when she'd been back in Ilsnare Palace, she had whiled away the hours—working at mastering her crow's body—looking over all the writings on birds, and how they flew. What had most surprised her, although why it had done, she wondered in retrospect was somewhat odd, was that in all of those *paragraphs upon paragraphs* there was almost nothing at all about the graceful, otherworldly sensation of inhabiting a bird's body. She wondered if any of those writers of those books had ever used anything but their eyes and ears . . . if they had ever deigned to use their *imaginations* . . . even if they weren't like her; with ice magic running through their blood. Perhaps *she* would be the one to write the book.

As she circled Ems'plot in the gloom down below, she took note of another figure. Not far away. She could see that the figure led a horse along the road. She sensed weariness.

Like her and Ems'plot, this traveller had journeyed far.

The traveller halted their progress, apparently having noted the torchlight which came from her and Ems'plot's camp. She stared for a long time, urging the traveller away.

If she had been in another situation, she might've attempted to speak directly into the traveller's mind . . . but with Ems'plot lurking nearby it would've been just as effective as shouting at the top of her voice. In the end, she only hovered above, watching the scene.

The traveller stood where they were, continuing to take in the torchlight, and then, right when Syre was certain that they would carry on along the road; that they would simply keep on going, they trudged toward the camp. Even in her crow's body, she felt her stomach sink.

She stared hard at the traveller with her beady eyes.

She saw how the traveller was walking right toward the spot where Ems'plot was crouched. Out of sight. Perhaps, as far as Syre knew, Ems'plot was working some sort of enchantment on the traveller's mind, urging him to come closer—apparently—of his own volition.

In the end, Syre acted without thinking. She allowed her wings to slink back into her bird's body and she plummeted out of the sky. Spiralling downward. Spinning around and around.

Directed at the flaky circle of skin at the centre of Ems'plot's scalp.

When Syre hit, there was nothing but a flash of light.

As soon as it happened, it was over.

And darkness consumed her.

A RESTLESS ARMY

L ou sat on his throne, turning the pages of one of the tomes which Veerna had brought him earlier that morning. It was one which he had read through several times before:
Ravensbark: A History.

Of course, this particular tome, having been among the Library stacks for decades, hadn't yet been updated to account for the sudden destruction of the monastery. Not that it mattered all that much. Lou's only interest was the past of the monastery. He really had no need to read about more modern events seeing that he had been so close that he could verily say that he had lived and breathed them. As he turned the page into another chapter, feeling a strange sense of vigour passing through his blood, he couldn't help but notice the footsteps sounding in the corridors outside the Throne Room. Even without needing to open his mind—even without having to use *magic*—Lou could tell just who it was who approached.

There was only one person about Ilsnare who would walk with that sort of purposeful gait:

The Captain of the Royal Guards.

The sound of boot steps should have summoned a sort of fear in him; they should have put him at an instant disadvantage. But, if that truly was the Captain's intention, then it was a mistaken one. Because, simply from sitting on his throne, Lou could already tell how many of them there were.

The Captain himself, of course, and a guard of four men.

Lou slouched a little back on his throne and turned his attention to the doorway, waiting for the knock. When it came, he asked the men inside. Almost instantaneously, he noted the musky scent clawing through the air; that stink of horses and manure which seemed to cling to anybody who spent any time at all with the Royal Guards.

He took in the men who stood before him; their silvery armour plates, how each one of them—the Captain included—held their helmets with both hands, neatly at their right side.

At first, Lou was a little dazzled by the reflection of the sunlight in the silver.

He squinted at this minor annoyance.

"Your Highness," the Captain said, with a slight bow.

He took a few steps forward.

Just like Veerna, Lou saw that the Captain had mousy-brown hair. He also had a neatly trimmed beard and a firm—*proud*—square jaw. This could quite easily be the sort of man who Veerna would grow into. Lou's eyes shifted away from the Captain, and onto the Royal Guards he had brought along with him. They wore their swords at their waists. Each had a crossbow slung over their shoulder. Already, again without so much as reaching out with his magic, Lou could tell that these men were on edge . . . that they were enjoying this impromptu visit to the Throne Room just as much as Lou himself was.

Lou turned back to the Captain who was now several steps closer, although still a good few paces away from the throne itself.

"Yes?" Lou replied finally, and then, in an absent-minded way he hoped would take the Captain off guard, he added, "What is it you want?"

The Captain swallowed hard, his Adam's apple bobbing in his throat. He met Lou's eye for a quarter of a second before shifting his gaze to where he—*apparently*—found it much more comfortable . . . onto the wall behind the throne. "Your Majesty," the Captain said, as if the first address hadn't been sufficient, "we have come here today—*I* with my closest of aides"—he flapped his arm behind him to indicate the Royal Guards at his heels—"to suggest that you re-examine this opportunity presented to us . . . a chance for us to launch a *pre-emptive strike* against the invaders."

Lou sat still for a long moment. He caught the eye of one of the members of the Royal Guards, and when he did, he gave the man a friendly smile. This seemed to catch the Royal Guard unaware more than anything else might have done and he quickly turned his attention to the tips of his—*well-polished*—boots. Lou turned back to the Captain, realising that this was the extent of the man's argument. He decided to be direct; that was his best chance of getting shot of them as soon as possible. "And?" Lou finally replied.

"And?" the Captain said, blinking rapidly, and then, seemingly unconsciously, glancing down to the tome on the history of Ravensbark. "Sire," the Captain went on, "perhaps you don't understand the significance of the opportunity presented us—that we shall never have this chance again." He took a quick breath and his shoulders arched back with his respiration. "The citizens want to see the Royal Guards *doing something* . . . isn't that why they pay their taxes?"

"I'm sorry," Lou said, cocking his head to one side, as if he might be having some trouble in hearing, "I don't quite follow you."

The Captain seemed on the brink of a sigh, but apparently thought better of it at the very last moment. "The people," the Captain said. "They're *afraid*, Your Majesty."

" 'Afraid' of what?" Lou replied.

"Of *war.*"

"I'd say they have every right to be *afraid of war*. It is destined to come to pass."

The Captain's complexion coloured slightly, and Lou couldn't quite decide if it was out of frustration or out of embarrassment; because it was quite clear who wielded the power here, in the Throne Room of Ilsnare Palace . . . and it most certainly *wasn't* the Captain.

"Then allow us to *try*," the Captain got out.

Lou stared back at the Captain for the longest time, and then he let out a sigh of his own. He turned to look at the other Royal Guards, then nodded to them. "What is all this?" Lou said. "Is this some sort of *ultimatum*?"

Again, as had seemed with pretty much the entire course of the discussion, this particular observation caught the Captain flat-footed. "An, uh . . . *ultimatum?*" the Captain replied.

"Yes," Lou said, rising from his throne now, and quite enjoying the way that the four Royal Guards at the doors cowered at this subtle gesture. "I mean," Lou went on, flapping his hand in the direction of the guards, "you come here with these *people* . . . all of you armed to the teeth, and you ask me . . . you *threaten* me into going against something which I have already made my mind up on." He turned back to the Captain, who was now looking a touch green. "Is that correct?"

The Captain didn't shake his head or—indeed—make any sort of other sound to deny this.

Which was a good thing, because if the Captain had done, then it would've been a lie.

What *else* was Lou supposed to read into this situation?

"If you intend to attack those encampments, you'll need to drag me from the throne." He turned to look at the four Royal Guards at the door—now discernibly uncomfortable. "Is that what you intend to do?"

A severe silence ripped through the Throne Room.

Lou drew breath and wondered if they would show some courage.

But, as ever, he found himself disappointed.

The Captain bowed once more, and took several steps back toward the doors of the Throne Room. "I . . . uh . . . *apologise*, Your Majesty . . . if I might have seemed *imprudent* . . . I hope that you shall find it in your heart to, ah, *forgive me* . . . yes?"

Lou watched the Captain all the way back to the doors of the Throne Room, and not once did the Captain turn his back to him . . . Lou wondered if he should think about writing a book on how to earn respect. Perhaps when he retired—if that day truly ever did come to pass . . .

The Captain lingered for only another moment before muttering an inaudible farewell beneath his breath. He promptly skulked out of the Throne Room with the four members of the Royal Guards on his heels. Before Lou had even picked up his tome again, he thought he could hear more footsteps out in the corridor. And he found himself hoping—*praying almost*—that Sully and Rut would return with their respective pieces of the keystone before too long. Without the leverage of the Webbing Armoury, he doubted his chances of resisting a coup.

Magical *or* Mortal.

FIRE AND ICE

"**Y**our Highness?"

Lou turned back to the doorway of the Throne Room. He saw that Hildie stood there.

Her red hair had been tucked into a bun around the back of her head, and she was wearing a looser robe; one which would normally be used by royalty to loaf about the Palace.

Once more, Lou felt the pendant Hildie wore about her neck drawing his attention.

It was the way that the sunlight which beamed in through the roof windows caused the golden grains embedded within to glitter and twinkle.

Her complexion looked a little darker. "What did those Royal Guards want?"

Lou gave her a smirk. "They think they can do a better job of ruling Shellacnass than me." He couldn't help but give a hard sigh through his nostrils as he slumped back down on his throne. "And I can't help thinking that they might be right."

"The Horrox encampments?" Hildie said, taking a few steps closer to his throne, each of her paces dainty and frail . . . Lou wondered if a medicine woman had been to see her, and had recommended that she take exercise about the Palace. More than likely, Hildie had decided to grant herself discharge from the bedrest inflicted upon her.

Lou nodded in reply. "Just as you said, the Mortals all want to launch a sneak-attack on the Horrox—to catch them in their beds." Here Lou found himself giving her a beaming, sarcastic smile. "And they have the nerve to call *them* the Creatures."

Hildie hunched her shoulders. "It's only what I've been trying to say for my entire life—it's a shame that there doesn't seem to be anyone willing to listen."

"It's probably because Mortals are the only ones you ever talked to . . ."

Lou's words hung in the air of the Throne Room for a long while, and neither Lou or Hildie thought to remark on them. After a decent amount of time had passed, and he could feel the slight annoyance that'd been aroused by that impromptu meeting with the Captain of the Royal Guards, and his cronies, he turned back to her. "How're you feeling?" he said.

Hildie rocked her head from side to side. "Better. Still not at full strength—but *better.*"

"Good. That's good."

As the two of them stood in the Throne Room, Lou half expected Veerna to come along at any moment, to break through the awkward silence as readily as a bucket of roasting embers might melt through ice . . . but, as always seemed to be the case, whenever he was *wanted* around, he simply never was.

"Lou?" Hildie said, finally.

"Hmm?"

"In my quarters, you were telling me"—Hildie broke into a smile; a *glorious* smile . . . one which Lou hadn't realised he had missed so badly until this moment right now—"I can't quite remember precisely, I was coming and going, dipping in and out of consciousness . . . but you said something about Ravensbark . . . you were speaking about *Damon.*"

Lou thought back to the meeting in Hildie's quarters. Even as he drew in the details, he thought he could feel the flicker of those flames up against his skin; threatening to bake him alive . . . to melt the ice in his blood. He was certain that the reason Hildie had fainted was because of him—because his influence, his *ice*, had been simply too much for her fire magic to bear.

From all that Lou had learned throughout the years—from all of his studies—he knew well that a fire and an ice mage could never be in close proximity for too long of a time. . . . And yet, it would be hardest of all to cast Hildie out again . . . it would almost be easier for Lou to let go of this mortal coil; to cast himself into the afterlife where he would cause no more suffering.

"Lou?"

Lou snapped back to the present moment. He pivoted around and took in Hildie; saw that she wore the same half smile clinging to her lips. Already, he found himself struggling with what he would tell her; as if he hadn't already made that decision, more than once now, to reveal the full extent of what he planned . . . of how he hoped not only to save Shellacnass from the destruction of an advancing army but to unite it forever more . . . or at least so that there might be peace for the remainder of Lou's own lifetime. Although he had felt as if he was a giant while he had fended off the Captain and the Royal Guards, he truly felt like he'd been cut down to size now.

As if he was nothing more significant than a worm.

"I . . . *need* you," Lou just about managed to get out.

He paused with his head bowed for a long while, unwilling to look Hildie in the eye. When he finally did, he saw that she was closer to him . . . he realised she wasn't wearing anything on her feet . . . when he had heard her footsteps advancing along the corridor, it must've been the *slap* of human flesh against marble. Or perhaps he had sensed her advance—without knowing—through his magic.

Lou met her crystalline green eyes.

"What for?" Hildie replied.

Again, Lou felt the knot form in his throat; it was all he could do to keep himself from throwing up his hands and telling her to forget all about it.

To forget that he had said anything at all.

But it was too late for that now.

He had to go through with his explanation.

In any case, he would have to open up to someone *sometime.*

"When we unite the Magical Fields," Lou said, "we'll need one to represent each one of the Four Corners; a magical practitioner for fire, ice, light and dark."

"And you had me posted as the *fire* Corner, I suppose?"

Although Lou could take no joy in being predictable, he nodded in reply.

"Who will be the others?" Hildie said. "I mean, I suppose that *you* will take ice . . ."

Lou held himself very still, already afraid of what he had given away. He knew it was stupid, that in his past he had had trouble with Hildie—with *believing* Hildie—that he shouldn't allow it to affect the present . . . and yet, it was so difficult for him to let go; to allow himself to trust *anyone* else. But, he supposed, if he was going to trust someone, then it might as well be Hildie.

"I thought about Syre, for darkness," Lou said. "And Flucknor for light."

Hildie held his gaze, and he felt a shudder pass through his blood.

When he looked into her eyes, he sometimes wondered if he could see down a never-ending well of memory; as if he could travel into the past somehow.

"Do they know?" Hildie asked.

"Who?" Lou replied, and then answered his own question, "Syre and Flucknor? No, they don't know yet . . . and they don't realise why they had to leave Ilsnare, either."

"Why *did* they have to leave Ilsnare?"

Lou turned his attention upward, to the sunrays which streamed in through the rooftop windows.

He knew it had been the architects' ambition that the sunrays would set the King—or Queen—of Shellacnass in a golden light; so that they might appear as a kind of demi-god when they sat upon the throne. He couldn't help but wonder what the architects might've imagined if they had known, one day, it would be a mage—rather than a *pure* Mortal—who sat upon the throne.

Lou's gaze finally settled upon the tome he'd been reading before the Captain and the Royal Guards had disturbed him. He eyed the gilt lettering on the spine:

Ravensbark: A History.

And then he said, "I had to preserve the sanctity—the *neutrality*—of the city." He turned back to Hildie. "Haven't you felt it for yourself? Haven't you felt the pressure I've been putting upon my own ice magic, trying whenever I can to downplay it? To shove it deep down into my veins as if it didn't exist at all?"

Hildie didn't nod that she had, but neither did she look away.

Lou calmed himself, feeling the sunrays pouring over his skin, making his ice magic prickle through his veins. "Listen," he said, "I had to keep this secret—I had to *make* this a secret—because I was certain that nobody would believe me."

This time Hildie did butt in. "Are you sure?"

He glanced back at her.

Lost himself again in those green eyes of hers.

Hildie went on, "Or is it because you wanted to control every-thing—that you wanted to be at the *centre* of this whole plan?" A slight smile twitched her lips. "Isn't that it?"

And as Lou felt Hildie closing in on him, as he felt the warmth from the fire magic within her veins seep out into the air and layer against his skin, he couldn't quite believe that this was all happen-ing. That this was all *really* happening.

He had hardly a moment to think as she pressed her lips up against his.

And even though searing pain burned through his heart—through his muscles—he couldn't help thinking that it was all worth it.

For a kiss.

ROAD TO NOWHERE

Flucknor felt as if the rhythmic beat of horses' hoofs was hypnotising him.

No, actually, it felt as if the rhythmic beat of horses' hooves had long ago *succeeded* in hypnotising him and now the sound was merely pummelling him into the damp earth which passed below. As if he had been buried alive in this cold, dank soil, and that he was waiting for the worms to come crawling over his body—readying to slowly digest him and return him to the essential elements he had once been.

The clouds bundled up above their heads. He could smell rain in the air.

He could feel the dampness of it against his skin.

He wished the downpour would come already.

The anticipation was always far more painful than the icy rains which would eventually tumble down from the heavens.

As Flucknor felt his body shifting about with the movement of the horse's flanks, clenched between his thighs, he found that he had to close his eyes; that the road ahead, the fog which draped over the land, concealing bogs and lowlands, sent a nauseous shudder through him.

He wished for nothing else other than blazing blue skies . . . the ones which he had come to grow familiar with in the early summer back at Ilsnare.

. . . The Crystal City . . .

It seemed so far away now.

And his escape, too.

When Flucknor turned, to try and catch a glance of Brotsboore, who rode on a horse nearby, he was aware of the Plarstark sneaking free of the pocket of his robe. Acting on impulse, he reached down for the button-like object, pressed it hard against his thigh so that it wouldn't have a chance of squirming free; of tumbling down through the air and landing on the ground.

He had long ago put aside the idea that he might be able to dispose of it somehow.

He had reasoned with himself that such a priceless object would have some means of recovery, and, if not, he couldn't quite find the strength in him to doubt that the Horrox would be able to inflict pain on him of an efficacy equal to the Plarstark.

He recalled what Arfklan had said about having been able to access Lou's mind through his own . . . and although Flucknor found himself often thinking about all Lou had done to him—how Lou had, in effect, exiled him from Ilsnare—he couldn't help but feel for the man who had been his best friend this last decade. Had either one really betrayed the other?

. . . Time would tell.

As Flucknor felt his horse lurching onward with the rest of the group, he was aware of Brotsboore bringing his own horse closer. When Brotsboore spoke to him, he spoke out loud, perhaps because there was little point in acting otherwise . . . after all, they were surrounded by Horrox on all sides.

"Flucknor?" Brotsboore said.

Flucknor turned his head to take in the sleek, lizard-like face: the black eyes and the horned, rash-red skin. The effect of the Horrox's appearance still hadn't quite become a totally everyday phenomenon . . . perhaps once this quest was through with it would have done . . .

"I was listening to what the other Horrox were speaking about; in their minds."

"What did they say?" Flucknor replied, staring between his horse's ears, to the bleak terrain which confronted them.

Brotsboore became a little fidgety. He spent a long while adjusting the reins of his horse in his hand, and then he shifted a glance back over his shoulder, as if all of the Horrox which surrounded them wouldn't be able to listen into their every word if they so wished.

"The encampments," Brotsboore said, "the ones back on the fringes of Ilsnare . . . they are intended to be a trap—bait, irresistible to the Royal Guards . . . they are supposed to launch a sneak-attack on the Horrox forces, and"—here Brotsboore paused for a long while before continuing"—it's supposed to be a *massacre*—to make up for the one which took place against the Horrox in the south, in Nor'tarth."

Flucknor thought back to what Arfklan had said to him; to how Arfklan had described what had gone on at the village in the tropics of Shellacnass, and close to the border of the Kingdom. "And what's happened?" Flucknor asked.

Brotsboore shook his head. "They haven't taken the bait."

Even despite the chilly rain which was surely about to fall—even though Flucknor was certain that he would be facing his death before too long—he couldn't help the warm glow which seized him from the inside out. His ice magic twitched through his veins with a fresh vigour, and his heart rapped strongly for the first time in days.

But, why?

. . . Why when he had left behind the Mortals so he might help bring about change with the Horrox? Was it his personal struggle—his personal *pain*—which had shifted his thinking?

He couldn't say.

And his thoughts were soon cut off by the sense of excitement which rippled through the group.

Apart from his control, Flucknor felt his horse quicken its pace, to keep up with the others. He managed to shift a sidelong glance to Brotsboore and said, "What's going on?"

Flucknor observed a slight smile take form on Brotsboore's face; in profile. "It seems," he said, "that we've come across what we were looking for."

As Flucknor set off after Brotsboore, he couldn't help a final glance back.

Flucknor was now one of the last of their group—lagging off the pace.

And it was now that he noted the strange creature which tailed them.

His heart bounced up to his throat, and tickled him.

He took in the floppy, velvety ears.

The squat little body with spry limbs.

And the round—*round*—eyes

Grey skin.

Flucknor thought he was imagining things, and, indeed, when, after turning his attention back to the front, he slipped a glance back over his shoulder once more, the Creature was gone.

He supposed that the constant physical exertion—the pain which'd been inflicted on him—meant that he had begun to *see* things . . . things which—*quite certainly*—were not there.

CHANGE OF THE GUARDS

Lou had been drifting in and out of a daze—it couldn't be called sleep—when he heard the definite sound of horses' hoofs against cobblestone.

Nearby.

His first thought, as he hurriedly threw his cloak about his shoulders and made his way through the corridors of the Palace, was that there had been a breach . . . that the Horrox forces had broken through the City Walls.

This idea was swiftly discarded, though, because Lou knew well that there would've been a *far* greater commotion if this was the case. The Royal Advisors—Royal Guards—would've been flooding every last nook and cranny of the Palace, caught up in the panic. And, in any case, the chances of the Horrox having run the gauntlet through the city, through the labyrinthine side streets which led off the Crystal Causeway and up to the Palace, was something resembling a farce.

Unless, of course, the Horrox had struck some sort of deal with the Royal Guards.

But Lou wouldn't allow himself to entertain *that* particular thought for the time being. It was better to think of the Royal

Guards as his allies until he was proven to be gravely mistaken. Having just woken up, he didn't want grave treachery to be the first thing to burden his mind.

Somehow, as if she hadn't ever been far away, he ran into Hildie.

She was fleeing from out of some side passage and she smiled at him when their eyes met.

After their meeting they had stayed together in the Throne Room for some time . . . until the sun had dipped on the horizon and night had arrived . . . the time when Lou's ice magic—no matter how hard he strove to push it down—would creep to the surface of his skin. He had no intention of dealing Hildie any further harm . . . nothing more than he had already *dealt* her.

The two of them, both in the casual robes they used when inside the Palace, made their way silently up the stone staircases, to the ramparts which offered a view out over the Crystal City.

Almost immediately, Lou found himself reeling from the sight.

The torches borne in hands.

Held up to light the way through the streets.

He looked to the Garrison nearby, saw that the gates had been thrown open, that the Royal Guards—on horseback—were being ordered through the gap.

For several moments, Lou stood stunned, resting his palms lightly on the smooth ramparts, unable to believe what he was seeing with his two eyes.

Treachery.

Treason.

They had defied him.

They had *defied* his wishes.

But what was he to do now?

As he stood there fuming, he was aware of Hildie beside him, and he was aware of the moon shining down on the two of them.

On instinct, he turned his attention off across the ramparts, and to the encampments on the hill opposite the Crystal City. Soon the Royal Guards would be proceeding toward them, on horseback, with nothing but their Mortal weapons . . . hoping—*desperately*—to vanquish these *Creatures*. He wasn't entirely certain how it had happened—although he greatly suspected the intervention of the Captain of the Royal Guards—but a story had been floating about the streets of Ilsnare, detailing the situation in Nor'tarth; that village to the south.

It was the same story which Hildie had re-laid to Lou, although, it seemed, the nuance of the Horrox having held themselves out for the slaughter had been skipped over in its retelling.

And, it seemed, the Royal Guards had taken the story to heart.

They had chosen their Captain over their King.

As Lou stood high above the streets below, he knew that there was nothing he would be able to do to stop them . . . the only chance he might have rested in the possession of the Webbing Armoury; but there had been no sign of either Sully or Rut, and while their return was delayed, there would be no fighting back for Lou. He doubted he even still had the strength.

When he turned around, he realised that Veerna stood there, that he had silently followed Lou and Hildie all the way up here—to the ramparts.

"Your Highness," Veerna said, his face left half in shadow by the moonlight. "The Royal Guards—they're attacking."

"I know," Lou said, glancing to Veerna. "There's nothing we can do about it now . . . it's too late for us to stop them—to have them see reason."

Veerna's eyes rounded. His voice became quiet as a whisper, and yet Lou could make out what he said perfectly well despite the constant *clatter* of horses' hoofs over cobblestones. "What'll happen to us?"

Lou glanced to Hildie, as if she might better know what he was supposed to say to a boy so young. Finally he realised there was nothing *to* say. In the end, he spoke so quietly that he hoped none of them would be able to hear. "I suspect we'll die."

TRACKING

The plains which'd surrounded Syre and Ems'plot for most of the trek so far had given way to rocky foothills. The afternoon heat had long ago reached its peak and was—thankfully—drifting down to more *habitable* temperatures. Soon it would be night again.

Syre felt the baking warmth which carried on the air. It seemed to send sparks jittering through her blood . . . she knew that it was in conflict with her ice magic; and that her magic wished for nothing save a total retreat from this place.

Truth be told, she would've liked to leave just as badly.

But not now . . . not yet.

Not until her 'master' Ems'plot declared that a possibility.

When she breathed in, she could smell sulphur on the air, and she knew that there must be volcanoes nearby. She could almost feel the warm ash of a recent eruption fluttering down like snow and settling on her skin. She turned her attention to Ems'plot, just in front of her, his stride showing no sign of flagging—let alone breaking—as he continued his incessant toil up the rocky landscape. She shook her head at herself, and perhaps would've muttered something under her breath if it hadn't been for the mule bringing up the rear; nudging its nose into her lower back . . . reminding her that even the mule was showing more resilience on this journey. The horses were a little way further back on the trail; apparently they had been bred for use on the plains and this landscape was something of a crass joke to them.

Reluctant, Syre took a deep breath of air—felt it fill up her chest—and then she exhaled and slogged her way onward. As she went on her way, she couldn't help but cast her mind back to what had happened after she had dived bombed Ems'plot . . . inhabiting the crow's body, and surveying Ems'plot while he stalked that approaching traveller.

It had all happened so quickly, but one thing was for certain:

Ems'plot had seen her coming and he had prepared himself accordingly.

She couldn't recall having made contact with Ems'plot before the entire world had been reduced to darkness . . . until she had felt her human body suddenly ripping through those bird feathers, and her *human* feet thickening and taking over from the talons.

When she had come back to consciousness, it'd been morning.

And she'd been lying beside the campfire.

Ems'plot had been whistling to himself; some gay little melody, as he cooked them up some berries he had foraged from close by . . . although Ems'plot's cooking wasn't close to being on par with that of the Glyph, she had to admit that his skills *far* excelled her own.

Knowing her luck, she would've starved out here if she'd been alone.

She knew, in the past decade, she had grown complacent; too used to the kitchens constantly stocked with food; the House Staff ready and willing to indulge her every whim.

They had said nothing more about the night before.

Nothing about her dive-bombing Ems'plot.

In any case, she had never truly intended to harm him . . . no more than she would intend to harm *anybody* . . . but she *had* wanted to stop Ems'plot from causing the passing traveller any distress.

And so she had acted.

She wondered what had become of the traveller.

Whether, once Ems'plot had dealt with her, he had turned his attentions onto the traveller; killed them, and buried them somewhere close by.

If Ems'plot *had* done that, then it surprised her that he hadn't stolen the traveller's horse.

And she had seen no sign of what Ems'plot might've scavenged off the traveller either.

. . . Then again, Ems'plot was notorious—if for nothing else—for travelling light.

The mule's saddlebags contained only a few tools: some rudimentary cooking utensils, a hunting knife. He was one of those people—one of those *mages*—who enjoyed being at one with the elements . . . taking on nature just for fun . . . just because he could.

Syre couldn't say that she had ever shared these sentiments. After having been forced to live out in encampments, when her hometown of Endmere had burned down, she could honestly say—*hand on heart*—that she would be blissfully happy living out every day, for the rest of her days until she died, in the unimaginable luxury of Ilsnare Palace. And now she thought of the Palace, she could hardly believe the situation she found herself in now . . . a situation which was of her own making. What had driven her to follow Ems'plot; what had *possibly* possessed her to follow him when he had told her to do so? She supposed that it was her own fault for having been so willing to follow his instruction. So open for suggestion.

Well, she was determined not to allow it to happen again.

When she glanced ahead, she saw Ems'plot was once more tilting his head back and sniffing at the wind. As would often happen, following a lull in their pace, Ems'plot strode on harder, as if there was something which drove him on . . . like a mongrel dog, left to ravish with hunger for days, sniffing out a nearby chicken coop.

Syre felt the muscles at the backs of her legs strain, and she urged herself onward, up the rocky slope. It caught her off guard when Ems'plot spoke into her mind:

— *Not too far now. Just around the corner, I believe.*

She was on the cusp of replying aloud, but, in the end, she caught herself and replied back into his mind . . . one less thing he would be able to scold her for this evening when they made camp.

— *What? What's just around the corner?*

Although he didn't so much as turn back to look at her, she could tell, just from how his words appeared in her mind, that his face was twisted in a smirk.

— *You'll see.*

She worked herself harder, dragging her weight up the slope, determined to keep pace with the elderly man; as much for her own pride as anything else.

Sure enough, the rocky land levelled out, and it brought them to a flatter surface.

She took in the igneous, reddish-brown rock. Even though the sight had been somewhat novel when she'd first laid eyes on the foothills—never having seen rock this colour before— that novelty had soon vanished after about twenty minutes of clambering up it.

Up ahead, she could make out caverns in the rock—darkened alcoves.

Having walked out into the middle of this flatter part of the hillside, Ems'plot stopped and glanced around. He *was* smiling . . . just as Syre had anticipated.

She listened for the steady *clip-clop* of the horses' hoofs behind them.

And the surer *trudge* of the mule's hoofs.

At one point, she had been sure that one—if not *both*—of the horses would fail to make it up the side of this rocky trail . . . but they had defied her expectations.

She glanced about, still unsure as to the merit of putting all the effort into reaching this spot. Then again, who was she? Some dumb, naïve girl?

. . . She certainly wasn't a mage.

"There, there," Ems'plot said, speaking aloud, having read her mind. "Don't be so hard on yourself, my dear."

Syre smouldered in silence and did her level best not to allow so much as a single thought to enter her mind . . . much more difficult than it first seemed.

"Now," Ems'plot said, again sniffing at the air, and then, apparently decided, pointed one of his knobbly, crooked fingers off in a certain direction. "*This way!*"

Syre slogged on behind him, with the horses and mule for company.

She had already failed to keep her loose thoughts in check, and they were tumbling about her mind; the most prevalent among them out-of-control fantasies which saw her putting Ems'plot to death in a variety of painful ways. She wondered if—in fact—when she'd been a crow, she very much *had* intended Ems'plot harm after all.

It happened so suddenly that Syre had no time to think.

After a whole day of relative inaction, she supposed she had some licence not to expect; and yet, when she thought on it later, she chided herself for having given into such Mortal failings.

Up ahead, she saw the figure emerging from the gloom of a cavern.

It took her another few seconds to realise who it was.

The *traveller* from before . . .

The one from the previous night.

Another moment later, and she finally twigged *exactly* who it was.

Why, she recognised him by his doughy cheeks.

His rounded belly.

But, most of all, that bright, blond hair; undimmed even after days of travel.

Rutterness. *Rut.*

Out of the corner of her eye, she was blinded by the flash of white light.

It shot out of Ems'plot's fingertips. Skittered through the air.

Caught Rut's throat. And Rut fell to his knees choking.

Choking to *death.*

She held still another second more. Then rushed Ems'plot.

A hundred different hexes spiralling through her head.

MASSACRE

Soon after Lou had witnessed the Royal Guards fleeing the Garrison—headed for the plains, intent on laying ruin to the Horrox camp—he had most of all wanted to descend the stone staircases to the Throne Room; to be left in *peace and quiet* . . . to await the report which Leona would surely later on bring him: The confirmed dead and injured, following the raid.

He would take no joy in hearing the information, of course.

Even though he had warned against such a foolhardy plan of action.

There was nothing *happy*—let alone *joyful*—to take from the destruction of life.

Whether it be the lives of Mortals or Creatures.

However, before he had had the chance to shift off his spot on the ramparts, where he had witnessed the charge by the Royal Guards, Hildie had reached out and taken hold of the crook of his elbow. He had seen her flinch at the touch. He knew that his ice magic was so powerful in the moonlight that it would be almost unbearable for her.

But she had held on for several seconds despite the obvious pain it inflicted.

She was no stranger to pain.

She had urged him to remain at the ramparts; that it was important he witness the scene.

Accepting this, he had then turned to Veerna, wanting at least to preserve the boy's innocence. But before he could mutter a word, Hildie had sunk her fingernails into his skin, as if in warning.

The message had been clear.

Veerna was to be allowed to witness what would unfold.

For some reason—unfathomable to Lou—Hildie believed it important that Veera see what happened . . . perhaps she wanted to prove the cruelty of Mortals to him. Or maybe she wanted to show him the power of *magic* . . . that which would be surely exhibited by the Horrox when the Royal Guards breached the camps. The Royal Guards would hardly reach the cusp of the camp before hexes began to soar through the air . . . before Royal Guards toppled off the saddles of their horses, gasping for the breath they would no longer be able to take.

Dying.

However, as the Royal Guards closed on the camps, there was no discernible response.

Again, Lou was certain that this was part of the Horrox plan; that soon enough the Creatures would emerge from the tents, flinging magic to all parts.

Ending Mortal lives.

But neither did that come to pass.

In the end, it was merely to observe; in the calm early morning—the gentle moonlight streaming down through the overcast skies—the Royal Guards striding about the camps, waving their swords and spears everywhere they dared.

And finding nothing at all.

Strangely, considering the anticipation which had come before, it had seemed an almost sad sight. To watch the Royal Guards returning from the encampments without having managed to capture a single one of the Horrox . . . let alone having managed to kill any.

The shabby formations with which the Royal Guards had returned to Ilsnare had communicated their utmost dejectedness at the situation; that they had failed to serve their purpose. That they had been unable to act as guardians for the Crystal City.

Lou had thought on what he might do next as he had finally descended the stone staircases to the Palace, with Hildie and Veerna alongside him, and he had already made the decision that disciplining any member of the Royal Guards would be a wasted gesture.

What would be the point?

Now that the Royal Guards had defied him once, he was certain they would do so again, no matter how many of its leaders he decided to kill. All he would leave was weeping mothers and squealing orphans. And he had no intention of doing such a thing.

He—*himself*—after all, was an orphan in this world.

When he reached the Throne Room—still with Hildie and Veerna tagging along—he felt the weight of their expectation . . . that he *should* do something about the Royal Guards; about their unwillingness to obey him. But he resisted this, too.

If there came a time for him to show his power then it would be for one final—*fatal*—moment . . . with the Webbing Armoury in his possession:

The Webbing Cloak wrapped around his body.

The Webbing Bow over his shoulder.

And the Webbing Blade snugly grasped in his fist.

Then they would know power.
Then they would know fear.
And they *would* obey.

ALL SKIN AND BONE

The night-time air was crisp and cold, and it sent a shudder passing around Flucknor's collar. His whole body felt as if it was drawn rigid. Lying on his side, on the bedroll he had been using throughout the journey for sleeping, he could just about make out the bleary figures of the Horrox standing around their prisoner. He hadn't been privy to the chase earlier that day.

But—from what he had heard, from the *sounds* he had heard—he had *known* it was a chase.

As Brotsboore had relayed to him, they had successfully managed to track down a human.

A Mortal.

It was then that Flucknor had noted something of a change in Brotsboore's voice . . . a kind of wavering tone . . . something like *emotion* . . . and he hadn't quite known what to make of it.

Flucknor wished there might be something he could do, and he had turned the Plarstark over and over in his hands, trying to work out whether or not he had the strength to put its power to use . . . if he could *really* fight back against the Horrox.

But, then again, he knew no details of the captured Mortal.

For all he knew, it could be some bandit the Horrox had picked up off the road; some ne'er-do-well who had been looking to make a fast few grung and had got themselves caught up in something *far* above their station.

Magic, after all, was the common thief's worst nightmare.

Worse even than a knife in the victim's hand.

Hearing a scream come from the captured Mortal—imprisoned between the Horrox all standing around—Flucknor turned and stared across the long grasses.

He wondered if he could do something.

If he could *help* in some way.

Wouldn't it be better to come to the Mortal's aid now and to ask questions of their character later on, once their life was assured? Although Arfklan would surely have Flucknor believe differently, he didn't much buy into the idea that they could trust one another just yet.

Trust took time to build.

And—for the yawning gaps in trust which lay between Flucknor and the Horrox—he could quite easily imagine that it would take several lifetimes.

Flucknor rose up and approached the Horrox encircling the Mortal. As always, the Horrox wore sable traveller's cloaks; a statement which seemed at odds with their ultimate goals . . . at least to Flucknor . . . their divine wish was for freedom and equality—that they might be *seen* by all.

Why then, out here, in the middle of nowhere, did they prefer to hide themselves.

Flucknor noted that Brotsboore was part of the circle of Horrox gathered about the Mortal.

Flucknor met the Horrox's eye for a moment, and then shifted his attention downward to the Mortal being held between them.

To begin with, Flucknor couldn't quite absorb the details which his eyes fed him.

Long, black hair.

A thin—*almost skeletal*—frame.

He recognised him. Of course he did.

It was Sulliman.

Sully.

One of Lou's best friends and most noble of allies.

But what was he doing here?

Out in the middle of nowhere.

It was then that Flucknor's eye was drawn by the object which lay in the long grasses, before him. When he finally saw what it was—a seemingly indistinct hunk of blue-grey stone—he couldn't honestly say what about it had stolen his attention.

Perhaps it was the white lettering engraved on the surface.

Had that lettering gleamed or was it a trick of the torchlight which illuminated the camp?

In any case, Flucknor could hear Arfklan speaking into his mind.

He listened to the words as they formed within his skull:

— *Ah, you have come to us, brother, that is good. That is what I had* hoped *for.*

Flucknor stood still. He gazed back into Arfklan's eyes, knowing that he would never fully grow used to the idea of having some other *being* speaking directly into his brain. He wondered how the Horrox ever became accustomed to the sensation . . . then again, he supposed that speaking within minds came as naturally to them as speaking through mouths came to Mortals.

Taking a deep breath, Flucknor replied to Arfklan, again within his own mind:

— *What do you want me to do?*

Arfklan chuckled within Flucknor's mind; a sensation which was so unworldly, so *unnatural*, that Flucknor felt a tingle skitter across the surface of his skin. And although he tried his best to hide his discomfort in his outward expression, he knew it would be for nothing. If Arfklan desired to know the state of his emotions he had only to reach out to his mind—to *feel* what Flucknor felt.

And that only served to send another quiver through Flucknor's gut.

More than anything, he wanted to escape the Horrox . . . but to where?

Not wanting to look at Arfklan as he spoke into his mind again, Flucknor turned his attention downward, onto Sully, on his knees before them.

— Now is the time to prove yourself, Flucknor. Now you shall show us the extent of your dedication not just to us, the Horrox, but to all Creatures throughout the world. Now is the time for you to show us, once and for all, which side you are truly on.

Flucknor's chest tightened.

His heart rapped several beats faster.

Every muscle seized tight.

Because he knew what was coming next—*somehow he knew what was coming next.*

Arfklan spoke into his mind another time:

— You have the Plarstark, do you not?

Flucknor felt for the pocket of his trousers. He thought—for a fraction of a second—about whether he might have lost it. Whether it might've slipped through his fingertips and into the long grasses . . . but, no, he still had it snug in his pocket. There would be no losing it, or so it seemed.

— Yes.

— Good, then I want you to kill *this Mortal here.*

Flucknor looked down to Sully, took in his body.

Nothing more than skin and bones, really.

Without looking at Sully's weathered face, it would've been hard to tell whether he was a young boy or a middle-aged man. Innocent or guilty. Something in between.

Flucknor knew that the hesitation would be what would get him into trouble; that it would only hasten his own demise. But, at the same time, he knew there was nothing he could rightly do in this circumstance . . . he couldn't simply kill another person in cold blood—for no discernible reason except for the fact that Arfklan told him to.

King of the Horrox, or not.

Even though Flucknor knew that he must answer Arfklan within the realm of his own mind, he felt his throat impossibly dry. He turned his mind to Lou, and he thought of all those he had killed throughout the course of his life—how Lou had burned down the Great Hall, back in Ilsnare, just so that he might prove a point.

That was cold-blooded.

Arfklan spoke into Flucknor's mind once more—for what seemed like the final time:

— I do not need to explain the importance of this act . . . or the consequences which shall come to bear should you fail to follow my instruction. Do not think too hard on it. Only do.

Flucknor again turned his attention to Sully, who held his head bowed throughout this encounter. Even though he couldn't hear the conversations which were happening only in the skulls of those who surrounded him, Flucknor was certain that Sully understood it all. Gripping the Plarstark tightly in his fist, Flucknor did his best to channel his ice magic to his solar plexus; that little piece of advice which he had often overheard, spoken between

Syre and her brother Lou . . . he just needed to concentrate. Concentrate on the Plarstark.

And the pain he would inflict with it on the Horrox.

Those surrounding him. Those *urging* him to kill.

But he wouldn't . . . he wouldn't . . . not even to *them.*

However, it seemed as if the luxury of freewill had been stolen from him, because an invisible hand, chilly to touch, seized hold of his wrist. All at once, he felt an impossible power—*magic*—course through his veins; a power which, once it had commenced, was impossible to stop. It flooded out through him, danced across the surface of his skin. And, before he knew it, when he looked down to the ground, he saw that Sully was writhing about in pain.

Paralysed by it.

Just as Flucknor had been.

Never before had Flucknor been so disgusted with himself.

And yet, at the same time, he was so *confused* . . . because it hadn't been his hand—*his magic*—which'd caused the pain in Sully.

But then whose *had* it been?

A ROOM WITH A VIEW

In the days following the failed sneak-attack on the Horrox en-campments, Lou spent most of his time between the Library and the Throne Room. He mostly worked under the cover of darkness—as he had been familiar with doing throughout his tenure as King of Shellacnass.

The strangest part of this routine was how Veerna and Hildie seemed to pop up at seemingly any given moment, appearing out of the darkness to ask him if he'd like a cup of tea, or else if he needed a helping hand with something. Each time this happened, Lou found himself shunting them away. Although he didn't want to come across as rude—let alone *ungrateful*—the truth of the matter was that, at this stage of his plan—the plan to unite the Magical Fields—there was very little that they could help with. Veerna, as Lou had discovered on more than one occasion when he had brought him books to the Throne Room, had only mastered the rudiments of reading. Often he mixed up his *z's* and *s's* or else got his *j's* and *k's* back to front. And Hildie, although she was certainly a powerful fire mage, even she couldn't doubt the fact that she had—*effectively*—been living outside of civilisation for the best part of a decade . . . and so she hadn't kept up with the latest developments in the area of magical studies.

Actually, Lou was fairly certain that his mental argument against Hildie was more of a cop-out than anything else since magical studies—the *understanding* of magic—had hardly gone through many seismic changes in the past century; let alone the past decade.

All the same, he couldn't allow her too close.

She might compromise the neutrality of the space he hoped to convert into his own personal Ravensbark. A location which would remain secret to all but himself.

And a location where he found himself headed right now.

As he clambered his way up the spiral stone steps of the North-West Spire, he wondered what it was that had drawn him to this particular location. He supposed he had wanted to find some part of the Palace which was little—*if at all*—used. And the North-West Spire was perfect.

To start with, one of the quirks of the design of Ilsnare Palace was that the only entrances into the North-West Spire were through a doorway from the Library or through another in the Catacombs.

One afternoon, Lou had collared an unsuspecting member of the House Staff and had them brick up the entrance from the Library; muttering something about the North-West Spire being structurally unsound. This had been a calculated gesture because Lou had counted on the famous Palace gossip turning this rumour into a solid-gold fact. As far as he knew, nobody else had yet discovered the entrance into the North-West Spire via the Catacombs. In fact, the entrance only existed in the older plans of the Palace; ones which would often be cast aside by anybody searching for architectural drawings for more modern versions.

So, he hoped his secret would be safe.

Of the history he had read of the North-West Spire, he had often come across stories of it being used to house fugitives; fleeing members of royal families adjacent to Shellacnass, and other such controversies. The entire point of the construction of the North-West Spire had been owing to a desire for secrecy. Making it known that the North-West Spire was structurally unsound wasn't even the first time in history *this* particular lie had been used. He had seen no reason to be creative with his tall tales when there were ready-made ones available.

Indeed, when he'd looked through the history books of the Palace, he had even noted that the structural soundness—*solid, or otherwise*—hadn't been commented on in more than a century. This seemed to suggest that the lie had finally been rubbished by some well-meaning architect . . . but Lou would admit no architects.

Once he reached the top of the turret, he felt the foul odour waft in with him.

Walking through the Catacombs beneath the Palace had hardly been a clean exercise.

There was a reason why they were sealed away from the rest of the Palace . . . and, before Flucknor had fled the Palace, and the city through the Catacombs, they had been well concealed behind a stone tablet. Now, though, since that tablet had been destroyed in the ensuing fight, Lou had had a door installed in its place . . . a sturdy door, and far more practical for the many visits which Lou planned to make down to the Catacombs, on his way to the North-West Spire.

Once up in the North-West Spire, Lou could tell, as he always did, why this was such a prized spot for secrecy. To begin with, there was a sturdy oak door with a hefty lock.

Lou had busted through this on his first visit.

He had been surprised how much it'd taken out of him to do so.

How much using his ice magic took out of him.

Beyond the door, the staircase continued, and spiralled upward.

There were three rooms: a washroom, bedroom on the lower level of the Spire, then the largest room on the upper level. There were no windows in the upper level, only holes in the stonework which allowed in the howling gales.

When he peered out of any of those openings, he could make out nothing of the Crystal City. The view from those slits was only of the sprawling, verdant plains beyond . . . the Crystal *Kingdom*: such a well of untapped, *limitless* potential.

Or, at least, that was what he told himself on more drab days.

Lou could tell, from the *rustic* state of the Spire, that there hadn't been any work performed on the location for decades . . . if not centuries. Even the architects, it seemed, believed the gossip.

Since he hadn't wanted to risk his health further by lugging books on up the spiral stone staircases to the Spire, he had had to memorise all the appropriate pieces of knowledge he would require before making the ascent. This had worked better than he had expected. His retention of details—*his memory*—hadn't faded as much as his will had.

Lou climbed to the upper level of the Spire. He took in the bare, stone blocks.

Even as he took in the sight, the crude chalk which he had marked—and then *remarked* when the rain had come and washed it away—on the stone floor.

He had clearly annotated the diamond.

The Magical Fields:

Fire

Ice

Light

Darkness

The Four Corners.

All of the positions were ready. Where they would each stand.

All that remained was to bring them here . . . to bring the *others* here.

And it was with that thought on his mind, with the gentle—*warm*—knowledge that this was probably the only part of the Palace which'd ever felt something like a home to him, that he felt the rumble passing up through the floor.

At first it was faint. Almost unnoticeable.

But then it was so forceful that he could only think it was an *earthquake.*

AN UNEARTHLY FORCE

L ou felt as if the foundations of the Palace themselves were shuddering beneath him.

That they might be in danger of coming loose.

He just about managed to catch himself against one of the stone walls as he fell.

When he caught up with his wits, he mumbled some carefully chosen words, and cast a protective charm about his body, to make it immune to being crushed . . . if the Spire *did* turn out to be as structurally impaired as claimed in the histories, and it crumbled with the force.

For about a minute, all he could do was hold himself flush against the wall of the Spire; to keep himself from tumbling down to the ground. When he gritted his teeth, he felt as if they might split beneath their own force . . . the force of the vibrations which pummelled his body and shook his bones, and which—*apparently*—refused to let him go.

He could smell smoke.

Thick and obvious.

It began to drive him crazy.

Was this some sort of trick?

Some *psychological* ploy?

Feeling the rumbling dying down, he shifted himself away from the wall, and, legs trembling from the force of the sudden earthquake, he peered out through one of the holes which looked down over the Palace. He stared at the Palace below, expecting to see that it had been reduced to rubble. His assumption wasn't far off . . .

Already, he could see gigantic cracks which had appeared in the rooftops; the glass ceiling of the Throne Room had collapsed beneath its own weight; unable to sustain its shape.

Lou felt *something.*

Not sadness.

And not anger.

Because he had never believed Ilsnare Palace to be his home.

He didn't even consider Ilsnare itself to be his home.

His home had long ago been destroyed . . . even if others had attempted to rebuild it from the rubble. What had once been his home—the part of his mind which *created* the feeling of a home— was forever broken. And it always would be.

He steeled himself, ready for further vibrations to pass up through the stone blocks beneath his feet. He knew, from experience, from what he had heard from Flucknor when he had described the final day that Ravensbark had stood, that there was always *something else* which could go wrong . . . something else which was ready to fall.

With that knowledge, he couldn't help but inspect his surroundings.

He stared at the stone walls with something approaching suspicion.

Would this . . . this *refuge* which he had built remain precariously balanced at the top of the North-West Spire, or would it take a tumble; fall down onto the wreckage of the Palace below?

At times like these, he wished he had ploughed more of his time—more of his *energies*—into working on transforming himself into an animal. If only he could turn himself into a crow, like his sister Syre . . . one of those many abilities which she believed she had kept concealed from him.

Lou knew everything there was to know about his sister; about Syre.

He would never have cast her out of the city if he hadn't believed her capable of surviving on her own . . . of seeking out her own journey of self-discovery and education.

He knew that, here, in Ilsnare Palace—the Crystal City as a whole—her ambition and potential had been stifled; like a bird with its wings clipped.

And now she was free.

So free, in fact, that Lou couldn't see how she could ever return.

Why *would* she wish to return?

What debt did she owe to the Crystal Kingdom, and to protecting its subjects from harm?

. . . Lou supposed he would see very soon.

If he survived this disaster, that was.

He held himself still, as if trying to second guess the North-West Spire, to sense whether it might buckle at its base and then suddenly lurch to one side or the other. He decided he needed to move off his spot. He had never achieved anything in his life by standing still.

What *had* he achieved in the past decade skulking about the Palace?

Just a whole bunch of words in his brain . . . most of which would never surface in his mind . . . which would never suggest themselves to him at the opportune moment.

He shifted away from the wall and off in the direction of the doorway.

He could make out the spiral staircase, leading downward.

That was the only way out of here.

He took a large lungful of breath and then bolted.

As he trotted his way down the steps, he felt as if he might slip and fall—*twist his neck* . . . and then that would be that.

But he held on strong and soon reached the bottom of the Spire.

When he got to the place where the member of the House Staff had demolished the door to the Library, and filled in the gap with stone blocks, he paused . . . and then realised that daylight was flooding in all around him. The wall had been demolished.

Dusty, torn pages floated about on the air.

He stood silently, gathering stock.

He looked around.

All the walls, all the ceilings, were falling.

The Palace was ruined.

It was then that he heard footsteps.

Coming up stairs.

He turned to face the doorway which led out of the Library, and down into the Catacombs. His heart rapped against his ribcage. But he held his concentration.

He stared into the darkness, to the Catacombs below, and prepared himself.

They were coming.

The Horrox were coming.

BATTLE

Syre could feel her whole body shaking.

But not with fright.

It was her ice magic which seized her . . . and which kept her alert.

She pressed her back up against the rock face, and then turned to her side, to look back at Rut.

Just to look at his blond hair, and his doughy cheeks made her feel as if none of this was happening. She couldn't believe that someone who looked like *Rut* could truly have set off on a quest like this one alone . . . and expected to survive.

But, then again, she had never truly been able to fathom her brother's motives.

Or to understand them on even a surface level.

She had attacked Ems'plot, and so disrupted the choking spell he had tossed at Rut.

The one which had sent Rut to his knees . . . gasping for air.

Then, acting quickly, she had cast a protective charm over Rut while she set about better disabling Ems'plot. Somehow she had succeeded. She had caught Ems'plot before he could get a hold on his senses again. She wondered if this had taken place two, three years before, whether the result would've been the same. Perhaps if Ems'plot had reacted only fractionally quicker, her efforts would've been futile.

That said, the most she had managed from her resistance was to buy some time.

She turned to look at Rut again, half expecting that he might have something to offer her by way of help here . . . however, she could see that the only thing he held in his possession was the stone with the white lettering etched on its surface. The same one which had leaped free of Rut's hands when Ems'plot had hurled the choking spell in his direction.

Syre breathed in deeply.

When she had disabled Ems'plot, she had worked quickly—had dashed off and grabbed hold of Rut's hand. Somehow, she had found the strength in her to drag him across the ground, and behind this large moulding of rock. Where they were right now.

She knew it wouldn't be long before Ems'plot regained his bearings.

And he would be coming right for them.

All along the journey, Syre had defied Ems'plot in little ways . . . she had even outright *attacked* him out on the plains; when Ems'plot had been lying in wait for the traveller . . . the traveller who, it turned out, had been Rut all along. Now, though, she had set out her stall.

She had stood up against him.

And she was going to have to deal with the consequences.

She felt the sting of ice magic moving through her veins and she hoped—*prayed*—that all she knew would be enough to at least afford herself and Rut an escape from Ems'plot.

Syre held herself still, getting her heartbeat back under control and then she shifted away from the wall. She inched her way across the rock face, and, taking care to keep her movements subtle, so that she wouldn't be noticed right away, she peered around the corner.

She saw Ems'plot, of course.

He was standing up again . . . the hex she'd hurled had, at the very least, knocked him to the ground . . . but it wasn't Ems'plot himself who drew Syre's attention the most.

It was the figure who now stood up beside him.

Syre took in the muscular body . . . much more muscular than usual.

The red, *red* skin.

Lizard-like jaw.

And she caught the scent of rotten eggs on the breeze.

A Horrox.

At first, Syre was perplexed as to what had happened; as to how this could be. But then—her eyes moving slowly before quickly skipping about the landscape—realisation dawned on her. She saw the pair of horses, where they had been left tied up. Each of them stirring their hoofs against the rocky ground, surely frustrated at being unable to find any purchase as they might do with soil.

And somewhat alarmed by the magical battle taking place in their vicinity.

It was then Syre understood the Horrox—using its shapeshifting abilities—had once been the mule . . . that apparently *tired, old mule* which'd followed Ems'plot all over the place.

Syre could clearly recall how she'd thought Ems'plot something of a curmudgeon for having trekked that mule along behind him . . . like a companion that he simply couldn't bear to let free.

More like a mongrel dog than anything else.

But it'd been an ingenious disguise.

Ems'plot and the unidentified Horrox swivelled about.

Their gaze—*as one*—snapped onto Syre.

And she knew she stood no chance.

That they had found her now.

And it would be a simple step to *destroy* her.

She retreated from the edge of the rock, and looked back at Rut, *hoping* he might have some idea of how they might escape. Just that piece of stone he held in his arms.

The white lettering etched onto its surface.

Before she had turned back around, she felt the *crackle* of magic pass through the air.

It brought the hair on her arms erect.

And sent a tingle down her spine.

Thinking quickly, she cast a protective charm about herself and Rut, knowing, even at the time, that it would all be in vain. That it wouldn't take any strain at all for the Horrox and Ems'plot to make short work of it . . . but what else was she supposed to do?

She thought back to the time when her people had been living in the encampments in the foothills of the Sable Mountains; and how, out on the plains, training with the rest of their impromptu defence, they had come across a band of approaching mages.

One of Ma'reygar's advanced attacks.

Supposed to act as scouts, of a kind.

Even then, without properly understanding the ice magic which cut through her—let alone the darkness which loomed over her— she had stood her ground and fought with all her might against the attackers . . . those who wished her loved ones agony.

And, with Lou's assistance, she had managed to repel them.

But then what?

It had taken so much of her energy—so much of her *health*—to feel her magic simply flow right through her as if she was nothing but its conduit. It would take a show of strength on par to that now. With this resolution firmly fixed in her mind, she turned to look out through the obscured bubble of air—the protective charm which she'd cast around herself and Rut.

She observed the Horrox and Ems'plot.

Stalking outside.

The two of them with their gaze firmly fixed upon Syre and Rut within.

Syre could feel the hundreds of hexes she'd learned through the years tumbling through her mind. There were so many of them vying for attention that she found it almost impossible to choose the right one . . . but which one would be the *Right One*?

Surely it would be the one which saved herself and Rut.

Before Syre could utter so much as a sound, she observed the Horrox and Ems'plot raising their hands. And she watched on as the colourful, neon sparks bounced from their fingertips, skittering along the ground. One or two of the sparks made contact with the outer shell of the protective bubble. She watched on in horror as they passed through the protective charm as if it hadn't been there at all, and—*worse still*—began to tear a much larger hole. She fired herself into life, shouting the incantations at the top of her lungs; as if the mere volume of her voice would have any bearing on the strength of her spell. She felt the pinkish-white light seeping out from her body.

Going to patch up the protective bubble.

Even as she weaved these charms, she knew it would do no good in the long run . . . that Ems'plot and the Horrox would be able to overwhelm her strength.

And so it was.

She imagined herself back on the boat—*Harver's Moon*—which had taken her and her brother away from Brinder Island . . . and the pursuing Ma'reygar.

At night, while her brother suffered from seasickness, Syre would take part in the arm wrestles with the sailors on the ship. They all knew she was different. Maybe they *knew* she was a Magical being . . . perhaps not . . . all they knew was that, when it came to arm-wrestling, she had a knack of beating all those who came to face her. Now, though, it felt as if she was on the other side of the table. The Horrox and Ems'plot simply overwhelming her resistance.

Gradually wrestling her fist down onto the table.

With a thick *slap* of flesh against wood.

This time, though, when the Horrox and Ems'plot broke through her protective charm, there wasn't anything so satisfying as that sound . . . it was only a gradual easing of tension—a weight being removed from her shoulders. And, just like that, the protective charm fell.

The warm, volcanic winds blew in over her.

Her breaths came shallow—*insufficient.*

She stared back at Ems'plot and the Horrox.

Knowing this would be the end.

"Get out of the way!" Ems'plot shouted at her.

Syre stood firm, shielding the cowering Rut with her own body.

Ems'plot swiped the air.

It was as if an enormous, invisible arm clawed Syre out of the way.

She flew through the air.

Pounded into rock.

As she raised her head, pain prickling all over her body, she stared out through bleary eyes and witnessed Ems'plot and the

Horrox standing over Rut. She didn't even have the energy to raise a shout from her throat . . . it became strangled; impossible to form in any cohesive way.

And, in any case, it never would've stopped those colourful lights—*the magic*—from fizzling about the hands of the Horrox and Ems'plot; bundling into a large ball.

From coming down with a *crushing* force.

FIGHT-BACK

Lou threw himself down against what had once been a stone wall of one of the corridors of Ilsnare Palace. He felt the sweat beading down the sides of his face. Although he had had an inkling that he was out-of-shape—that he'd not put in the requisite practice to keep his magic sharp—he'd believed that he would have more resistance than this.

Stone dust clouded the air.

He could feel it settling on his face.

And catching in his airways.

Making his throat as dry as anything he might imagine.

He took another moment to catch his breath, and then glanced up, over the wreckage of Ilsnare Palace. He could see the Horrox— *dozens, hundreds?*—they streamed out of the door to the Catacombs . . . it was obvious that that was how they had made their way in . . . but *how*?

The only entrance Lou knew of into the Catacombs—from outside the city, the only one which remained—was down on the banks of the River Ils. That was one of the first tasks Lou had set his architects; to find out all the possible ways that enemies might find their way into Ilsnare . . . was it possible there were other entryways he hadn't considered?

His wandering thoughts were curtailed by the magic which sliced through the air.

And which caterwauled into the remainder of the stone wall he shielded himself behind.

A piece of rock flew *hard* into his chest.

As hard as if the projectile had been aimed at him with extreme purpose.

For a couple of moments, he lost his breath.

But he forced himself up, into a crouching position.

Doubled-over, he remained behind the still-standing portion of the stone wall.

He hoped the Horrox wouldn't find a lucky strike.

While he trudged his way along, he muttered a protective charm into being about his body. He felt the crackle of magic bringing all the hairs on his body erect. And it caused his stomach to sink.

As he went along, he listened to the hexes bouncing off the protective charm he had cast.

He didn't turn to take in the perpetrators.

As far as he cared, they could remain faceless.

Nameless.

At this moment in time they were only *enemies.*

He sensed himself free of the immediate grouping of Horrox when he turned the corner. Up ahead, he eyed what remained of a stone staircase. It was only now that he felt his heart leap into his mouth. He thought of Hildie and Veerna, and he wondered if they were okay . . . or if they had been crushed by the earthquake which'd shaken Ilsnare Palace to its very foundations.

His first priority was to get clear.

To get clear of the *Palace.*

He found himself on cobblestones now. He could see the Palace Walls.

They remained very much intact.

He couldn't help thinking of the irony; that the Palace Walls which'd served to keep the King safe were now responsible for casting him into grave danger.

He eyed the main gates, and knew there was no other way.

If he ran with all his strength, he might be able to make it out to the snaking, labyrinthine streets located in the lead-up to Ilsnare Palace . . . the ones which would eventually take him to the Crystal Causeway, and to the City Gates themselves. But first he had to breach the Palace Walls.

He recalled the countless times he had witnessed Syre—without her knowledge—transform herself into a crow and—very simply—flutter up and over the walls.

Now, though, this option wasn't available to him.

It was only when he reached the walls themselves, and came to a standstill, that he realised he had no plan for getting over the top. And, worse, that he would be cornered by the advancing Horrox.

He was certain that they would make him a prime target.

What could send a better, more domineering message, than the death of the King of Shellacnass?

How would the Garrison fight back against the Horrox then?

From what Lou could tell, from the frightened voices—*at full pitch*—on the other side of the Palace Walls, the Royal Guards hadn't yet realised what had gone on.

That the Horrox had managed to breach the city.

Seeing no other way out of the Palace, he toyed with the idea of crying out for help . . . but this seemed a cowardly and ineffective solution. He knew well that—in a time of crisis—in an *emergency*, the very worst that a person could do—with survival in mind— was to follow the herd.

For several seconds, he lost himself in the remembrance of a story he had overheard from a hobblesman . . . about a flock of sheep, so dizzied by their numbers, and by their surroundings, that they simply followed one another—*one after the other*—over the edge of a cliff; falling to their collective doom. No, he needed a better solution.

It was then that—out of the corner of his eye—he caught some movement.

Nothing more than a vague motion.

He realised that it was a block of cobblestones.

Lifted up ever so slightly.

A gap wide enough only for a pair of eyes to peer out.

Thinking quickly—in truth *not* thinking—he sprinted over to the block of cobblestones, dropped onto his belly, and then yanked it upward. He cast a final glance about himself, just in time to see a pair of Horrox turning the corner, their inky-black eyes searching for a victim.

He slipped in through the gap. Dropped down into the hole.

Darkness swallowed him.

INVISIBLE, MURDEROUS HANDS

I t had been a long ride for them to return to Ilsnare.

A week . . . more?

Flucknor had felt as if a cloud, full of rain, thunderous—and ready to burst at any second—had been hanging over his head. He still couldn't escape what he had done . . . what he had *done* with his own two hands . . . In his mind, he could still see Sully's eyes peering up at him:

Pleading with him.

Wishing for mercy.

And yet, those invisible, murderous hands—he could term them whatever he liked, but they would *always* be his own—had squeezed the Plarstark tightly and inflicted the greatest, most terrible power that he had ever experienced. It had flooded through him as if he had been struck by lightning. Never before had he expected to possess such power.

Had it even *been* his own power?

He supposed he learned something new about himself every day of his life . . .

He could still feel the form of the Plarstark in his pocket, seeming to weigh him down as he plodded along on the back of his horse; among all the others.

All of them headed for the promised land of the Crystal City.

Flucknor wasn't sure why he had retained the Plarstark, or, better still, why he hadn't turned that impossibly strong power upon the Horrox who had surrounded Sully; who had been so determined to see him writhe in pain—*to suffer to the maximum*—while he was killed . . . and to think, with these sorts of thoughts floating about his mind, that others had once considered Flucknor to 'wander in the light'.

. . . If that had been true before—*if that had ever been true at all*—then he knew that he unmistakably 'walked in the darkness' now.

He had joined Syre in that way.

Perhaps that could give him some comfort?

Flucknor sensed the pace of the group of Horrox on horseback quicken, and—to begin with—he paid the sensation no mind. He was lost among his own thoughts . . . lost in his own world of the past . . . and his past memories. One thing was for certain, he would never shake the terrible image of Sully's dying expression from his mind.

Finally, he glanced up.

And he saw the glass rooftops of Ilsnare.

The Crystal City.

The setting sunlight caught the glass. Reflected its golden rays all over. Its light almost blinding.

Next, he took in the impossibly long—impossibly *tall*—pit-black City Walls which surrounded the capital of Shellacnass. Although it had only been weeks he had been away, it felt as if he had left this place behind decades ago. He only realised now he had expected never to return.

Maybe he had thought the Horrox would kill him rather than use him.

Perhaps, in a way, they had done both.

As it had for the past few days, he could feel his horse limping. He could recall a moment when his horse had slipped on a piece of loose ground, apparently turned its ankle. Ever since then, it hadn't been able to walk right . . . to walk *soundly.* Although his horse attempted to keep up with the others ahead, it was soon reduced to limping along . . . unable to continue at the same pace.

The result was that Flucknor steadily felt himself being left behind by the rest.

Even Brotsboore, riding amongst the other Horrox, set off away from him at a brisk trot.

Flucknor wondered if the Horrox would notice at all if he quietly slipped away—if he decided to disappear into exile . . . to go somewhere he would never be found.

He had proven himself to them, after all.

He had shown the extent of his dedication.

He had *killed* a fellow human being.

Surely that would be enough to satisfy their bloodlust?

It was only when the Horrox had disappeared out of his line of sight, down the hillside which would lead onto the verdant plains which surrounded the Crystal City, that Flucknor—for the first time he'd left Ilsnare behind—felt truly alone. Truly alone with his thoughts.

A chance to look himself in the eye.

No matter how unpleasant that might be.

Feeling his horse staggering now—apparently having done itself serious harm trying to keep up with the others—he allowed himself to gradually slide down the leather saddle. He landed with his feet an even shoulder-width apart then stood and watched as the horse trotted away; after the others, freed of the burden which it had had to lug about on its back for day after day.

He breathed in deeply, taking in the fresh air.

He had heard the news, of course, relayed to him through the Horrox.

He knew that Ilsnare had fallen.

And that the Horrox had seized control of the Crystal City.

If the stories which'd got to him were to be believed, then it was true that the Horrox had brought Ilsnare Palace to the ground . . . reduced it to rubble. When he had heard that, related to him as a cold, hard fact, he had felt a profound sadness descend over him. It seemed almost as if—while he had been reeling from being stabbed in his heart—somebody had decided to cut off his feet.

His home, what had become his home, was now gone.

Everything was forever changed.

Although he had heard no news as to the fate of Lou, he could only suspect the worst. He could tell, from the body language of the Horrox, how they seemed to have a fresh vigour injected into their step, that they believed they would return to Ilsnare to claim their victory. Despite the warm weather which'd draped over them for the past few hours of their journey, he was certain that he could feel a cold front moving in. It was an almost *moist* sensation, up against his skin. He thought he could hear the rumble of thunder on the horizon, perhaps moving in from the Sable Mountains.

Ready to roll in over Ilsnare.

A mist, too, was beginning to descend.

Strange that this touch of winter was coming to the plains when it had been stifling hot for so long. But, then again, he supposed that was just the dice which nature threw . . . as casually—*as wantonly*—as an old, blind beggar down a back alley.

It was out of the mist that Flucknor first began to see the form.

Stout.

Spry.

Grey.

Flucknor squeezed his eyes shut, hoping to shake any delusion free from his vision.

But when he opened them again, it was only to see the same figure from before.

Out there.

In the mist.

He gazed about, realising that the sun had set completely now, and that night had very much come to bear on the landscape. He felt a shudder pass through him. He tried to tell himself that it was because of the cold, though he admitted that this figure, out there in the mist, had caught him off guard. Just when he had believed himself alone . . .

When he had thought he might have a moment's peace; just for himself . . .

It would teach him to be so presumptuous.

The figure drew closer, and he was better able to make out its grey skin, even in the fading light . . . the last glimmers of sunshine giving way to moon glow.

A strange creature.

Like a goblin . . . or a gremlin . . . or—at least—what he had *heard* of them.

Finally, the grey, little creature stood before him.

It took Flucknor another second to realise that it clutched something in its hands.

A grey piece of rock.

With scrawled—*glowing*?—writing across it.

Flucknor waited for the words to appear in his mind, and was glad when the Creature actually spoke aloud . . . in Flucknor's own tongue:

"I thought you might require this," it said, holding the object to him.

Flucknor stared long and hard at the piece of stone. He shook his head. "I . . . what is it?"

The Creature gave a vague smile. "That which the other Mortal was seeking." The Creature gave a wide grin, exposing its many, white, sharp teeth. "I stole it from one of the saddlebags, when they weren't looking."

Finally, because the Creature was so insistent, shoving the piece of stone into his chest, he took it off him. And now he was *certain* the white text was glowing.

He felt a sinking feeling in his stomach.

He looked back to the Creature. "What *are* you?" he asked, only realising how rude and pointed the question seemed after he had uttered it.

The Creature, however, didn't seem put out.

"A Glyph," it replied. "Or, I suppose, *the* Glyph . . . since I haven't seen another around lately." The Creature—*the Glyph*—cocked its head to one side and squinted with its round, large eyes. "You haven't seen another like me, have you?"

"I . . . uh, *no*," Flucknor finally got out, shaking his head too, as if this might help make the statement more emphatic.

The Glyph glanced about itself, and then its eyes dived downward, to Flucknor's trouser pocket. It then reached out its skinny, grey fingers and pointed. "I would like to exchange," it said.

Distracted from the stone in his hands for a moment, he glanced down.

Down to his pocket.

And then he remembered the Plarstark.

A shudder passed through him.

Remembering what it could do.

Flucknor glanced back at the Glyph. "Why?" he said. "What do you want it for?"

The Glyph gave a shrug, its same easy smile clinging to its mouth. "I shall make sure it never finds its way into the wrong hands again."

He held himself still for a long—*long*—while . . . and then, gently, slowly, he reached down to his pocket and produced the Plarstark from within. He held the sky-blue object, gleaning dully in the moonlight, tight between his index finger and thumb, as if it might attempt to squirm free of his grasp. "You mean *my* hands, don't you?"

The Glyph remained silent for several moments, and then it reached out for the Plarstark. It took it from Flucknor, grasped it for a few seconds . . . and then it was gone:

It simply disappeared into thin air.

The Glyph replied, finally, its tone a touch dour now, as if reflecting the long journey which they had all made, "I wouldn't be so certain that they were *your* hands."

After wallowing in wonder at the Plarstark's disappearing act for a couple of beats, Flucknor finally snapped himself out of his daze. He stared hard at the Glyph. "What do you mean?"

"I mean, that those weren't *necessarily* your hands—*your powers*—which committed murder."

"*You?* But *how?*"

The Glyph remained still, taking on an almost melancholic air now. A slight smile tugged at the corner of its mouth. It glanced up at him one more time. "It was the way it had to be. I could see no other method . . . no other method," it repeated whimsically.

" 'No other method' . . . for *what*?" he replied, feeling impatient, relieved and terrified, all at the same time.

The Glyph remained steeped in silence for a long while longer, the mists rolling in on them, and sending a fresh shudder through Flucknor—cutting him right down to the bone. And then it said, "No other way to keep the Webbing Armoury in good hands . . . in *safe* hands."

Flucknor allowed those words to drift about in the air a moment or so longer, and then the sheer importance of what the Glyph claimed hit him like a punch to the back of the head.

UNDERGROUND

L ou felt all around him.

Whenever his palms came into contact with the wall, he felt the dampness . . . the *moss* which clung to the stonework. He breathed in the earthy scent of it; felt it weaving its way into his bones . . . matting the insides of his lungs. He wondered if he just stayed here—*just stayed here*—in the darkness, in these underground chambers which ran beneath the River Ils, the world above would go away. If the Crystal Kingdom would go away.

It was a childish urge; for him to simply shut his eyes and make the whole of existence vanish. And, as with most childish urges—most childlike *desires*—it had zero probability of coming true.

But that didn't stop Lou from hoping. He had always been a fool for such things . . .

". . . Lou? . . . Lou?"

He heard his own name, drifting along the tunnel.

Drifting to his ears.

Out of shadows.

He recognised the voice, of course—*her voice.*

Hildie.

And he knew why she had been sent.

He had gone missing from the cavern.

Others were worried that he had come to harm.

Realising there was little point in keeping up this childish game of hide-and-seek, he allowed his ice magic to swill to his finger-tips. A searing white-blue glow illuminated the world around him.

He looked to the stone walls, and then to the earth ceiling above him; the ceiling which seemed as if it was *far* too low for any normal, standing person . . . but, then again, these caverns hadn't been dug out for those such as him; Magical beings had been here centuries before, making their homes beneath the plains. When they had left, he really had no idea.

There was so much of the Kingdom of Shellacnass which went undocumented in the Palace Library . . . or it *had* gone undocumented before the Horrox had consigned Ilsnare Palace to nothing more than rubble.

He turned his attention to the end of the tunnel, to the corner.

It was unnerving, being underground.

It was as if a damp cloth was pressed into each of his ears—stuffed up his nostrils.

Even his taste, when he breathed in, seemed to be affected by the earthy scent which clung to everything. He knew that the bed of the River Ils was close by. He could smell it. He would've thought, after being underground for weeks—or had it been months?—he might've grown accustomed to these sensations . . . but, if anything, they had only grown more pronounced.

Rather than becoming part of him—part of his sensory image of the world—they had grown larger and larger, like a group of unwelcome houseguests who—no matter how strong the prompting—were determined never to leave.

At the end of the tunnel, he made out Hildie's form.

She wore her red hair in a tidy bundle, at the back of her head, as most of the women underground did. And, like everyone else, her cheeks were matted with clay, and earth, and other elements which encapsulated the living conditions beneath the level of the soil.

When her eyes met with his, she gave an easy smile.

One which took Lou off guard.

He had grown so used to the beaten-down expressions of those who dwelled underground; the decrepit postures, all of them hunched over from being forced to bow their heads so that they might simply walk through the tunnels dug out by dwarfs, or who-knew-what-else.

Hildie approached. Somehow, in walking, she retained her grace. Perhaps it was her being of a shorter stature than most. Surprising to him, her smile didn't let up as she got closer to him.

This had to be *really* good news . . .

"I just got word," she said, "from scouts on the surface."

Lou thought about how things had worked out. How a community of them had come to live underground . . . while up on the surface the Horrox were committing Mortals to slavery.

Lou could still recall the first days, the constant sound of *crumbling* from above—the constant *rumble* through the ground—as the Horrox demanded the buildings of the city be demolished.

In those first few days, those among them considered most trustworthy—not to mention brave—had been sent to the surface tasked with bringing news; what they heard, what they *saw*, of the Horrox's regime coming into being above. This 'news' had been predictably bleak.

It was just as he had imagined it, just what had kicked him into wanting to study as hard as possible so that he might avoid war . . . at the very least, he supposed that he had avoided that.

From the news they'd gathered from the surface in the days following the Horrox's destruction of Ilsnare Palace, the Royal Guards had surrendered in short order.

It appeared that the Horrox had emerged in other places about the city too.

From out of the Catacombs.

A sneak-attack.

Lou had wryly wondered whether the Captain of the Royal Guards had been taking notes all the while . . . perhaps he could learn something from this manoeuvre for the future.

Lou fixed his stare back onto Hildie—onto those brilliant green eyes of hers.

The icy-white glow emanating from the palm of his hand.

"What do the scouts say?" Lou asked.

"They say the North-West Spire is still standing."

Lou felt a thrill through his chest. It'd been such a long time since he had felt anything at all. It was difficult to feel anything underground. But this was something . . . this *was* good news for him.

It meant that the area he had conserved—the area which he had strived to keep neutral, the area in which he had placed his hopes of uniting the Magical Fields—was still standing.

And yet, did it even matter any longer?

From all the reports he had heard, he knew as well as anybody else that the Horrox had seized control of Ilsnare, and, by extension, the administration of the Kingdom of Shellacnass. Then again, other reports went into detail about how there were already rebel groups—being whipped up from the Northern Villages, among other places—and it was believed that in a matter of days there would be a wave of resistance against the new self-appointed rulers of the Kingdom.

That would mean *more* death.

More suffering.

If only he could make the Mortals see that they had no hope of beating back these Magical beings . . . the Horrox were—*quite simply*—operating on a plane far removed from that of Mortals. They played by different rules. The only way to beat the Horrox . . . the only way of embracing them . . . would be through Magical means.

And Lou was determined not to allow that hope to die.

Not quite yet.

"Is there anything we can do?" Lou said, meeting Hildie's eye.

For the first time in their conversation that day, Hildie's expression turned away from its rampant positivity. She averted his gaze. "We need to bide our time," she said. "We're still working on a way out . . . perhaps there will be a means for us to escape."

That was right. Although Lou had remained detached from the plans, he had been obliged to be present in body. And he couldn't help having some of the details penetrate his brain . . . he had heard stories of a group of them doing their best to dig out another tunnel; to perhaps link up with the Catacombs which ran beneath the entirety of the city.

To find a way out onto the plains.

But Lou couldn't see what that would achieve.

By now, the Horrox were certain to have the surroundings of the Crystal City *stifled* by patrols.

An escape of that magnitude—let alone what others were planning: bringing those on the surface down through the tunnels so that they might escape to the plains—just sounded impossible to Lou.

But, at the same time, he understood the need for hope. These people needed to be able to believe in something. And if this kept them occupied—kept their hopes *alive* in the meantime—then there was little Lou could think of to fault them.

Hildie gave him a parting smile, as if acknowledging the truth they both understood implicitly—that Lou had come here, to this part of the tunnels so that he might be alone.

She trod away; disappearing around the corner before he could have the chance to say anything else. Not that he would've said anything at all.

Now he could only wait. Wait for the right time. And place his trust in others.

Sully.

Rut.

Flucknor.

Syre.

The only ones who mattered any longer in the Crystal Kingdom. At least where Mortals were concerned.

TRAPPED

Syre stared out through the bars of light which held her imprisoned.

She scolded herself—*time and again*—for getting trapped like this.

But, when she'd seen the flurry of lights—the pummelling power with which Ems'plot and the Horrox had snuffed out Rut's life—she had quite simply lost the will to live.

Never before had she suffered a loss so badly.

Not even the death of her mother and father.

At least then there had been something to fight for.

Survival itself.

The strife against the hidden danger—against the cursed animals . . . and against nature itself which threatened to leap up and rip out her throat at a moment of its choosing.

Now, though, things were much simpler.

Syre was a mere prisoner. Only now did she see the true purpose of the purloining of the horses earlier in their journey. They had been intended for the three of them.

For herself.

For Ems'plot.

And for—what had once been—the *mule.*

But which was now a Horrox.

The third horse had been acquired at Rut's expense; the very horse with which he had travelled to this particular spot in the Kingdom. Ems'plot and the Horrox, for some indiscernible reason—other than perhaps spite—had decided she should be the one to ride Rut's horse.

Then again, she supposed that if any of them were going to be riding Rut's horse then it might as well be her. It was all that was left of him.

The bars of light hung around her, conjured out of thin air. As soon as Ems'plot had cast the charm, she had tested out its strength and had soon ascertained that she could—*quite easily*—break through it. But she had decided against doing that. For one, she had nowhere to run to . . . and, for another, she couldn't quite get shot of the feeling that she, Ems'plot and the Horrox were all headed for the same place. They were all returning to Ilsnare.

The Capital of Shellacnass.

The Crystal City.

As she sat on the back of Rut's horse, she could see the glass rooftops of Ilsnare coming into view. For the first time since she could remember, her stomach sank at the sight—an *actual* feeling at seeing the city as if it might represent something more than a mere collection of stone walls and artfully placed glass. Was it because of what it represented—what it *had* represented?

That, for the past decade, anyway, it had been something of a refuge for herself and her brother?

After all, she had passed so much time in the luxurious throes of Ilsnare Palace.

Most likely she had become spoiled and accustomed.

Only now, on the outside of the pit-black walls which marked the circumference did she realise the truth.

That Ilsnare was as good as home to her.

The closest thing she had to a home.

Ems'plot and the Horrox continued on their way forward, and Syre's horse followed their lead. She was surprised when, acting on instinct, she looked in the direction of Ilsnare Palace and found that it was no longer there. All that remained was a single spire.

The North-West Spire, if she recalled accurately.

What had happened here?

As if the gods decided to answer her question, she turned her gaze to the ramparts above the City Gates and saw the Horrox which stalked about.

They had no weapons, of course.

They needed no weapons.

They had the advantage over all humans.

Simply from their status as Magical beings.

Even as she moved beneath their gaze, on horseback, with Ems'plot and the Horrox leading the way, she couldn't help but feel a shudder pass over the surface of her skin.

There was something so profoundly *unnatural* about all this.

Something unspeakably *cruel.*

These Horrox using their powers to reign over Mortals . . . the same way, Syre supposed, that Mortals had once reigned over them.

Syre recognised the Crystal Causeway when they turned onto it, but not before. All the buildings leading up to the cobblestones which ran along the bank of the River Ils had been decimated . . . it seemed much worse than if the city had simply been under siege. No, this was more a case of the Horrox moving—*systematically—*

between each building and making a point of grinding it into the dust. Until there was nothing left.

What was it that the Horrox were trying to prove?

Trying to achieve?

Did they hope to banish Mortals from the face of the world and— in their place—create some new order . . . some new civilisation with no memory of the old?

Syre, not privy to the Horrox's thoughts, couldn't say.

As they continued on up the Crystal Causeway, she caught sight of several humans—*Mortals*—moving this way and that; their clothing ragged and torn as they lugged pieces of stone back and forth at the whim of the Horrox. When some of them looked over, when some of them saw her face, she turned away. She didn't want to be the one responsible for the punishments which would surely be meted out by the Horrox for slacking off duty.

If it had been a strange feeling passing through the City Gates, then it was a much stranger one still when they plodded on into the Palace courtyard to an audience of Horrox on every conceivable side, standing at every conceivable angle.

She breathed in the thick, heady stench of rotten eggs which floated about everywhere. She couldn't help thinking of Tineoots . . . of when he had assumed his true form.

When he had shown himself to her; and to the world.

As they trod into the centre of the courtyard, she realised that— amongst the rubble of what had been Ilsnare Palace—one of the Horrox had decided to remove the throne from the Throne Room . . . to bring it out here, into the middle of the courtyard.

And to act the *King.*

It was only when Syre's horse came to a halt, behind Ems'plot and the Horrox, that she recognised who sat on the throne. She had seen him before, of course. The self-proclaimed King of the Horrox: Arfklan.

It was then that her gaze shifted upward, to Arfklan's shoulder.

Her chest tightened as the realisation dawned over her of who it was standing there.

Brotsboore.

The Horrox who had been a friend of Flucknor.

One of those who had made up the *Outcast*.

The white lights keeping her prisoner in the saddle of her horse gave way.

Releasing her.

Even as she slipped down off the saddle, and landed on the cobblestones of the courtyard, she could hardly believe what she was witnessing. That this was truly happening.

It all seemed so . . . *unreal*.

She thought of how the Council of Wisemen had spoken of the Outcast at the time; how they hadn't taken the Outcast seriously . . . how they had believed them to be an organisation of little consequence. She couldn't help wondering what the Council of Wisemen might think of them now . . . but, then again, the Council of Wisemen had perished.

Perhaps that said it all.

At any moment, she expected to see Flucknor show his face.

It wouldn't have surprised her.

But the only faces—her own and Ems'plot's aside—were those of the Horrox.

Those lizard-like features.

The inky-black eyes.

And that unquenchable *stench* of rotten eggs.

Ems'plot hung back while the Horrox—the one who had transformed himself from the mule—approached Arfklan, sat on the throne.

Syre held her breath in her lungs as the Horrox knelt down before Arfklan, bowed his head in his presence. She wouldn't have minded admitting aloud that she held just about as much reverence and respect for the royal duties of other Creatures as she did for Mortals . . . which was to say that she held none at all.

Arfklan rose up from his throne, having acknowledged the Horrox before him. He shifted his gaze from Ems'plot onto Syre. Then a sly grin emerged on his lizard lips. "Princess Syre Dorf," he said, at least having the manners to speak aloud, rather than directly into her mind . . . perhaps there was hope for Mortals yet . . . "Or, as is probably more accurately said these days, *Syre*."

Perhaps it was the fatigue of the many days of journeying, or maybe she had simply lost her wits, but she found herself bowing her head to Arfklan.

She expected this gesture to be greeted with gloating.

That there would be a whole chorus of shrill laughter at her expense.

But there was nothing.

Just the slightest of hints of Arfklan's smile widening.

"Wonderful to see you," he said, and then turned to Ems'plot.

His expression transformed into more businesslike pursed lips. "I presume that you have brought it with you? That you have fulfilled your part of the bargain?"

Ems'plot, himself with a sly grin, was holding the piece of stone with which Rut had emerged from one of the caverns. Unlike before, Syre couldn't make out any of the white text glowing . . . perhaps it was because of the time of day . . . because the sun was shining down on them.

For the first time, she realised that the stone wasn't cleanly cut; that it had a ragged edge to it.

When Ems'plot stood right before Arfklan, still holding tightly to the stone, he said, "And where is *your* end of the bargain?"

Strangely, she noted that Arfklan became fidgety at this probe.

And she hadn't long to wait to find out why.

"We've . . . ah," Arfklan began, "had some *troubles* . . ."

This time Ems'plot tilted his head to one side. He held the stone to his chest. "Well, then, I don't see that we have a deal."

Arfklan remained where he stood, and then he cast a glare at Syre. "She will be mine—you've brought her to me . . . you *promised* . . ."

Ems'plot gave a shrug. "But a promise is only as good as your word, and I don't trust you."

Syre felt the world swirling about her. She realised what Arfklan was saying; what was going on here. That Ems'plot had struck a deal with Arfklan to bring her to *him.*

. . . For what purpose, she was afraid to ask.

Not that it would've made any difference.

For a start, she wasn't Ems'plot's to give away.

Ems'plot looked to Syre, and spoke to her through gritted teeth, "Come on," he said.

However, even as Ems'plot turned his back on her and made to exit the courtyard—and the Palace—Syre watched on as the muscular Horrox, the one who had been in the form of a mule throughout the journey, blocked his path.

"Let me *through!*" Ems'plot said, sounding more curmudgeonly than ever.

The muscular Horrox stood firm.

When Syre glanced back to Arfklan, she saw that a fresh sly smile had appeared on his lips. "You didn't think we would allow you to take her away once you'd brought her to us, did you?"

Ems'plot glanced to Syre, suddenly looking somewhat sheepish, and then he turned back to Arfklan.

Syre felt the tension taut in the air.

Her heart rapped against her throat.

And her ice magic pricked her veins.

She knew it was now or never.

So, clenching her fists down at her sides, she allowed her magic to get the better of her.

She pictured her ribcage splitting open.

And all her magic pouring out from within.

A NEW HOPE;
A DISMAL TRUTH

As always, Lou kept himself to the fringes of all discussion of strategy . . . especially when it came to deal with *escaping*. He was glad to find that Leona, the woman who'd acted as his High Representative, and—previously—as the Speaker of the Council of Wisemen, had taken his place.

It was widely acknowledged, if not outwardly stated, that Leona was as good as the voice of the King of Shellacnass. And Lou couldn't have cared less. He had his own plans to work on; and to put in the requisite mental fortitude, he needed as little interaction with others as possible. At least, the others living underground seemed to intuit this, and they tended to leave him alone. He wondered if this was some kind of misplaced *respect* for him as the King of Shellacnass; perhaps they felt sheepish about the fact that he could no longer hide himself away behind the walls of the Palace . . . keep his presence out of the grasp of mere *subjects.*

No matter how many twisting turns Lou took through the tunnels—and no matter how many times he tried to search for new spots for hiding—he would find, without exception, that either Hildie or Veerna would locate him with ease.

Whenever they did they were undoubtedly reverent, and clearly only wanted to be *close* to him . . . and, to tell the truth, Lou was glad to have the company.

Another useful factor of their company was that they would often bring him various news items; the stories which would be shredding through the rest of the underground and yet unremarked upon by the King himself. His mind clearly wrapped up in other things.

The news which came was not often cheery, but it was usually easily ignored by Lou; making neither a negative or positive impact on his outlook . . . one day, however, changed all that.

Lou had shut himself off in one of the countless disused tunnels, and he was putting his mind to work on some matter of uniting the Four Corners when he heard the giveaway *shuffle* of footsteps.

Almost as if he had been poring over some dusty tome, he looked up from the patch of earth he had been staring at in the darkness and brought a sliver of ice-white flame dancing up on his palm.

It was Veerna who emerged from the cloaked shadows.

His features were boyish, as always—fine and chiselled . . . but still lacking refinement. He knew that, as the boy grew into his body, he would grow into those features. And it would be a most familiar face. At least to Lou.

"What is it?" Lou asked, sounding much icier in his tone than he had intended.

He supposed that all the time he spent alone gradually chipped away at what remained of his good manners; piece by piece.

Veerna became fidgety and it was then that Lou knew that the news he had to deliver was very grave indeed.

"Go on," Lou said, turning away, shifting his focus back onto the earthy wall, as if he might be able to soften the blow of whatever it was that was about to come.

He could hear Veerna's tiny, snatched, boy's breaths.

The way he would breathe all the way in only to suddenly exhale ... as if the latest breath wasn't sufficient to get out what it was he had to say. "It's about Sully and Rut," Veerna said.

And before Veerna said anything more, Lou could feel his heart dropping in his chest.

So many times he had second guessed his decision to send the two of them away.

But there had been no other way.

The truth was that the only ones who knew how to recover the keystones—the means to gain access to the Webbing Armoury—were the two of them.

Nobody else in the entire world knew of their existence.

Lou prepared himself for the worst, and when Veerna spoke the words, confirmed that Sully and Rut were dead, Lou only felt a hollowing sensation in his chest ... as if some invisible hand had managed to suck all the warmth out of his body; never to allow it to be restored.

His entire body went numb. The icy fire which Lou held in his palm flickered.

Almost went out.

He lost track of his thoughts.

"Your Highness?" Veerna said. "Are you ... okay?"

Lou continued to stare at the earth walls of the tunnel and he wondered just what they were doing down here, underground. What they were hoping to achieve was undoubtedly impossible. So why should they keep on trying? Why not just turn themselves over to the Horrox?

The Webbing Armoury . . . without the keystones, it would be lost forever.

And even Lou had to admit that he wouldn't place the last of his hope in Syre and Flucknor . . . in *himself* somehow managing to bring this plan of his together.

It had been doomed to fail from the start.

Why hadn't he been able to see that sooner?

Lou turned to Veerna, his voice firm, and his tone unshaking . . . *hard* almost. "Go. You need to *go*."

Veerna held still, as if he was rooted to the ground, and then—with a barely discernible nod—he took off along the tunnel, leaving Lou behind.

Only when Lou was alone did he allow sadness to grip him totally.

Only then did he allow his feet to sink down into the earth below . . . to feel as if he might just keep on sinking forever and ever . . . until the end.

Although he hadn't wished to admit to himself before, the chances of the Horrox allowing him access to the North-West Spire—let alone him, Flucknor, Syre *and* Hildie—would be next to none.

They simply wouldn't believe him.

That his intentions were *good.*

They would see it as simply another case of Mortal trickery.

And wasn't it?

Because, in the end, Lou's endgame—his hope for the future—was to restore balance to the Kingdom; and what, exactly, did that 'balance' entail?

. . . Mortals at the top of the chain, of course.

As it could only be from his perspective—from *any* Mortal's perspective.

Now Lou could see why his plan would never work.

But was there a solution?

Although his heart told him that surely there was—*undoubtedly there was*—he couldn't help but second guess himself . . . what if he failed yet again?

What if more lives were lost?

What if a compromise could never be found?

Was it simply the fate of the world that one race was destined to be the master, and the others—*at best*—the slaves?

THE COVER OF DARKNESS

Flucknor spread himself out on the long grasses.

He could feel the damp soil from the rains which'd come earlier on in the day.

He could feel the moisture passing through the thin material of his tunic and bringing goose pimples out onto the surface of his skin.

His heart thumped percussive and hard.

Blood pumped about his skull.

And the ice magic tickled his veins.

At any second, he expected to feel the sting of a hex pierce his skin; fire into his body. He knew it would be a quick death. Most likely the sentries which were posted up on the ramparts of the City Walls would have been given clear, unambiguous instructions . . . to *kill* or *be killed.*

Down at his side, he clung on tight to the stone which was engraved with white text. He was glad that it wasn't glowing in the darkness; that would've made it too easy for the sentries watching the plains for any sign of movement . . . any excuse to let their magic free.

Behind him, he could see the Glyph moving—turned invisible, at least to his eyes—and crawling about close to his ankles. He felt strangely tickled by the image as it cropped up in his mind.

They must've looked a ridiculous pair.

He remained expressionless as he crawled on his belly knowing that one false move—perhaps so much as the cracking of a smile—would be enough to alert the sentries . . . and thus blow their attempted entrance into Ilsnare out of the water.

The only way he knew into Ilsnare was the way that he had left.

Through the Catacombs beneath the Palace.

First, though, they needed to wade through the River Ils, through the stream leading downward, seemingly into the earth . . . and then, if he and the Glyph managed not to get themselves knocked over by the powerful currents, they might succeed in reaching the door concealed below.

He could say one thing for their plan, and that was it was simple. *Clear-cut.*

And yet, as the Glyph had explained to him, Flucknor wouldn't be able to open the Webbing Armoury with the piece of stone he had. First he would have to find the other half.

He got the creeping feeling that it wasn't going to be as easy as it sounded.

That was the problem with simplicity; it had the knack of *over-simplifying* things.

As he got himself wet, wading into the stream, he was aware of the stirrings above. Up on the ramparts. He knew it was near impossible not to make a sound when entering water.

He glanced back to the Glyph and thought of how it had promised him there would be nothing to worry about . . . that he needn't worry about making a sound when he entered the stream . . . those calming words seemed to have been spoken a long time ago now—almost in another age.

Flucknor felt his ankles sink into the mud of the riverbed. He kept tilting his head upward, to the ramparts, perhaps in the hope that he might look his executioner in the eye; because there was nothing he could do to avoid being put to death . . . to being consigned to a watery grave.

Slowly, he allowed himself to move further downstream.

Further into the rivulet leading off from the river.

He reached out and felt for the banks, guiding his way in, not wanting to lose his footing or his sense of direction.

That would get him, and the Glyph, drowned.

When he finally had to duck his head under the surface of the water, he felt his stomach give a groan. He knew his body was fighting him, but his ice magic urged him to continue . . . to push himself *harder* . . . if he would just keep on going under . . . if he could just reach the door . . . then all would be well . . . all would—

The first indication he received that all was *not* well above him, was a sharp tug from the Glyph behind him, followed by the words spoken directly into his mind:

— *Quickly! Move quickly!*

Flucknor wasn't sure how he could move any faster through the water, but he did his level best.

He kicked hard with his feet, propelling himself along maybe a half-step faster than before. He felt the air in his cheeks pushing to be expelled.

He went deeper into the stream, and he felt the currents pummelling him downward.

He risked opening his eyes.

The door.

He could see the door!

Light blazed all around.

Filling the water.

And his head filled with a low note . . .

But he kept on going.

Kicked his legs.

His vision centred on the doorknob out ahead.

He reached for it.

Took hold.

Grasped tight.

And *twisted* as hard as he could.

At first, there was no give.

The resistance of the water was too much.

But then . . . but then . . . all at once, as if he was shifting years' worth of muck from the mechanism, the doorknob turned. And the river gushed all around.

Hurling him through the doorway.

When he landed within—a subterranean channel in the Catacombs—he gripped the stone tightly, determined not to allow it to slip from his grasp; and neither to allow it to drag him under into the oily, black depths. He glanced about, searching for the Glyph. Finally, he located it, floating nearby, using its arms to keep its head above the surface of the water.

It was only when he met with the Glyph's round, large eyes that he absorbed the look of shock inherent in the Glyph's face.

Flucknor looked around.

Saw they were surrounded.

Surrounded by Horrox.

PLAN INTO ACTION

L ou could feel the sunlight pouring in through the gap above. Through the block of cobblestones which he pushed up with all his strength.

It was surprising how his muscles had atrophied while he'd been underground.

Although he had never really believed he used his body all that much throughout his day-to-day activities in the Palace, he supposed that he had used them more than he imagined. As he peered about the street above him, to the plaster walls of the houses on the dead-end lane, he wondered if the coast might be clear. If he could safely pop his head out through the gap.

But he held back.

Suddenly unsure.

He turned his mind back to the news; that which Hildie had relayed to him this morning. It had been passed onto her, on good authority, that his sister—Syre—was back in the city . . . and, more to the point, she had caused something of a fuss at the Palace a few days back.

A 'fuss' was probably to put it extremely mildly.

From the stories which had been relayed to Lou, he had heard that she had near enough wiped out the entire population of the Horrox who'd been gathered about her in the courtyard. Hildie had told Lou that it'd caused chaos throughout the city—that the Horrox had left their guard posts and their human slaves had taken the chance to escape their captors.

Many of them had fled the City Walls to the relative safety of the plains surrounding Ilsnare.

Believing that he was free to move, that there was nobody in the street above, Lou peeked up through the gap in the cobblestones. He stared about the deserted houses.

Took one more moment.

And then hauled himself upward.

As he dragged himself up and over the edge of the hole in the street, he felt a strain across his chest and shoulders. His muscles burning hard. But he disregarded the feeling, telling himself that there would be time enough for self-pity after this was over.

Whatever that meant.

Although the news of his sister—*Syre's*—disturbance at the Palace had acted as something like a catalyst, he had decided ever since he'd heard of Sully and Rut's deaths that he couldn't afford to wait any longer. The possibility of being able to access the Webbing Armoury had slipped away from him ... perhaps forever ... and, worse still, it most likely meant that the keystones had slipped into undesirable hands. Hands which would use those weapons for ill will.

Either to slaughter Mortals.

Or to slaughter Horrox.

No, the only chance that Lou saw for an end to these conflicts rested on the plan which he had hatched so long ago ... and which would need to be hurriedly put into place now.

He straightened up and replaced the block of cobblestones. He tapped them flat with his foot and found it remarkable how the entrance to the tunnels below the city disappeared so easily. If he hadn't just emerged from the darkness, he would never have believed there was really an entrance just here. He wondered how many others secrets Ilsnare held in store.

Most likely more than he would be able to unearth in a lifetime.

He kept himself close to the plaster walls of the houses.

He cast an invulnerability charm about himself; a charm which was designed to keep him concealed from the most cursory of inspections . . . he couldn't risk using up more magic on a stronger charm; he would need all the strength he possessed for what was to come.

He peered around the corner of the house, and across to the Crystal Causeway.

Deserted.

Eerie.

In all his life—all the time he had spent in Ilsnare—he had never seen the Crystal Causeway so deathly silent . . . it was such an unnatural state.

He drew back from the sight, flattened his back against the wall.

He wondered how he was going to do this.

And—more to the point—whether or not he would be *successful* in even getting as far as the next street over without being spotted.

He thought about Hildie, about how he had instructed her to come up using a different passageway from the underground, and to meet him within the North-West Spire.

Only now, standing up here, on the surface, did he realise how many things could possibly go wrong with that plan. He had put trust in Hildie to make her way alone . . . and, even then—*even if they managed to ascend the Spire together*—they would need to deal with the fact that they had no darkness, no light. It would simply be fire and ice. And there was no telling what might occur.

. . . For all Lou knew, it might create much greater damage than the Horrox might inflict on the Mortals; or the Mortals might inflict on the Horrox.

But there was no other way.

There was no other plan.

Lou fixed his attention on the Crystal Causeway and knew that he was heading into the unknown.

And that, quite possibly, his life would end in the next few moments.

HIDEOUT

Syre drew her soaked head up from the wooden bucket, filled with warm, soapy water.

She felt the steam rise against her skin and open up her pores.

It had been so long since she had felt warm water that it was almost as if she was caught up in some kind of feverish dream.

When she reached out for the fluffy towel, wrapped it about her hair, so that it might dry, and so that she wouldn't soak the loose tunic she wore, she glanced around and looked to Ems'plot.

He crouched at the wide-open window, peering into the streets below.

Syre rolled her eyes. "You do realise how suspicious you look in that position?"

Ems'plot didn't turn away from the wide-open window. His eyes continued to trace the details down below . . . *what* exactly, Syre wasn't entirely sure. The streets were as deserted as they had been for days. Ever since she had *blown up* at the Palace.

She turned her attention to the rustic, cobbled-together wooden table which sat across the room, against a wall without a window.

On top of the table sat the stone with the white text etched into its surface . . . the *fragment* of stone which Rut had been retrieving.

The stone which'd cost Rut his life.

Once they'd made their escape from the Horrox at Ilsnare Palace, Ems'plot had explained to Syre about how this stone fragment represented half of a key to access the Webbing Armoury . . . Syre would've liked to have said that she was surprised to hear this fact; but, as it was, she had managed to intuit as much from the face-off between Ems'plot and Arfklan. Sometimes she wondered if there was *anybody* in the world who thought of her as anything but a poor, uneducated—*unintelligent*—peasant girl who had risen too far above her station . . .

Syre trod across the bare, well-worn floorboards of the upper floor apartment in which she and Ems'plot had taken residence. "In Mortal society it's seen as something of a *faux pas* for an elderly man to skulk about the chamber of an unwed lady . . . not to mention a *princess.*"

Ems'plot remained very still.

Continuing to stare out the window.

Into the street.

Finally he murmured, under his breath, "You're no princess."

Syre suppressed a sigh. She had no idea how Ems'plot was managing to give himself airs; after all, wasn't he the one who had attempted to *trade* her for the other half of the keystone?

For the key to the Webbing Armoury?

Well, at the very least, she knew what she was worth.

She knew where she stood. Not many women could say that much.

Syre busied herself with the rest of her clothes, settling on a warm robe to wear over her top half. That done, she glanced about the room and thought again how much she would like to walk on the street—to be out in the open air. She had been so shut up here, in this apartment, that she almost felt as if she was back at Ilsnare Palace. Perhaps that fact would've been bearable if Ems'plot had been in the slightest of moods to speak with her . . . to provide her with some sort of entertainment.

He did, after all, owe her *some* grace following his attempts to trade her away.

"What now?" Syre said, her eyes lingering over Ems'plot.

Ems'plot remained silent before answering, as he was in the habit of doing. It seemed that he enjoyed making her wait for a response . . . some sort of *geriatric* quirk no doubt. " 'Now' ?" Ems'plot replied, finally turning to look at her. "Well, that depends."

"Depends on what?"

"It depends on what you want to happen here—if you want the Horrox to take control of the city, or if you want to wipe them out in one swift swoop."

Syre's chest tightened. Her heart rapped against her ribs. "What're you talking about? Have you got the other half of the keystone?"

Ems'plot gradually shook his head. He broke off eye contact with her and turned to look back out the window. "No, not that. But I've just seen your brother—"

Before he could continue, her heart beating wildly, she stalked across the room and lingered over him. "Where?" she said, her voice almost snapping with tension.

A slight smile crossed his lips. "*Skulking* along this lane, that's where." He reached out with his knobbled fingers and indicated the direction. "Looked like he was headed for the Palace."

"To do what?"

Ems'plot slowly turned to her. Again met her eyes with his watery stare. A slick, wry grin seized hold of his cracked lips. "Do I look like I can read minds?"

ILSNARE PALACE

Lou felt his whole body going rigid as he spiralled through the back lanes approaching Ilsnare Palace. He couldn't help wondering to himself—considering the amount of time he'd spent in the Palace, the past decade or so—if he should better know of the illicit passages in.

But, for all his study, for all the time he had spent in the Library, or else in the Throne Room, reading his way through the Magical Fields—trying to better understand the Four Corners Theory of Magic—he had neglected better getting to know the Palace itself. He supposed that the greatest extent of his knowledge of the Palace's architecture had come about when he'd turned his mind to using the North-West Spire as the centre of his neutral place . . . the area which he planned to use for the gathering of fire, ice; light and dark.

Or—as it would be for the time being—simply *fire* and *ice*.

If the streets had been deserted until this point, then they had become comparatively crowded now. He took in the several Horrox, pacing back and forth, their robes hanging off their spry bodies; and their lizard-like faces and alert eyes stretched back to take in whatever there might be to take in.

One thing was for certain, he knew the Horrox would prize his capture—the King of Shellacnass—above all others . . . he would be a worthy bargaining tool, indeed.

Perhaps one which could put a stop to any of the resistance in the area surrounding the city. Something which would convince those who had fled to lay down their weapons once and for all . . . and to embrace their new masters.

Their new slavery.

It was only when he reached the gates to the Palace that he realised that he had no plan at all in mind; and that the best he could come up with was burning through his ice magic to sneak past the Horrox guards. As he drew closer to them, he breathed in the stench of rotten eggs.

The odour *clung* to the air. And it sent a quiver to his gut.

As he inched his way past the pair of guards, his invulnerability charm still doing the trick, he couldn't help but reach out and *feel* the guards' thoughts . . . feel their very *being* oozing out through their bodies.

He felt no anger.

No malice.

No sense of injustice.

This pair of guards had, quite simply, been led here.

To the Palace.

So that they might keep their people safe.

And wasn't that what everyone—Creature or Mortal—in the Kingdom wished for?

Perhaps . . . but it was also far more difficult to sell peace to a people than *war*.

Lou slipped past the guards, leaving them unaware.

And he eyed the North-West Spire; still standing proud amongst the rubble of Ilsnare Palace.

RECAPTURED

Flucknor had believed that the Horrox would instantly put him to death.

That there would be some sort of order out against him . . . that ever since he had gone missing on the plains outside the city, Arfklan had decided that he had once more become an enemy.

Flucknor wasn't certain what he *wanted* to think.

What he wanted to *happen*.

All he wished for now was a quick and relatively painless death.

Was it wrong that he wished for a better end than that which Sully had had?

That which Sully had suffered through?

Flucknor had believed, too, that the Horrox would have better searched him.

That they would've better searched his surroundings when he and the Glyph had been captured . . . that they might've taken a look down into those oily waters of the Catacombs' channels so that they might find the fragment of stone he had allowed loose from his grip.

The fragment he had allowed to sink to the *bottom* of the channel.

But none of the Horrox had said anything about it.

He had simply been brought, wordlessly—not even a single word uttered so much as into his *mind*—to this windowless room, one of the few left standing, within Ilsnare Palace.

There were guards, of course. A pair of Horrox outside the bolted door.

But that was all.

He glanced up at the Glyph squatting in the corner of the room.

They had hardly spoken a word between them since their capture, more because of the fact that Flucknor could think of nothing at all to say given the circumstances. He supposed it was customary to attempt to console one another, to give one another some sort of assurance that there *would* be light at the end of the tunnel.

The Glyph, though, remained with a slight smile clinging to its lips.

Utterly unmoved—or so it seemed—by the turn of events.

Had the Glyph seen this coming?

Was he keeping secrets from Flucknor?

Making it so that there would be all sorts of surprises awaiting him further down the road?

Flucknor could honestly admit that he wouldn't put anything past the Glyph.

The Glyph appeared to have tricks up its non-existent sleeves to spare.

Flucknor had drifted into an uneasy sleep when he heard the voices in the corridor outside. He had quickly shifted into a standing position, more out of a desire *not* to be thrust into some new pain while slouching on the floor. He had his self-respect. That surely had to count for something.

And so, standing up straight, he turned his attention to the doorway.

He noticed, out of the corner of his eye, that the Glyph remained crouched down.

No doubt it was still smiling too . . .

Flucknor dreaded the day when the Glyph would feel fear and openly show it.

There was the sliding of a bolt on the other side of the door and then it swung open. Standing there, in the doorway, Flucknor was surprised to see Hildie. She stood alongside a Horrox.

This one looked more muscular than the others which Flucknor had previously met.

And Flucknor had never seen him before . . . this Horrox hadn't come along on that journey of theirs; the journey which'd culminated with Sully's death and the retrieval of that piece of stone . . . that piece of stone which now lay on the bed of the channels in the Catacombs.

For several moments, he couldn't put the image together; he simply couldn't make sense of it even with his brain working at full speed. He wondered if it was some mistake.

Some delusion.

Or if he had allowed himself to be fooled . . . if *Lou* had allowed himself to be fooled.

It was no secret that Hildie held something of a . . . *power* over him.

Hildie glanced behind her, out into the corridor, and then, with the Horrox beside her, she stepped into the room; Flucknor and the Glyph's makeshift gaol cell.

Already, Flucknor could feel a panic setting in.

He wondered if Hildie had made Arfklan promise to allow her— and *only* her—to be the one who would snuff out Flucknor's life. Some wreckless act to illustrate a lesson for Lou.

"We're going up to the North-West Spire," she said, without missing a beat.

As if Flucknor was unable to unglue himself from the spot where he stood, she shunted over to him, grasped him firmly by his forearm and led him toward the open door.

"Wait!" Flucknor said, and then looked over his shoulder, to the Glyph.

It seemed the Glyph, too, was coming with them.

Flucknor shifted his attention back to Hildie. "What's going on here?"

Hildie's eyes narrowed to slits and she grasped him tighter. "There's no time," she said. "*Move!*"

But Flucknor stood firm, doing his best to ground himself on the stone floor.

This time he looked in the direction of the Horrox. "Is *he* going to do away with me? Is he the one who Arfklan's going to use to *kill* me?"

Hildie and the Horrox exchanged glances. And then Hildie looked to Flucknor. "His name is Inta," Hildie said. "And he doesn't intend to *kill* you."

Flucknor's eyes darted between Hildie and the Horrox—*Inta*—but no matter how hard he tried he still couldn't find any trust. He was sure that one—or both—was out to trick him somehow.

To lead him—unwittingly—to his demise.

Before Flucknor could protest any more, he felt Inta take hold of him.

That scabby, red skin scratched against his own.

A shudder ran down Flucknor's spine.

His heart bobbed up to his throat.

But he maintained his straight-backed pose.

Determined to remain noble until the end . . . if this *was* the end.

It was only then that he heard the Glyph speak into his mind.

He felt that reassuring—*calming*—tone.

Instantly, Flucknor felt himself relax; not all the way, but at least now his blood didn't feel like it might stream free of his veins at any second:

— *Trust them, Flucknor. It's true. Their intentions are pure.*

With all three sets of eyes on him now, Flucknor couldn't help feeling that *he* was the unreasonable one . . . that he was the one who was causing the fuss.

And yet, with these three powerful magical practitioners surrounding him, Flucknor knew—in reality—there was very little, if anything, he might do to resist them.

So he acquiesced.

A TORMENTED ASCENT

Lou had no idea how he managed to reach the entranceway into the North-West Spire without being discovered. There were several moments—when he had turned side-on in the corridors, held his breath deep in his lungs as Horrox guards had passed by—in which he was certain he would be discovered. But his invulnerability charm had remained intact.

It had protected him from discovery.

The charm—along with the steadily falling dusk—had aided him on his way.

Now that he had left the ruins of the Palace behind, and that he had reached the torn-open entrance to the North-West Spire—that large hole in the side of the stone which had come into being with the Horrox's invasion—he allowed the charm to fall about him . . . it was an act committed as easily as the casting off of a cloak after a long day's journey.

The only difference here was that the journey still lay ahead.

Lou clambered his way up the stone spiral steps, keeping a firm grasp on the rickety wooden banister which ran the length of the structure. When he had closed on the North-West Spire, he had worried that the Horrox might've taken over . . . that they might've posted sentries at the top of the building so that they might keep a lookout across Ilsnare. However, now that he had arrived to the North-West Spire, he saw no Horrox around. It was only, having reached the top, feeling the sweat drooling down the sides of his face, and his limbs aching all over, that Lou had a chance to gaze out at the plains surrounding Ilsnare. And it was then that he saw that night had fallen.

But it wasn't night itself which attracted his attention.

As he surveyed the surrounding plains, looked beyond the glass rooftops of the Crystal City, he saw that there had sprouted hundreds—*or were there thousands*?—of torches.

And from all directions.

As he leaned himself up against the sturdy stone wall of the North-West Spire, he watched on as his breath left his lips as steam; as the night drew in chilly and unfeeling. While he stood there, he thought he could hear the shouts of warmongering, and he knew that these were the promised Mortal rebellions. And he knew, in that moment, that this was their final stand—their final *strike back*—to reclaim that which they believed their own.

Their attempt to return Ilsnare, and the Kingdom of Shellacnass, to their hands.

It didn't matter to the Mortals that they were overpowered.

That the Horrox could wipe them out in a single stroke.

No, even if they had known—even if they *did* know—they would keep coming.

Because they had nothing else.

They were desperate.

And their hearts were set on freeing their imprisoned brothers and sisters.

Their purloined homes and businesses.
This would be their last hope.

DARK AND DANGEROUS

Syre had entered Ilsnare Palace the same way she had done for most of the previous decade . . . under the cover of darkness. And in the form of a crow.

Quite simply, she fluttered up over the Palace walls, and down into the courtyard. Her inky, midnight-blue feathers the perfect cover against the incoming darkness.

Not one of the Horrox blinked an eye at her waddling her way across the cobblestones and through the corridors. What she had most feared, while transformed into a crow, was that one of the Horrox might unintentionally step on her. That would, indeed, be an ignoble end for what she had begun to see would be an increasingly noble act.

Perhaps they would write this in their books.

Or, if it was the Horrox who eventually reigned the Kingdom of Shellacnass, maybe they would speak this history down through future generations . . . stoking the same sense of wonder—and *terror*—which ripped through her body now.

She had surprised even herself when she had spotted her brother Lou. He had been concealing himself using a rather rudimentary—and quite *weak*—invulnerability charm. It was one which she herself would have easily been able to cast . . . but, then again, she had always believed that she possessed a raw magical power far in excess of that which dwelled within Lou's veins.

He was more consistent, that was all.

She tailed Lou all the way through the rubble of the Palace to the North-West Spire. When she watched him slip through the hole in the side of the building, she couldn't quite believe her eyes. The North-West Spire, it seemed, was about the only part of Ilsnare Palace which hadn't succumbed to . . . whatever had happened . . . however the damage had been brought to bear on the Palace when the Horrox had invaded.

She turned her mind back to Ems'plot, thinking of him hiding out in that apartment, not too far from the Palace, and she wondered if he had known more about what was going on.

If he knew about what it was Lou intended.

Because—and she knew it for a fact—Ems'plot could *most definitely* read minds.

Syre bounded up the spiral staircase, all the time expecting to hear the crumble of rock around her as the Spire finally tumbled down to be among the rest of the rubble of the Palace.

But, somehow, it held itself together.

When she reached the top, she peered in through the doorway, and there she saw Lou.

Standing in the middle of a raised platform, surrounded by the stone walls.

She cast a quick glance over the stone floor, and the chalked outline there.

And then, with the briefest of glances to her brother, she turned her attention to one of the windows which looked out over the plains . . . the view beyond the City Walls.

Torches.

Hundreds—*thousands*—of them.

REUNITED

Lou stared long and hard at his little sister.

At Syre Dorf.

Somehow, although it had only been a matter of months since he had seen her last, he thought that she had grown *years* older. He recalled how, once upon a time, her hair had been a fairer shade. Not quite *blond*, but not too far off either. Now, though, there was no doubting that it was black. As black as the walls which surrounded Ilsnare. As black as the coal which the House Staff used to keep the kitchen stoves burning away. As black as the feathers of the crow's body which she inhabited. Syre fixed her eyes onto him now.

Lou felt a shifting down deep in his stomach.

She trod closer.

Then, only a few paces away, she stopped.

Lou felt as if all the words had been stripped from his tongue. His throat became impossibly dry and seemed to close up on itself. He could only think of what he had said to her—how he had cast her away from Ilsnare, and into the wilderness . . . now, though, *now* he could explain why that was. He could explain *everything . . .*

If only Hildie would arrive.

So that he wouldn't have to repeat himself.

It was somewhat appalling for him to acknowledge that he had cast so many others away . . . but he never would've done so if it hadn't been strictly necessary.

There had been no other choice.

He had taken the hard—*and correct*—path.

He was sure that it would all be worth it now.

That if he could only hold himself together—if he could only get the others to follow his instructions—then they could save so many lives.

He was almost thankful for the present events, the torches closing on Ilsnare outside.

It at least provided a distraction for their meeting.

He followed Syre's gaze as she looked on out through the windows, to the plains beyond. He could see now that the Horrox were forming up on the ramparts of the Palace . . . he knew that they had noticed the advancing rebels. Surely they would strike sooner rather than later.

They couldn't take risks.

If they allowed these rebels to get a foothold then they would relinquish the firm, unshakeable grasp with which they held the Kingdom of Shellacnass.

The Horrox response would need to be brutal.

Final.

And that could only mean death on the largest scale.

A tragedy which was still within Lou's power to prevent.

Lou turned away from Syre, hearing more footsteps sounding on the staircase.

Both of them turned to look; their attention drawn to the doorway.

This might be it . . . everything could easily be over before it had started.

And death and destruction would reign.

As he observed the bodies make their way inside, he counted them; one by one.

First there was Flucknor—*safe and sound after all!*—and then there was Hildie.

The ones who followed, though, put Lou on edge.

He felt his whole body seize up.

The penultimate was a Creature which Lou had never seen before; a dirgy grey body with slick, almost slippery-wet skin. And large—*large*—round eyes.

Something . . . a *voice* . . . deep from the recesses of his mind told him the Creature's name:

A *Glyph*.

Although this particular Creature—this *Glyph*—was something of a curiosity, the next who passed through the doorway was far more of an obvious danger.

A Horrox.

Large.

Muscular.

A clearly *unwieldy* strength.

Unconsciously, Lou backed up a step.

Two steps.

And he felt his mind reaching for a hex which might knock back the threat.

Which might keep their hopes of avoiding tragedy alive.

Or so went the theory.

Apparently noticing the shock on his face, Hildie spoke up.

"Wait," she said. "I can explain."

Lou, unwilling to take his eyes off the Horrox, hoped very much that she could.

AN EXPLANATION

Hildie felt faint after climbing up the spiral stairs, although she was loath to show it outwardly. She knew that the time for weakness—both physical and mental—had long ago passed away into the realm of luxury. After this was over . . . then—*and only then*—would she have the licence to allow herself to relax. She turned to the Horrox who she had brought along with her; the Horrox who, it seemed, had risen from the dead.

Inta.

When she had stolen into the Palace, she had noticed him.

Luckily he had been alone.

Merely pacing his way down a corridor.

Hildie had had a terrible sensation that she was mistaken when he had finally set eyes on her, and there had been not one tiny shift in his expression. She had believed that he would attack her.

That he would *kill* her.

And she had almost wished he would.

Then, though, she had realised who he was.

And where he should've been . . . *dead* . . .

Yet he was here, still among the living.

Once they had thawed the silence, and Inta had established she was who she *said* she was, Inta had gone on to explain how the people of Nor'tarth—at the last minute—had decided to spare his life . . . they had decided that there needed to be a *survivor* . . . one Horrox who could spread the story to the others. That was how the news of the massacre had spread to the north.

To the Winter's Moan.

To Arfklan.

Inta, of course, had been embraced by his fellow Creatures.

Welcomed back into their home.

And brought onside for the extracting of their revenge on the Mortal menace.

Throughout their conversation, when Hildie had met with Inta down in the rubble of the Palace, she had tried her best to emphasise that she wanted to find some means—*some compromise*—which would avoid the need of the coming war.

And she had been surprised at how patiently Inta had listened to her.

Even more surprised still when he had agreed with her.

Asked to help.

For it seemed that Arfklan was now beyond hearing reason. He was so drunk on the idea of drawing Mortal blood that he could see no other solution. And so Hildie had asked for Inta to bring her to where Flucknor was being held prisoner—she had heard off the scouts that he had been captured—and he had done exactly as she had requested.

So here they were.

Hildie looked about the upper room of the North-West Spire again, and she could hardly believe what was about to pass. The entire room was in near darkness now, although she didn't think to ask if she should light the torch which hung from one of the walls.

She knew now was a time for reverence.

That Lou had expended—she couldn't tell *how much*—of his energy, of his physical wellbeing on assuring the neutrality of this spot.

And Hildie was determined that she wouldn't be the one to destroy it.

She wouldn't be the one to bring about destruction again.

Not if she could help it.

Her hands seemed to work apart from herself as she relayed all that had happened—about her relationship with Inta; about how he wasn't an enemy, but, *rather*, an ally.

She stroked the Almber's Glass which hung around her neck and felt something like a warmth emanating from within. The Glass itself represented a time of peace . . . a time which was in the past now; *untouchable* . . . and it also served as a reminder that any peacetime could come to an end as swiftly as the heavens might break and a rainstorm might erupt.

She had learned that lesson, it seemed, time and time again.

And she didn't wish to learn it once more . . .

But only fate could tell if that was a possibility.

She turned her attention back to Lou, to Syre; and then to Flucknor, Inta and the Creature which she had learned was known only as the 'Glyph'.

Now was the time for them to put their trust in Lou.

It was the only hope of avoiding war.

THE FOUR CORNERS

Lou crouched down in the fading light at the top of the North-West Spire.

He grabbed hold of the block of chalk in his fist.

That done, he worked to thicken out the outline he had drawn so long ago.

And which he had traced and retraced more times than he cared to remember.

Once he had gone over the form another time—drawing out the diamond and then the cross between each one of the Four Corners—he straightened himself up and tossed the chalk to one side. If this went to plan then he would never need that chalk again.

He tilted his head up and looked to Hildie.

She stared back at him.

Her green eyes almost pulsating from their sockets.

He could feel the *flicker* of her fire magic straining to be released from her skin.

That was good . . . *strength* was good . . .

And yet, it was his worst nightmare that he would be unable to match her power.

That she would overwhelm him.

It was what he had feared all along.

And that which he had *hoped*—during the longest nights; the longer days—would not come to pass. Not now. Not with so many lives on the line.

Lou moved into position, taking up one corner of the diamond.

The Corner which he had dedicated to ice.

And then he met Hildie's eye . . . indicated that she should take up the opposing Corner; that which corresponded to fire.

The two of them, each in their own Corner of the diamond, stood their ground.

Lou stared into her green eyes, almost lost to the fading light of the Spire.

And then he held up his hands.

Hildie did the same.

Mirroring him.

Outside, Lou heard the first forays of arrows skittering about the ramparts . . . the *whistle* of crossbow bolts through the air; ducking and weaving. He closed his eyes and hoped that the Horrox wouldn't respond with hexes.

Not yet.

He just needed a little time.

That was all.

Just a little time.

As Lou stood up in his Corner, in the Corner of Ice, he reached out with his mind.

He could feel Hildie's aura.

The heat which seeped from her skin.

So much strength.

So well contained.

So well controlled.

And, right now, she would need all of the control she could muster.

If either one of them—Lou or Hildie—began to lose control then it could cause a destructive force far stronger than anything the Horrox might use against the Mortals.

It would leave Ilsnare an enormous, smoking crater in the earth.

A simple pockmark in the plains.

As Lou felt the two of them closing on one another, he pictured in his mind a cloud of ice, bundling into the air above his head.

From Hildie, he pictured a twisting, turning blaze.

Its shape ever-shifting.

Impossible to comprehend.

Lou felt the weight across his shoulders.

Pushing him downward.

Into the stone blocks beneath his feet.

As he felt his influence mixing with Hildie's, he found that he could *see* her thoughts; that he could see the story which she had told . . . about Nor'tarth . . . and the slaughter which the people— the *Mortals*—had led on the Horrox encampments.

He felt her anger, confusion . . . but, above all, *sadness.*

Lou crooked open an eye.

He looked to Syre.

Saw that, as with the others—Flucknor, the Glyph and Inta—she stood to one side engrossed by the scene. He could only imagine what it looked like from their point of view.

Syre caught Lou's eye and he motioned for her to go and stand in the Corner which he had marked out as representing darkness.

She did as he gestured.

As she joined with the diamond, Lou reached out to her mind.

And he saw Inta . . . and another . . . a *mage?*

Lou stood powerless, in a volcanic-looking landscape.

From a distance, he witnessed Inta . . . *the mage* . . . standing over Rut's body . . . ready to bring all of the force of their magic down upon him.

To end his life.

Lou felt a sadness ripple through him.

. . . So that was how it had happened . . .

Wiping that image from his mind, knowing that he couldn't afford to have external memories interfere with his duties, he turned his attention to Flucknor. When he first made eye contact with Flucknor, Flucknor tried to look away, as if his glance wasn't intended for him at all.

Even beneath the burning burden, the constant struggle which Lou exerted with Hildie . . . his ice magic battling with her *fire* . . . he managed the slightest of smiles. Lou hoped that it would be an encouraging smile, but realised, in reality, it more than likely came across as a grimace.

In any case, it did the trick.

Flucknor took up the final spot on the chalk outline.

Standing on the spot—*the Corner*—which Lou had intended for light.

When Flucknor stood in his Corner, the final one to complete the diamond, Lou felt an extra energy pump through them all . . . it made the hairs at the back of his neck rise up, and sent a tingle down his spine. A *thrill* through his blood. And he reached out to Flucknor's mind.

This time it was a different feeling . . . when Lou had witnessed the death of Rut, he had sensed an overwhelming sensation of impotence . . . now, though, now when he looked through Flucknor's eyes, into the past, down onto the cowering Sully below, he felt only panic—*terror* . . . and yet, as Lou witnessed it, he saw that it was Flucknor who was the one responsible for dealing pain.

The one responsible for sending Sully into spirals of pain.

This time it was harder for Lou to free his mind from the sight.

It, quite simply, dominated him.

Lou wasn't certain if he'd be able to draw breath ever again without *seeing* Sully's face—tormented in pain . . . or to feel that new level of terror which soared through Flucknor.

Really, Lou had made great demands on his friends.

Demands which they—*surely*—expected him to repay.

He hoped that the salvation of the Kingdom . . . sparing so many innocent lives . . . would be enough for all these *enormous* sacrifices.

Once more, as Lou had done with Syre, he stepped back from the memory.

He cast it into shadow.

Into some corner of his mind where he could contain it.

Control it.

Within his mind's eye, he pictured his cloud of ice mingling with Syre's darkness, and with Flucknor's light . . . he imagined the colours.

Hildie's; fire-red.

Syre's; a bruise-purple.

Flucknor's; a creamy-white.

And his own; a cool, crisp light-blue.

They all swirled together, entangling with one another.

Lou waited for something to happen.

What he had in mind, he really had no idea. Perhaps he believed that some sort of elemental blaze would fire free from their union, lavish the world around them with its benevolent glow.

But everything seemed caught up.

Static.

It seemed as if their mixing Magical Fields had ceased to churn together. And then, opening his mind further, doing his best to understand that which was binding all four of them, he realised that it was Hildie's fire-red cloud which was retreating. He opened an eye.

Saw that she was wilting beneath the force.

That lines of expression sketched her face.

And that her cheeks were puffed out.

It took another few moments—another few moments when all four of them could hold the magic flowing between them.

. . . And then it simply collapsed.

DEVASTATION

Lou broke off his own magical connection soon after Hildie collapsed. He rushed across the chalked outline which joined them all—and which was now glowing a bright-white.

All over his body, he had a stinging sensation.

It seemed like he had to exert a great amount of energy simply to keep his eyes open. As if his eyeballs themselves could not cope with the strength of that which passed between them.

When Lou reached Hildie, when he crouched over her, took hold of her limp hand, he could only feel the very faintest of pulses. And he felt the tickling warmth of her fire magic up against his skin . . . and the familiar *burn* of his own ice magic in his veins.

It told him to run.

To leave this behind.

To save himself.

Lou glanced up. He was surprised to see that the Horrox—*Inta*—had deserted them now.

That he had merely slipped out.

Lou's first reaction was confusion. And then the full force of suspicion struck him.

Rising to his feet, leaving Hildie's now-frail, and unconscious, body behind, he turned to the Glyph with an accusatory stare. "Where did he go?!"

The Glyph stared back at Lou with those round eyes.

It didn't shift from the spot or reply.

And that served only to further enrage Lou.

He found it almost impossible to stand those who ignored his commands.

Perhaps it was his role as King of Shellacnass which'd left that particular mark on him.

He spun around.

He caught both Flucknor and Syre's eyes—would he ever be able to look at them the same way again after he had seen his two best of friends die in their memories?—and then he sensed the sounds of war taking place outside.

The sounds of screams.

A constant *whistle* of arrows and crossbow bolts.

And he was certain . . . *yes* . . . the *crackle* of magic through the air.

It was too late.

They had failed.

Pain had arrived.

And defeat—*devastation*—would arrive soon after.

Lou breathed in raggedy breaths now, realising himself how much this entire charade had exhausted him. And all for nothing. It didn't matter now that the Horrox—that *Inta*—had gone to fetch his allies. His *Horrox* allies. In a matter of hours—perhaps only minutes—every last Mortal . . . every last *Creature* which wasn't Horrox . . . would be put to death.

Lou felt as if his mind had become frayed about the edges.

The sharpness was completely gone.

He had given all he could . . . and he had nothing left.

It was then that he heard the Glyph speak into his mind:

— *Don't give up. Not yet.*

But Lou felt as if he already had.

RETURN

As Lou was hunched over himself, listening to the sounds of the battle raging outside, he was aware of the quieter—*closer*—sound of footsteps coming up the stone stairs.

But he held the sounds at an arm's length . . . afraid of what they might mean. That he was going to be slayed in the most horrific manner imaginable because of his temerity to call himself the King of Shellacnass. Slowly, he straightened himself up from where he knelt down on the floor.

He glanced about.

To Syre.

To Flucknor.

The two of them still standing on their Corner of the diamond.

At least *they* would remain loyal to the end . . . but who did Lou have to remain loyal to?

His people?

The people of Shellacnass?

. . . He supposed that they would look to him at this time of crisis . . . and—just as Veerna had done—they would expect him to emerge from near defeat with the Webbing Armoury about him . . . a phoenix out of the ashes.

But there would be no Webbing Armoury.

The keystones had never returned to his possession.

And Lou would know only the bitter sting of failure.

He could feel his heart wrenching when he turned to look at Hildie. He saw how she lay flat on the ground, her chest rising and falling with her strained breaths. He could tell she was close to death . . . that the energy and strength which'd been demanded of her in forming the Magical Fields had been too much . . . her fire magic would slowly choke her out of this world and into the next.

Into the one which her father inhabited.

Even as Lou thought of it, he couldn't help a wry smile sneaking onto his lips.

What fresh new horrors might Hilda and Ma'reygar wreak upon the afterlife?

. . . He supposed that he would have to wait himself to discover.

Once more, he heard the Glyph speak within his own mind:

— *Get up. Now is not the time to rest. Now is the time to* act.

But Lou did remain where he was.

Defeated.

Through the ground, Lou felt forceful vibrations. They rattled up through the Spire, shaking the very stone blocks which formed the building. But the Spire continued to stand.

Another smirk sprung to his lips to think that he had chosen his spot well . . . that he had chosen the place where he might create this diamond to unite the Magical Fields somewhere even the hardiest of forces couldn't quite knock over. He wondered if the North-West Spire would go down in Shellacnass mythology for its hardiness; for its ability to resist all attacks against it.

Another tremor passed through the ground.

This time stronger.

Lou felt a trickle of stone dust fall from above.

He tilted his head back to look.

It was raining down on him now—on *all* of them.

Perhaps he had been a touch foolhardy to believe that the North-West Spire would indeed remain standing . . . perhaps it had simply been intended as the encore to the Grand Destruction of Ilsnare Palace all along. Only the gods could know these things.

Out of the corner of his eye, Lou sensed movement in the doorway.

He turned to look.

And felt his heart nearly freeze.

The Horrox . . . the one from before . . . he had returned . . . *Inta.*

Now, though, there was another Horrox standing alongside.

A Horrox who Lou didn't immediately recognise.

With a scar down his left cheek.

Then he turned to look at Flucknor, saw the spark which passed between the two.

And then Lou *did* recognise who the Horrox was:

Brotsboore

The Horrox with whom Lou had done battle.

He recalled how they had each replicated themselves . . . performed that same parlour trick . . . and that, in the end, Brotsboore had escaped with Flucknor.

The two of them had simply slipped out of Ilsnare.

Under Lou's guidance, of course.

But what was Brotsboore doing here?

Was this some sort of a revenge tactic?

That the Horrox wanted to be the one to finally kill him?

If that was the case then he would have little trouble . . . Lou had no strength left in him . . . to have gone head-to-head with Hildie—to have matched her magic with his own—it had almost left him dead . . . just as it had almost left Hildie nearly dead.

But, no, that didn't seem to be it.

If the Horrox—*Brotsboore*—had intended to kill Lou then why was he wasting time?

Why not simply slay him now . . . while he had the chance?

. . . Before Lou regained something of his strength . . . just enough to *resist*.

Lou felt his heart beating weakly as he heard Brotsboore speak into his mind:

— *I have come to take her role, brother. I believe that I could create an equally powerful fire Corner to the Magical Fields.*

Lou shook his head, feeling the tears stinging his eyes.

A Creature!

A *Creature*!

. . . Even as the thought skittered through his dizzy mind, he knew that it was the most ridiculous thing he had ever heard . . . and yet, he couldn't quite shift it.

Hadn't he been looking for some means of uniting the Kingdom?

For Creatures to stand shoulder to shoulder with Mortals?

Might not this be the solution?

. . . But Lou knew that he had nothing left in him . . . that his strength had deserted him . . . he wondered if he might ever recover it again. As that thought tumbled through his mind, an almost unsupportable ringing filled his skull. It rebounded about, inside his head. Made him nauseous. He felt a warmth at his nostril. He reached up and touched the spot with his fingertips.

Blood.

Red.

Dull.

Sticky.

On his skin.

It was then that Lou became aware of the Horrox—Brotsboore—standing over him; and, a little way off, still standing up by the door, he saw the other one, Inta. When he stared up into Brotsboore's impossibly black eyes, it was all he could do to stop himself from grinning all over like a maniac. This was just all so *ridiculous*!

They would all be *killed!*

Brought tumbling down when the Spire finally *fell!*

Somehow, Lou found the strength to utter something.

"I . . . can . . . can . . . I *can't!*"

Brotsboore remained still, towering over him.

Would he make some show of his dominance?

Would he simply crouch down and twist Lou's neck?

Bring the world to an end with a gut-wrenching *snap*?

. . . That might well be the appropriate end for the Hitchking; the one who had *hitched* the Kingdom away . . . stolen it out of the rightful hands.

It would be a lesson for all.

Lou heard another voice in his mind—this time not Brotsboore . . . no, it was that odd, grey Creature from before . . . *the Glyph.*

— *I shall act in your place. As ice.*

Again, Lou had the urge to chuckle out long and hard.

To shake his head in some bout of exasperation.

How . . . how . . . *how* . . . could this *Creature* possibly take *his* place?

His . . . *place*?

Louson Dorf, the Greatest Ice Mage of his Time.

. . . He had put off that phrase for so long in his mind; had never wanted to admit so much to himself; but what was truly gained from *not* speaking the truth?

He had nothing left . . . no strength . . . and yet he couldn't quite *bear* this Glyph taking his place in the diamond . . . taking up the spot which was *rightfully* his . . .

The Glyph spoke into his mind one more time:

— *You still have your use. I understand what you are attempting here, to balance the Magical Fields, to centre the power of the Kingdom in this one place . . . and so to strip absolute power away from any one group of Magical beings. A noble endeavour; and but for one factor it would be a worthy one.*

Here he really did feel as if he had to laugh.

Who was this *Glyph* to be speaking to him in such tones?

He had spent the greater part of the last decade in perfecting his understanding of the Magical Fields—in attempting to scour the depths of the Four Corners . . . in bringing about the day when he could concentrate all this magical power in one spot and bring peace for all kinds . . . for all races . . .

The Glyph spoke to him again; once more in his mind:

— *Do not take my words for rudeness, Your Highness, you have already achieved so much, simply by uniting these people together. However, your design . . . it lacks a balance . . . a point of focus; the centrepiece of the Magical Fields.*

Finally, Lou found his voice. "A sacrifice," he said, his tone deadpan.

The Glyph nodded dolefully in reply.

THE SACRIFICE

Louson Dorf felt a moment of clarity set in over him.

For several long moments, he felt as if the madness which brewed all around ceased.

Gone was the *crackle* of magic in the air; the constant *groans* of pain on the ramparts . . . all the trimmings of Mortals and Creatures putting one another to death.

Locked in deadly battle.

A fresh strength entered Lou—not a *physical* strength—but a clean, clear-cut mental sharpness. When he glanced up, he saw that both Brotsboore and the Glyph offered him their hands. He reached out and allowed them to help him to his feet.

When he stood, Lou was surprised to find that his balance was solid.

That he had neither the urge or the frailty to tumble back down to the floor.

To land on the stone blocks.

To pummel his fists against the ground and disappear . . . for his impotence . . . for all he had wished for and yet failed to achieve.

First, Lou went to Flucknor, his trusted ally; the one who had stood by him for the best part of a decade . . . and all while Lou had kept him a safe distance away—just as he had kept *everyone* at a safe distance . . . those with magic in their blood could only serve to compromise his plans . . . whatever those plans were now.

He looked deep into Flucknor's icy-blue eyes, and past the well-defined cheekbones, sure that he could make out the boy he had once met underneath; the boy with whom he had travelled to discover his master; Auch'ray . . . the man who had taught Lou so much about 'walking with weakness'. He supposed that Auch'ray, at least, would be proud of Lou for doing that now.

With nothing at all to say, Lou reached out and took hold of Flucknor's shoulder. He gave him a light squeeze, feeling the manly muscle there. He knew he had made the right choice when he had appointed him High Representative; and that he had also made the right choice in sending him away—*in allowing him to go.* Flucknor's magic was greater than Lou could even appreciate.

He saw that now, if he hadn't before.

For the final time, he broke off Flucknor's gaze. He gave him a brotherly pat on the shoulder and—somehow—knew that all would be well. That Flucknor would 'walk in the light'; that his magic would show him the noble path.

Next, Lou went to Syre; seeing the tears were already streaking her cheeks. Her whole face seemed made out of porcelain, fit to break with the slightest of cracks . . . and yet she, too, had shown herself more than Lou's equal; that she held a wild—*perhaps untameable*—power within her . . . and that, however she chose to use it in the future, she would do the most remarkable good with it now. Lou supposed that Syre had taught him to believe that 'walking in darkness' didn't necessarily equate to 'walking in evil'.

His hands shook nearly uncontrollably, and he found no strength to mutter so much as a word.

When he tried to step away from her, she surprised him by lurching forward and throwing her arms about his waist. Tugging him into her. Locking him with an embrace that made it almost impossible to breathe. When she finally let him go, he could still feel the moisture from her tears dampening his tunic. He could smell the slightly salty scent clinging to him.

Last of all, he looked to Hildie.

She lay on the ground, crumpled in a heap, to one side of the diamond drawn in chalk on the stone floor. Her eyes were shut tight and her fingers bundled into tight fists. As she slept—if what she did could be called that—her whole body twitched and jerked . . . he knew that Hildie wouldn't spend much longer in this world than he himself would. He wondered if he'd ever really believed that the two of them might live so closely together; and then die at the same time . . . it seemed like some kind of macabre dream.

Except it was reality.

Lou crouched over Hildie, feeling her warmth; the fire magic still stirring in her veins as it would continue to do until the hour when her heart itself stopped.

He leaned in and planted a single, soft kiss on her forehead.

And then he backed away.

When Lou stood up straight, he felt all the sounds from outside return to the tight room at the top of the North-West Spire . . . he could hear all the sounds of life, and death; all of the cruelty so crudely wrapped around all that was beautiful.

Now—*now* was his time.

He would pay the ultimate price.

And he would do his ultimate duty.

All four of them stood in place.

Lou saw that Inta had retreated from the room; that he had made himself scarce.

He looked to Flucknor one last time; standing in the light.

Then to Syre; in the Corner of darkness.

And then to the Glyph, in Lou's place, in the Corner of ice.

Finally, he turned to Brotsboore, who stood in the position of the Magical Field reserved for fire.

All of them together.

Though there was no chalked-on cross in the centre of the floor, Lou could draw it on with his mind. He could see his place; between all of them.

Right in the centre.

The *sacrifice*.

He held his head bowed as he trudged over to the preordained spot, and when he stood there he felt a warmth encapsulate his body that he had never before imagined; something which he had never before believed *possible* . . . but there it was . . . every day of his life he had learned something new; why should this day—the last day of his life—be any different?

As he stood between all Four Corners of the Magical Field, he experienced the united force of their magic washing over him; leading him upward, to a higher plane. And, before he even really knew what was happening, the light became too bright for him to bear.

It became too bright for his *Mortal* body to bear.

And so he rode into the clouds.

DEATH'S DECEPTION

E**ven for weeks later,** Syre could still feel the magic tingling over the surface of her skin.

It was the most powerful sensation she had ever experienced.

And she knew that she would never experience anything quite like it again.

By the time her brother Lou's funeral arrived—on the day when his remains were to be cast into the Royal Crypt—Syre hadn't many more tears to shed.

It was the result of everything . . . all that had gone on in the past few weeks.

How she, just like any other subject of the Kingdom, had taken to picking up the pieces and—standing shoulder to shoulder with their once-aggressors, the Horrox—putting right that which had almost torn the entire world apart.

It was an incredible turn of events by any measure.

She could hardly recall the order of how it had happened.

It'd all been so fast.

Of course, she had vivid recollections of the night up in the North-West Spire; that building which somehow still managed to cling to its foundations, and which stood up proud among the now-cleared rubble of Ilsnare Palace. What would be the last standing piece of the original Palace when it was eventually rebuilt.

She recalled standing in the chalked diamond.

Concentrating her powers.

Channelling them through Lou's body with the others.

And bringing out of Lou an impossibly bright light.

When Syre closed her eyes, she thought she could still see the red marks left behind from the exposure to such a bright light and she couldn't help wondering if she would continue to see the trace of that night until the day she died.

Whenever that was.

Once it was over, Syre could hardly believe the simplicity of the ceremony . . . how, when she strained her hearing for the sounds of fighting outside the North-West Spire, she had heard nothing . . . only sustained silence.

Word had spread.

To Mortal and Horrox alike.

They had all heard the peace within their skulls.

That little voice which told them to down arms.

Being involved in the ceremony itself, Syre hadn't had the opportunity to experience first-hand the voice speaking in her own mind, but she had seen its aftereffects. It had been the Glyph, in the end, who had brought an end to their uniting of the Magical Fields; the bridging of the Four Corners . . . it had told them that what they had accomplished would be enough.

That it would do the trick.

How the Glyph had become so wise—how it had learned so much about the management of the Four Corners of the Magical Fields—Syre had not the faintest inkling.

In a way, she had been kept in the dark all along.

Once Lou's funeral was over and done with—as overwrought as she might've expected with seemingly every single street of the city shut for the occasion; and sable, pit-black banners strung from all the windows of the previously abandoned homes—she was glad to get away from it all.

Syre knew well that the event wasn't made for her.

That it was made for the general population.

Lou had been the symbol they had required—the *hero* they had required . . . and he had more than fulfilled that particular role . . . his name would live on in the memory of every man, woman and child born into the Kingdom of Shellacnass.

And, perhaps, beyond.

At Lou's funeral, Syre only began to feel normal again once she was on her own . . . relatively speaking. She still had Flucknor at one shoulder and Lou's manservant Veerna at the other.

The clothes which'd been picked out for her by the House Staff consisted of a stiff, inky-black dress. Something which she never would've chosen for herself. And which, she was sure, Lou would've treated with riotous laughter. But she tried not to let such a small matter as discomfort distract her from the sombre nature of the occasion.

Once through the gates of the Palace—a route through the rubble had been cleared—they proceeded down the stone staircase into the Catacombs, where the Royal Crypt was located.

They passed through what had once been the Library, no doubt trampling the flaky remains of centuries-old books beneath the soles of their boots.

An elderly member of the House Staff led their way, while the Royal Guard charged with carrying Lou's remains—nothing more than a pot of ashes—solemnly trudged along on their heels. Syre eyed the set of chunky keys which hung down from the belt of the elderly member of the House Staff, and, almost as if she controlled his hands with her mind, he reached for the keys, brought them up in his hold and then inserted the thickest, rustiest-looking one in the hole in the iron door. When he turned the key, there was an unbearable *screech*, and Syre had to crunch her teeth together in order to keep herself from crying out in pain.

All her senses had seemed to become a thousand-fold more sensitive in the past few weeks, following the ceremony in the North-West Spire.

As she stepped into the dank air of the Royal Crypt, breathing in that dusty scent which clung to nearly everything—the odour of decay—she could still make out the faint, rhythmic pounding of the drums in the town above her.

The achingly slow March of Death.

It felt almost as if the entire event had been designed so that it might depress her, so that, with each one of those drumbeats, she would be pounded further down into the ground. At least she didn't have the citizens of Ilsnare standing by the side of the road, staring at her. Seemingly attempting to drive some sort of reaction out of her . . . and, at the same time, Syre had felt as if they might be judging her, for not crying; because how could she cry any more tears when she'd spent the last few weeks cooped up alone sobbing to herself?

No, she knew she had cried enough.

When the member of the Royal Staff arrived at one of the rectangular holes cut into the wall—already prepared with wispy-grey velvet lining the base—he made an elaborate turning around gesture before standing with his back to the wall; his gaze averted.

Staring upward, into the roof, at seemingly nothing.

Syre stood to one side, too, allowing the Royal Guard past with Lou's remains.

Flucknor and Veerna paused their advance a few steps away from Syre.

The Royal Guard approached the hole in the wall, the pot in his hands, and Syre took a moment to admire the ornate, flowery design over the top of a sedate, beige-coloured porcelain. The Royal Guard bowed his head and then slotted the pot in on the shelf within the wall. He bowed one more time before retreating, leaving the Royal Crypt behind.

Next, the elderly member of the House Staff turned to where the pot lay in its final resting place and bowed as the Royal Guard had done. When he made his way out of the Royal Crypt, he stopped before Syre. Flucknor and Veerna then bowed also.

Once Syre was certain that they were all alone; that all of these hangers-on had left them in peace to mourn her brother, she approached the pot.

. . . Somehow she couldn't find it in her to refer to it by its proper name:

An *urn*.

For several seconds, feeling her heart bobbing in her throat, she stood before the pot, stared at the flowery design, and was unsure how to square this image with the memory of her brother. How was it possible for a person to be reduced to such a simple object?

The simple answer to that was that it *wasn't* possible . . .

Lou would remain with her forever.

In her mind.

In her memories.

And in her *heart*.

Feeling strangely empty inside, she moved away from the pot. She felt drained. There was—*quite simply*—nothing left for her to pour out. She was a husk.

Once Flucknor had looked in on Lou, Syre was surprised that Veerna lingered so long. That Veerna continued to stare at the pot . . . apparently attempting to put all the pieces of this puzzle together in his mind. Finally, with a slightly pale complexion, Veerna turned away, and looked to Syre. He met her eye, his gaze unshaking despite the circumstances.

Despite the fact that he was looking at the *Queen* of Shellacnass.

"I don't understand," he said, finally, his voice sure and steady, yet kept to a volume appropriate to the setting of the Royal Crypt.

Syre felt a pang of exasperation. She glanced to Flucknor as if he might be able to help, but he seemed just as lost as she was. Realising that she needed to answer the boy, she turned back to him. "What don't you understand?" she asked.

Veerna remained still, in silence, for several moments. "I don't understand why the fighting stopped . . . I don't understand what you *did* up there . . . in the North-West Spire . . . how you managed to stop the invaders; the *Horrox*."

Syre allowed Veerna's boy's complaint to fill the Royal Crypt. She toyed with how she should answer it. Finally, Flucknor was the one who spoke up. "Listen, Veerna, this really isn't the time, do you think?"

But Veerna remained focussed on Syre, and Syre knew that there was no way that she could deny the boy . . . as with everyone throughout Ilsnare; Shellacnass . . . the whole of the Crystal Kingdom . . . he deserved an answer.

She breathed in deeply, cast another glance to the pot which contained her brother Lou's remains and then fixed her gaze on Veerna. "What we created is nothing short of what might well prove to be a lasting solution for peace—a means for Mortals and Creatures to live side by side without causing one another harm."

"But didn't they live in peace together before?"

Syre shook her head. "Creatures were often forced into living *among* Mortals, but they had always to be carefully disguised. They needed to live by their customs—their *rules* . . . and, in most cases, to take on their appearance."

Veerna continued to stare up at her, and Syre couldn't tell how much of this he had heard before and how much of this was completely new . . . but she felt that if she stopped now then she would never be able to start up again. So she continued, "You see, the issue has always been that the Creatures have possessed great power . . . their *magic* . . . if they had wished—as the Horrox attempted to do—they could simply reach out and *crush* Mortals . . ."

"And what stops them now?" Veerna replied.

Surprising even herself, she felt a slight smile spread across her lips. "For many years, the Creatures showed great restraint . . . in most part because of Herimyre, once the Captain of the Royal Guards, and another King of Shellacnass . . ."

"The one who Louson slayed?" Veerna put in.

Syre nodded. "That's right, one of the three who Lou slayed."

Here she couldn't help but sneak another glance to the pot which contained Lou's remains, and wonder if from somewhere—*somehow*—Lou might be spying on her, and silently chuckling to himself about her obvious discomfort in explaining the unexplainable to a young boy.

"Herimyre possessed a magical artefact—Tysron—a weapon which was capable of repelling magic . . . with that weapon alone, he was able to wage war against the Magical world, and to relegate it to the shadows." Syre paused, unsure whether or not Veerna was taking all of this in, and then she added, "And that was where the Magical beings stayed for such a long time . . . to have Magical blood—to be *different*—it was understood that those things would bring unwanted and *perilous* attention to any being."

"Why didn't the Magical beings return?" Veerna asked. "After Herimyre was slayed by Louson?"

"Because," Syre replied, "they had made their homes in other places; in the fringes of the Kingdom . . . in the Winter's Moan, or else in the Sable Mountains."

Expression lines scored Veerna's forehead. "Does that mean they'll return now?"

Syre shrugged, then shot a glance at Flucknor. She turned back to Veerna. "We don't know what it'll mean, that'll be up to them . . . perhaps they're comfortable in their homes; or maybe, like the Horrox, they wish to integrate with Mortals. What we have done is create a balanced centre of magical power . . . a single location which draws the strongest magic together and which shall spread its protective spell across the land; allowing Mortals and Creatures to live in peace. At last."

There was a long pause while Veerna apparently absorbed this detail, and then he opened his mouth to speak again. "And what . . ." But Veerna stopped himself before he'd even got started.

He flushed a touch.

"Go on?" Syre prompted.

"What you did . . . in the North-West Spire, does that mean that we'll be safe . . . that the Magical beings will no longer be able to hold dominance over the Mortals . . . that Mortals shall no longer be able to hold dominance over the Creatures?"

Syre smiled back at him, feeling a warmth spreading through her gut. There was something about the innocent, inquisitive nature of children which acted as a sort of cure-all . . . it seemed to strip away her sadness; to see that the world wasn't such a bad place after all . . . that wounds, given time, would heal. She looked to Flucknor one more time, and then back to Veerna.

"We hope so," she said. "And that's all we can do."

A NEW FUTURE;
A NEW WORLD

When Syre emerged** from the Catacombs, and back into the daylight, she noticed that Arfklan was awaiting her. He stood at a reverential distance, his head bowed and his claws clutched at his waist. Although Syre knew little of politics and governance, she realised that, following her brother Lou's burial, she was, as of this moment, the reigning monarch of the Kingdom of Shellacnass.

There would be meetings to attend to.

Deals to be struck.

An indomitable mountain of procedure for which she had always believed herself inadequate ... but just who else was going to do that work for her? Just look what had happened when Lou had decided to entrust a large amount of the Kingdom's administration to Tineoots ...

Syre could also see Brotsboore and Inta standing nearby; a sort of guard to Arfklan.

Despite having remained somewhat distant from the business of the Horrox, and their continued integration with Ilsnare, she had heard rumours that both Brotsboore and Inta had been given roles close to Arfklan . . . and she supposed that the incoming meeting would make such matters clearer.

When Arfklan raised his head once more, Syre gestured for him to follow.

The House Staff—and a legion of builders—had been working on reconstructing the Throne Room . . . the executive decision had been made somewhere along the chain during Syre's mourning that since it was the centrepiece of the Palace it would be the most important area to have back in functioning order. She led Arfklan, Brotsboore and Inta along.

The Glyph, too, appeared out of seemingly nowhere.

She could also hear the footsteps of Flucknor, who she had asked to accompany her for the duration of these meetings. She had hoped that he would make things smoother. That he would prevent her from becoming emotional. But, truth be told, she didn't feel that emotional at all . . . in fact, she felt that she held her sanity together quite well. Then again, perhaps she wouldn't know that for sure until she had been posed some deliberately incendiary question by Arfklan.

As she paced over the emerald-green marble floors of the Throne Room, she found that the High Representative—*her High Representative*—was awaiting her:

Leona.

The woman who'd once been the Speaker of the Council of Wisemen.

Before *that* particular organisation had died a death.

Just like her brother Lou.

Within the Throne Room, there was already arranged a series of chairs.

Syre allowed the others to sit before she did.

That done, she closed the doors to the Throne Room and took her place among them.

An uneasy silence settled on the room.

It was difficult to know where to start, she had so much to thrash out with the Horrox—so many different areas for them to define . . . and then there was the fact that however they arranged things, whatever agreements they eventually arrived at, would be used as the basis for all other Creatures looking to better integrate them-selves with Mortals.

Which was to say, those who wanted to interact *at all* with Mortals.

Finally, it was Arfklan who spoke up.

"I wish for this discussion to be brief. Already, over the course of the past few weeks, we have laid out our position . . . worked out how we would *fit in.*"

Syre tilted her head to one side. She still had thoughts of the funeral on her mind, of course; of all the sable draperies in the streets. And she couldn't help thinking that the mourning hadn't simply been for Lou himself—for the King of Shellacnass—but also for all those who had fallen in recent times; either trying to defend Ilsnare, or else attempting to win it back.

Perhaps she had wanted a little longer . . . perhaps she had want-ed more time to mourn . . . but, as she well knew, all matters of state—of the Kingdom—had been put on hold while the repara-tions of Ilsnare had taken place. Many matters had been allowed to slide. And the fact was, now that Lou had been bid farewell, these things couldn't be put off any longer.

A kingdom needed its *queen*, after all . . .

"We believe," Arfklan said, looking over both Brotsboore and Inta, "that it would be in the best interests of Shellacnass to build the new system of governance around the Four Corners . . ."

Here Syre felt her chest tighten. She cast a glance over Brotsboore and Inta. She saw that their expressions were somehow smug, and she could tell that this was a point which'd been discussed at great length . . . and which, no doubt, had brought on a great deal of conflict between the Horrox themselves. For Arfklan to cede power so easily . . . just like *that* . . . well, it seemed unprecedented. As if acknowledging this truth, Arfklan raised a thin-lipped smile.

He met Syre's eye cautiously and went on, "The four; that is, Brotsboore, the Glyph, Flucknor, and, yourself, Your Majesty, shall be put in sole charge of deciding the matters of the Kingdom. However"—here Arfklan thrust a finger up in the air—"I also propose that, beneath the Members of the Four Corners, there be a group of . . . shall we say *lesser* talented practitioners." Arfklan glanced about them all, meeting everyone's eye in sequence. "A way of keeping those above in *check* . . . a sort of *Shadow Council*, if you will."

Syre considered this.

While it was possible to read Arfklan's statement in a variety of ways; that he was perhaps looking for some way to hold onto control through some means of puppetry with the Members of the Four Corners—to keep control through Brotsboore, no doubt, the only Horrox Member—she knew that what he proposed was more than fair. After all, Syre and Flucknor would be *two* Mortals serving as Members of the Four Corners, with the other two being Creatures . . . one a Horrox, and the other . . . well, whatever it was that the Glyph was.

"So," Arfklan said, arching an eyebrow, "what I propose is that each Member of the Four Corners shall choose another . . . to serve beneath them."

It was here that there was no mistake to be made, he turned his attention directly onto Brotsboore, who nodded in reply. Brotsboore cleared his throat. "I elect *Arfklan* to serve beneath me."

Syre had seen that one coming. She turned to look at the Glyph, who appeared to have become awfully uncomfortable all of a sudden. Without meeting her eye, the Glyph said, "And I nominate Inta to serve beneath me."

The tightness across Syre's chest grew more pronounced still. Her pulse rapped faster. And her heart jigged against her ribs. But she did her best not to show her shock or surprise . . . that this had been a *clearly organised* campaign against her . . . or, perhaps, a pre-emptive strike against Mortals; an attempt to keep the Horrox with at least fifty-percent control of the Kingdom.

But, then again, she and Flucknor still had their own choices to make.

Next, Flucknor said, "I select Gdandra to serve beneath me."

Syre stared at Flucknor for a moment before realising that this made perfect sense, that Flucknor had chosen his mentor to be his fall-back option. It didn't make Syre's choice any easier, though.

Try as hard as she might, she couldn't think of a single person who would be appropriate to serve beneath her . . . and then her gaze settled on Leona . . . and a smile formed on Leona's lips . . . Syre knew—*both of them knew*—that there would be no other way.

Finally, Syre raised her own voice. "And I nominate Leona to serve under me."

Leona flashed Syre a smile before taking on a more neutral expression.

Arfklan rose to his feet, apparently bringing an end to these discussions, despite *him* being the guest in the Throne Room of the Queen of Shellacnass. He approached Syre, still sitting, and outstretched his clawed hand for her to shake.

"Then it is decided," Arfklan said, "those who shadow the Members of the Four Corners shall be charged with giving advice where they can—with representing the *people*: Mortals and Creatures, through the Kingdom."

Syre reached out and took Arfklan's hand.

It was cold, and scaly.

She felt a shudder pass through her blood and couldn't help wondering if she hadn't just made an enormous mistake. But it was too late now . . . and what price *wouldn't* she pay for peace; even if it was to last for only a short while?

Syre watched on as Arfklan, Brotsboore and Inta filed on out of the Throne Room.

The Glyph hung about sheepishly for a few moments, before approaching Syre. He attempted a smile, but it came off a little unconvincing. "I apologise for what must seem like a misunderstanding," it said, "and while it's true that I anticipated the Four Corners—the uniting of the Magical Fields—I can honestly say that I did not see this coming." It blinked several times and then added, "I shall serve as best I can—as *fairly* as I can."

Feeling a refreshing warmth pass through her blood, Syre nodded by way of reply, and the Glyph excused itself.

Once Leona, too, had slipped out of the Throne Room, bowing to Syre and thanking her for the confidence she had shown, it left Syre alone with Flucknor.

When she turned to look at him, she stared into his deep, icy-blue eyes.

"Did you even think to ask Gdandra whether she'd be willing to take on such a role?"

The corner of Flucknor's mouth turned up in a smirk. He gave a shake of his head. "She's always going on about being lonely—I thought this might be a good way to get her better involved with the world of the living." Flucknor reached out and lightly touched her forearm. "Come on," he said, "I want to show you something."

A little taken off guard by this tenderness, among all the stuffy formality, Syre made to follow Flucknor out of the Throne Room; out of that which would be her domain until the day she died . . . or the day when she decided to up and disappear . . . to leave the Crystal Kingdom to the vultures . . . to those who *wanted* it . . .

THE COURTYARD GARDEN

When Syre turned the corner, she could already hear the playful sounds of splashing water. She could feel it in the air. Overhead, soaring blue skies stretched to the horizon.

Not a cloud in sight.

When she breathed in now, it wasn't to inhale stone dust, wood chippings; all of the evidence which presented the case for a city being rebuilt. She caught the scent of flowers, and of lush, long grasses. Even with these hints, it surprised her to turn the corner and see—spread out before her—a veritable garden; decked-out in a deep-blue marble and with flourishing, verdant plants blooming all over. A pair of members of the House Staff were down on their hands and knees, tending to the fledgling flowerbeds, their bare hands pleasantly covered with the ever-so-natural layers of soil. There was a wooden bench there, too, and Syre could see that it had been freshly varnished with a walnut polish. She allowed Flucknor to take her by the hand—the way that a young prince might take the hand of a princess—and he led her over to the seat.

The two of them sat down, and Syre felt the wooden planks of the bench creaking beneath her weight. It was a pleasant sensation, the two of them there, sitting in the stillness, and calm, among all of the relentless industry taking place throughout the Palace . . . throughout the city. Syre could feel the *thrum* of her ice magic moving through her veins, pumping through her, giving her heart some extra *kick*—a much-needed sense of optimism for the future.

For what was to come.

Over the top of the wall, she could make out the North-West Spire, towering over everything.

In the new designs for the Palace, the North-West Spire would feature prominently.

It would dominate all else in the Palace . . . and the skyline for miles around.

She thought of how, from the plains, it would be easily spotted even from the horizon.

Even from the land which surrounded Ilsnare.

A means for any being—Mortal or Creature—to see the beacon of neutrality, of *justice*, which held sway across the land . . . uniting magic, and making it stronger . . . allowing it to be used for good . . . and to keep power over their minds. Somehow, Syre had always believed that Mortals—that *all* beings—at their heart required a higher power to look up to. They needed something to fear. She decided that the reason for wars was not strictly down to evil, but it had more to do with the ambitious not being put in their place . . . shown that the world would *not* simply roll over for them. That it wasn't some virgin pearl for the taking.

She felt Flucknor move his fingertips over the back of her hand.

It sent a shiver across the surface of her skin.

She slipped him a sidelong glance.

He remained focussed on the fountain—intently staring at the water as it gurgled its way through the mechanism. Perhaps one day—one day when she was in need of distraction—she would ask Flucknor *how* exactly a fountain functioned. She wondered if it would be a strictly mechanical explanation or if there might be a—*more wondrous*—Magical reason.

But that was something to ponder for another day.

"So," Flucknor said, "have you had any thoughts about king-making?"

At first, Syre was confused by the question. "What do you mean?"

Flucknor turned to look at her.

Met her eyes.

"I mean, are there any eligible suitors . . . someone to share your throne?"

"And what makes you think that I want to share my throne with *anybody*?"

Flucknor shrugged, then grinned. "Just an idea."

Syre rubbed her thumb and index finger together and brought forth a flicker of ice fire. She tossed it into Flucknor's lap. There ensued a brief bout of flapping as Flucknor struggled to put the fire out. Syre rolled her eyes and looked away from him.

When she dared to look back, she saw that Flucknor was staring at the fountain again. She followed his gaze, realising that he was now regarding the top of the structure. It was then that she noticed the jewel adorning it . . . it *was* a jewel, wasn't it?

She screwed up her eyes.

The way the sun caught the clear mineral, it made the golden flakes within glimmer.

She had seen it before.

Around Hildie's neck.

That was the piece of glass she had worn.

Syre turned on Flucknor, confusion surely sketched all over her face. "What is this?" she said. "What's this *about*?"

For the first time in their visitation of the courtyard garden, Flucknor became a touch flustered ... well, aside from the time when Syre had tossed ice fire into his lap. "I ... well," Flucknor said, and wouldn't meet her gaze. "When they came to me ... asked me what I should do ... I couldn't ... I mean, you were ..."

"You're not making any sense," she said, standing up, no longer wanting to sit beside him. "What *is* this?"

All of a sudden, Flucknor seemed to get himself back together. "Listen," he said, "when Hildie died, the House Staff had to know what to do with her ... and since they wouldn't allow her to be buried in the Royal Crypt with Lou—for *obvious* reasons—I thought that this would be a more appropriate place."

Syre stared at the fountain.

And then to the ground beneath.

The *marble.*

She turned back to Flucknor. "You mean to say that she's *buried* here?"

Flucknor nodded in reply. "Her ashes were scattered across the soil."

Syre allowed this fact to drift over her. She felt a strange humming in her chest but she wasn't quite sure what to make of it. Of course, she had every right to be angry with Flucknor.

He had *deceived* her ... in a way.

And yet, at the same time, Syre couldn't help but feel that he had done the right thing. Here, in this courtyard, Hildie would catch the morning and afternoon sun. It would send its glow ploughing through the earth. Warming her ashes.

Syre turned to look at the fountain, and to that glass pendant which was embedded in the top. She supposed it was by far the most fetching headstone she had ever seen.

She breathed in deeply.

Brought her emotions back under control.

Then glanced back to Flucknor.

Finally, she managed to raise a smile. "Thank you," she said. "Thank you for taking care of it." She paused, searching for the right words, and yet, at the same time, knowing that they simply wouldn't come. "I'm sure she'll be happy here—*comfortable* here."

Flucknor smiled back at her.

And then he reached for Syre's hand.

Gave it a squeeze.

Against all her best efforts, she found herself blushing.

Was it because she was Queen of Shellacnass that she felt ashamed of such exploits performed shamelessly in front of the House Staff? Anyway, the two members of the House Staff didn't seem to notice as they tended to the flowerbeds on their hands and knees.

She turned back to Flucknor and leaned into him, planting a simple—*soft*—kiss on his lips.

Over his shoulder, she noticed Brotsboore and the Glyph, moving through the corridors, headed for the North-West Spire.

She knew that it was time.

Time for them to send their good vibes out across the land.

"Come on," she said, squeezing Flucknor's hand back. "We've got work to do."

Flucknor turned to look, acknowledged the Glyph and Brotsboore.

Then he looked back at Syre.

"When I asked about you choosing a King," he said, "I meant *me.*"

Syre smiled back at him, and then led him on, in the direction of the North-West Spire. "I know," she said, and felt her heart flutter up to her throat.

Although she didn't look back on the courtyard garden, she could still picture that piece of glass glimmering in the sunlight; embedded in the top of the fountain.

It truly was a lovely reminder.

But not just of Hildie . . . of Lou too . . . and all that was beautiful.

It would act as a monument—*a line in the sand*—for the bringing of the time when all things would be beautiful once again.

Because, now that the darkness had passed, lightness must flood all over.

Even Syre could hope for that much.

THE CATACOMBS

Veerna felt the darkness surrounding him.
It seemed to poke and prod at his skin.
But he wasn't afraid.

His eyes had grown accustomed to the dark by now. He had been down here, in the Catacombs, for the best part of an hour; ever since Queen Syre Dorf and Flucknor had departed the courtyard just above. As he paced alongside the channels, he peered downward, to the dried-up silt beds where the overflow from the River Ils had run.

From what he had heard—the stories he had witnessed firsthand—Flucknor and the Glyph had entered Ilsnare through the Catacombs . . . they had gone through a door around here somewhere; a door which would lead to the River Ils itself. It surprised him over and over again when he thought of all the secrets which Ilsnare Palace held in store, and he could only thank his lucky stars that he had managed to make himself such a preferred member of the House Staff.

The only other member of the House Staff who had been allowed to tag alongside Queen Syre and Flucknor on the day of Louson

Dorf's funeral had been the elderly Heither Jopf . . . the locksmith of Ilsnare Palace. All Veerna had ever wanted, from the moment that he had been taken off the street, and put into service as a member of the House Staff, was to have some sort of purpose:

To *mean* something.

And, of course, he never wanted to suffer from thirst—or hunger for that matter—ever again.

There was no doubt about it, he had landed on his feet.

Veerna listened to the odd, *schlick-schlick* sound as the soles of his boots trod in and out of the damp mud at the sides of the channels. He breathed in the stale, yet *pungent* air. He had never been afraid of the dead . . . of being *around* the dead . . . in the streets, in Ilsnare, he had often come across corpses here and there. It wasn't that he had become *desensitised*—whenever he did come across a corpse, he couldn't ever prepare himself for the overwhelming smell . . . and neither could he prevent the goose pimples breaking out over his skin.

But he had learned to take death in his stride.

To pull the collar of his tunic up over his mouth and nostrils to shield himself from the worst of the smell; and to move on quickly from the sight so as not to retch up whatever little sustenance he had managed to scavenge earlier. For some stupid reason he had wanted to test his resolve . . . to see if he still had the inner-steel he'd possessed out on the streets of Ilsnare . . . and now he had accomplished that feat. He still had it, whatever *it* was . . .

Veerna was on the cusp of turning to leave the Catacombs—of leaving the darkness behind—when something caught the corner of his eye.

He pivoted.

Turned to look.

Lying there, on the dried-up bed of the channel, Veerna saw a whitish glow.

He took a few steps closer to the light.

Then crouched down on the bank of the channel, trying to get a better look.

It was writing ... *glowing* white text on a fragment of stone.

Often in the Palace Veerna had been chided by various *senior* members of the House Staff for touching this, or that, priceless object. Right now, though, there was nobody around but himself.

With a quick glance about to ensure that his suspicion was the correct one, and seeing that—*indeed*—there was nobody around, he eased himself down the bank of the channel and dropped down onto the dried-up silty bed. He only thought of his wispy-grey uniform—the uniform of the House Staff—several seconds after he had landed . . . it would take some serious scrubbing to get the stain out, but, then again, one of the washerwomen had taken a shine to him in that motherly way older women seemed to do.

The stench was stronger still, now that Veerna was standing down on the dried-up bed of the channel—the smell of mud, and manure ... *blood*?

It was no secret to Veerna that dead bodies were often disposed of by simply hurling them into the River Ils.

Once he had got over the queasy feeling in his gut, he approached the stone fragment then bent down over it and picked it up.

Heavy.

Heavier than he'd imagined.

Just about comfortable to hold, though.

When he had first come to the Palace, he recalled how he had been so scrawny that he'd been unable to lift so much as a bag of coal for the fire without breaking sweat ... and yet it'd only taken a few weeks before he had comfortably been chopping woodpile after woodpile.

He had grown into his muscles soon enough.

He squinted at the glowing white text etched onto the stone fragment.

Some language he didn't understand.

Hearing some sound off in the distance of the Catacombs—a *scutter* or something like it—he turned to look. But saw nothing at all.

Most likely it'd only been a rat . . . the Catacombs were known to be *crawling* with rats.

When Veerna turned his attention back to the stone once again, he realised he wasn't going to be able to make anything of it. He knew the sensible course of action would be to take the stone to some wise man; one who might be able to tell him what it was for. But there was a large risk that he would have the stone taken *away* from him, and that, to be quite frank, was unacceptable.

Now that he'd got hold of this mysterious object he could hardly bear to let it go.

Decided that he would take it back to his sleeping quarters and stash it somewhere, a voice came at him from out of the darkness.

"What's that you've got there?"

Veerna's whole body seized up.

His *throat* seized up.

And he couldn't make so much as a *squeak*.

He stared into the darkness, but saw nothing.

"Who's there?" Veerna asked.

No answer.

He gripped the stone tighter.

When the voice sounded again, it was closer.

Behind him.

"Say, would you like to see what *I've* got?"

Veerna turned around again, becoming giddy with these jerky motions.

He stared into the darkness . . . thought that he could just about make out a form.

Finally, the figure took a pair of steps forward:

A man.

An *elderly* man.

It was then that the white glow commenced from what Veerna supposed to be the elderly man's chest. And it took Veerna another second to realise that the elderly man held an object like the one in Veerna's possession . . . no, he held the *other half* of the object . . .

Veerna's fear wavered, replaced by curiosity. "What are these?"

There was a long, drawn-out pause, as if the elderly man was working out the exact way to phrase his reply. It got Veerna thinking back on how Syre had spoken to him so haltingly, when she had described how peace had finally arrived to the Kingdom.

"These?" the elderly man said, a hop in his voice. "These, my child, are two halves of a keystone . . . the keystone which unlocks the Webbing Armoury."

It felt as if the blood froze in Veerna's veins, and he could only utter a husky, "*What?*"

" 'The Webbing Armoury', my lad, come now, I'm sure you've heard of it."

Veerna remained impossibly still for a long time, and then finally replied, "Yes—yes, I have."

"Here," the elderly man said, thrusting the stone fragment at him.

For a while, Veerna wasn't sure what to do with this gesture. He was still getting over the fact that he'd uncovered *one* such wonder . . . and to find out its secret so soon . . . and *what* a secret! He took the other stone fragment from the elderly man, who now turned away from him. "Wait," Veerna said.

The man halted.

But didn't turn around.

"Where're you going?" Veerna asked.

"Me?" the elderly man said, as if the question was completely unexpected. "I'm leaving Ilsnare—for *good.*"

Holding the two fragments of the stone, feeling them weigh down his hold, Veerna found himself speechless once more.

The man shuffled on another few steps.

"Stop!" Veerna called out, the desperation shredding his voice now.

"Hmm?" the elderly man said, glancing back over his shoulder.

"Who *are* you?" Veerna said.

A long pause, and then the elderly man answered, "My name is Ems'plot—a very fine mage . . . *once.*"

Veerna shook his head. "You should give these keystones to someone else . . . I'm not even Magical . . . and, in the Palace, I'm not really . . ."

The silence hollowed out between them.

The elderly man butted in.

"What?"

But there was nothing Veerna could say by way of reply.

The elderly man's face—*Ems'plot's face*—came better into view in the dim light of the Catacombs. He was smiling lightly, the leathered skin of his cheeks creasing. "Tell you what, son, you do whatever it is you think's right with the keystone." He winked. "See that it gets into the right—*responsible*—hands, hmm?"

Veerna stood stock still, and he watched the elderly man retreat. He wanted to call him back so that he might explain further but the truth was that Veerna was so stunned to find himself holding the *key* to the Webbing Armoury that it stole away his very breath. And by the time he had regained something of his consciousness, he sensed that the elderly man, Ems'plot, was gone.

When Veerna had clambered his way back up the bank of the channel—and no doubt dirtied his uniform all the more—he felt himself shuddering slightly.

As he made his way back toward the staircase which led to the surface, he paused, looked around, and then glanced back to the Royal Crypt.

Heither Jopf—at his old age—was often forgetful.

And Veerna could see that he had left the door to the Royal Crypt wide open.

Acting quickly, Veerna stole inside, found a spare hole in the wall, and then laid the fragments of keystone within. He stood back, thought about what he was doing—what he was *really* doing—and then he brought the iron door shut.

Concealing the fragments of the keystone inside.

As he climbed the stone stairs, back up to the surface, Veerna told himself that he had hidden the keystone to the Webbing Armoury for the good of the Kingdom . . . it was better that such power could not fall into restless hands. And yet, as he surfaced, blinking away in the setting sunlight which dribbled in over the Palace, he knew that it wasn't the whole truth.

Because, after all, he had—in effect—made *himself* the caretaker of the Webbing Armoury.

He was the only one who could get access.

As he headed toward the service quarters where he would get a washerwoman to see to his uniform, he consoled himself with the fact that he didn't even *know* the location of the Webbing Armoury.

Not yet, anyway.

THE END

AUTHOR'S NOTE

Thank you for picking up and (hopefully!) enjoying one of my stories.

When it comes to reaching readers in the modern era, reviews mean everything to authors. This is where you can help out. If you have a spare moment I would really appreciate it if you could leave an (honest!) review on the sales page for this title.

To hear about my latest releases — and to get your hands on some free fiction (!) — you can sign up for my newsletter: www.raymondsflex.com/readers

Thank you so much for reading!

Raymond S Flex

ABOUT THE AUTHOR

Raymond S Flex:
Science fiction. Fantasy. And everything in between!

Among tales of laser blasters, crazed sprites and diabolically minded executives sits the Crystal Kingdom epic fantasy series. Join Louson Dorf — and a burgeoning cast of characters — as he strives to piece his crumbling world back together again.

Get free fiction, notification of the latest releases, and more, when you join Raymond S Flex's mailing list:
www.raymondsflex.com/readers

COMPLIMENTARY DIGITAL EDITION

A complimentary digital edition is included with this book.

To download your epub, mobi & PDF versions of this book, please navigate to www.dibbooks.com/digital-editions/ and when prompted for a password enter the following:

louson